A GUY WALKS INTO A BAR

SPACE ROGUES

BOOK 7

JOHN WILKER

Rogue Publishing

CONTENTS_

PART ONE

CHAPTER 1

CHAPTER 2

CHAPTER 3

CHAPTER 4

CHAPTER 5

PART TWO

CHAPTER 6

CHAPTER 7

CHAPTER 8

CHAPTER 9

PART THREE

PART FOUR

PART FIVE

To my readers. The fact I'm still able to tell the stories of Wil and the crew of the Ghost is fantastic. Thank you for your support!

PART ONE

CHAPTER 1_

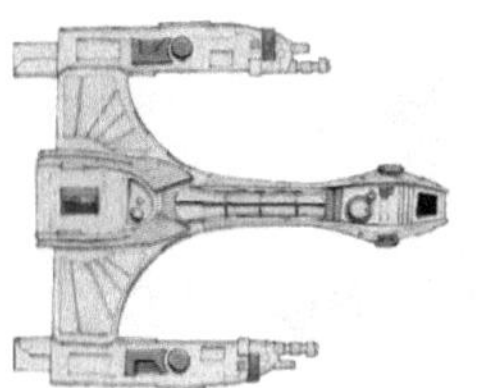

WIL CALDER, BOUNTY HUNTER_

"I THOUGHT he'd put up more of a fight," Zephyr says, looking up from her station.

Cynthia looks over at her friend. "I mean, he beat the dren out of Wil, so…" she shrugs.

Wil spins in his command chair. "Hey, not fair! He took me by surprise!"

Bennie makes a barking laugh sound. "He's a Partherian. The only thing he's sneakier than might be a rock."

Wil waves the Brailack hacker away. "Whatever, dude. He's stronger and faster than he looks."

He turns back to his console, then to Cynthia, who nods. "We're cleared, so let's take off. Let's get off this planet and get paid."

"Won't make us forget your ass kicking," Bennie says without looking at Wil.

"I will throw this Kel statue at you," Wil replies, patting the small blue bear-like creature affixed to his console.

Maxim chimes in, "I'm not thrilled about going back to Partheria. The sooner we get there and get off-planet, the better." From her station, Zephyr is nodding slowly.

Wil looks at his first officer. "Yeah, I'm sorry I didn't think this job through better when the offer came in."

Zephyr smiles, her eyes locking on Wil's. "It's fine. It was a long time ago now. The Partherians were pawns. It's not like they were part of the conspiracy. They were just doing what they were told."

Wil nods, pushing the repulsor lift power lever forward. The *Ghost* shudders and tilts slightly as she leaves the duracrete of the spaceport, lifting straight up into the sky. He reaches over and presses a button. The sound of the landing gear retracting echoes through the ship.

Wil pushes the controls forward, tilting the ship slightly so she'll drift out of the spaceport's airspace.

Minutes later, the telltale boom from the aft of the ship and the g-forces that accompany it announce the *Ghost's* imminent departure from the atmosphere.

On the main display, the pale blue clouds and salmon colored sky fade to black as the *Ghost* clears the atmosphere. Wil switches from atmospheric engines to sub-light and looks around the bridge, eyes settling on Maxim. "You know, maybe a little sparring wouldn't hurt." He raises an eyebrow at his tactical officer. "Interested?"

Maxim smiles. "In kicking your butt? Yes." He stands and heads for the bridge hatch. As the hatch opens, he holds an arm out to Wil to let him leave the bridge first.

Bennie hops out of his seat. "This should be good."

WIL HAS CHANGED OUT OF HIS NORMAL SHIPBOARD JUMPSUIT and into a tank top and shorts. Maxim is similarly dressed. The big Palorian looks at his captain, a head shorter than him. "I'll go easy on ya."

"It hasn't been that long," Wil says defensively.

Maxim tilts his head. "Do you even remember the last time you trained?"

"Well, no. I mean, I don't mark it in my calendar or anything."

"Almost eight months." Maxim points to Wil's midsection. "You've also gotten fat."

From the side of the training mat, Bennie cackles until Cynthia smacks him on the back of the head.

Wil swings his bo staff in a wide arc, attempting to get in a shot at Maxim before he expects it. The big Palorian dodges to the side, Wil's staff missing him by inches, whistling as it sails past. In the same move, he brings his own bo staff around, catching Wil in the ribs.

Wil takes a step back, readying his staff just in time to deflect an overhead swing. He twists at his hip, bringing his staff down, dragging Maxim's with it. He opens his mouth to comment but clamps it shut just in time to twist further, narrowly avoiding a blow to his head.

Maxim spins quickly, bringing his staff low to take Wil's feet out from under him. Wil jumps just in time, bringing his staff up to catch Maxim on the chin. The two of them separate a few paces.

Maxim tilts his head side to side, cracking his neck. "It's on."

Wil swallows. "Oh, shit."

Bennie rubs his hands together.

OLD MEMORIES_

"He did better than I expected," Maxim says as he and Zephyr get ready for bed. The *Ghost* is en route to Partheria, and after the sparring match, the crew had hamburgers and turned in.

Zephyr leans out of the small refresher in the corner of their quarters. "Yeah, I was shocked when he got that shot in on you." She waggled a finger. "Maybe he's not getting better, you're getting slower."

Maxim drops his undershirt and pulls her out of the refresher. "I'll show you slow," he growls.

"Breakfast, loser," Wil says as he walks into the *Ghost's* small brig. Their prisoner sits up, watching Wil approach.

As Wil slides the breakfast tray through the small slot at the bottom of the door, the Partherian says, "What is it?"

"Eggs, toast, a little bacon." Wil inclines his head. "Bacon is getting pretty low, sorry." Wil stands up to leave but stops when their guest clears his throat.

"Why'd you come after me?" The Partherian man stoops to pick up his breakfast tray.

Wil turns as the doors to the small brig open. He leans in the doorjamb. "Well, you broke the law. But real talk, we got paid." Wil smiles, adding, "Handsomely."

"Low life bounty hunting scum," the Partherian growls, taking a bite of bacon. He chews, then says, "Dren, this is good. What did you call it?"

Wil smirks. "I won't take that first part personally." He turns to leave. "It's called bacon. Enjoy." The doors slide shut, sealing the brig off.

Wil walks into the lounge area. Everyone is at the kitchenette table. Bennie looks up. "I can't believe you wasted bacon on our prisoner."

Cynthia slaps the Brailack on the back of the head. "We're not monsters." She looks from Wil to Bennie. "Well, not all of us." She turns back to Wil. "He have anything interesting to say for himself?"

Wil shakes his head, walking over to take a seat. "Nah, just the usual 'bounty hunting scum' stuff." He scoops up some scrambled eggs, their blue tint giving away their not being from a chicken.

Maxim smiles. "He didn't mention kicking your butt?"

"Or you falling into the river?" Zephyr offers.

Gabe, standing off to the side per usual, raises a hand. "While I am not an expert on humor, that was, I believe, one of the funnier things I have witnessed in several cycles. I have saved a recording for later watching."

Wil blushes. "The log was slippery, and he sucker punched me." His voice is now several octaves higher than normal.

Maxim grunts, "Okay, laughing at Wil aside..." He taps his wrist-comm, and the large display in the seating area comes alive with a recording of Wil and their Partherian guest on a large fallen tree over a sizable river. Something is said and the two grapple briefly until Wil stumbles and falls first on his butt, then slips off the log into the river below. "What's the plan when we arrive on Partheria?" His face makes it clear he hasn't moved on as well as Zephyr. "I'd rather not spend long there."

Wil nods once. "Yeah, I don't blame you. We're supposed to drop homeboy off at the Hall of Justice in the..." He taps his wristcomm, flipping through screens of information.

Before Wil can find the information he is looking for, Gabe says, "We are expected at the Hall of Justice in the Leojirn Province."

Lowering his arm, Wil looks at his mechanical friend. "Show off." He turns to Maxim. "We get in, drop off the dillhole on the brig, get our money, and get off-planet."

Maxim looks down. "I know I shouldn't be so angry about it—it's been cycles—but I just can't. The Partherian security service took the Peacekeeper tip without a second thought, snatched us off the street, locked us up, and then threw us on that battleship." He shakes his head.

MEETINGS ABOUT MEETINGS_

After breakfast and two episodes of *ALF*, Bennie's choice, the crew splits up to take care of their various shipboard duties. Wil heads for the bridge with Bennie and Maxim to work on something, while Cynthia and Zephyr head to the cargo hold to work out. Gabe retreats to engineering.

Zephyr twirls one of her two bokken. "These are nice." She holds one up and examines it, feeling the balance. "Solid core? What kind of wood?"

Cynthia twirls both of her short, wooden training swords. "A gift from Barbara." She bows to Zephyr.

Zephyr bows, then strikes a ready stance. She paces to the side, her eyes glued to Cynthia. "You two really bonded."

Cynthia launches into a flurry of slashes with both wooden swords. Between swings she says, "Yeah, we've stayed in touch since that whole Farsight thing." She ducks to avoid an overhead slash, continuing, "I never knew my parents and the matron of the orphanage was anything but parental." She makes a jab with her left sword. "And most certainly not matronly." She moves to dodge another slash but is a split second too late, catching a stinging hit on her right shoulder.

Zephyr tilts back just in time to avoid Cynthia's counter strike but fails to adjust in time to avoid her opponent's less powerful right-handed strike. She grunts as she gets clear. "That must have been tough." As she parries quickly, the sound of wood on wood echoes through the hold. "Did they die? Your parents?"

Cynthia makes a double-handed swing, bringing both of her bokken fiercely against both of Zephyr's, the impact making both women's hands tingle. "No idea. I was left at one of the municipal orphanages. As I understand it, I was passed around the first few months. State run orphanages on Tyr aren't that big and are usually overcrowded." She sidesteps, quickly spinning backward, one of her bokken whistling through the air. It misses Zephyr by an inch. "I ended up in something called the Yadro program." She jumps over a low slice. "They take orphans and make 'em, well, me." She tilts back then lets herself fall so she can raise her feet to kick her opponent in the midsection, driving her away.

Zephyr stumbles back two steps. "Is the program still in operation?"

Cynthia is about to strike but stops dead in her tracks, lowering her bokken. "I... I don't know."

"Good evening, everyone," Gabe says to an array of faces on the large display in the engineering space that usually shows an animation of the status of the *Ghost's* systems.

A Tarsi man with gray hair bows. "Is it also evening where you are, Representative Gabe?"

Gabe shakes his head. "No, I was being polite. We are in transit; it is ship's midday."

One of the other Galactic Commonwealth councilors chuckles. The first councilor clears his throat. "Yes, polite. Let's get down to business." Everyone on the screen nods, as does Gabe.

Gabe says, "I am happy to hear that progress is being made on determining the best approach for integrating droid civil liberties into the greater Galactic Commonwealth constitution."

"Thank you—" one of the councilors begins to say.

Gabe holds up a hand. "However. It has been two standard months now, and my guiding committee reports that they are still routinely excluded from planning sessions. That is unacceptable."

"These things take time, Gabe. I'm sure you can understand that," another councilor says, this one an Olop woman. "A social movement such as this, causing a change to the core of the GC—that doesn't happen fast."

Gabe inclines his head. "Of course. Our initial agreement, however, was that my aides would be involved in my absence and that that involvement would be absolute in terms of the issue of droid civil rights."

"Please understand, Gabe, that the exclusion of your aides has not been intentional."

"I, in fact, do not understand. They are onsite, they do not require sleep. They can meet at any time of the day that is convenient." Gabe raises his hand once more. "I will consult with them shortly, but please do not take my absence as an opportunity to renege on our agreement or in any way stall."

A Tygran man dips his head. "Please forgive us. I better than them know the importance of this issue and apologize for our slowness and poor behavior. It will not happen again."

Gabe smiles. "Please see that it does not."

NEWSCAST_

"Good evening, I'm Mon-el Furash."

"And I'm Klor'Tillen, and this is GNO *NewsTock*," the Brailack co-host says.

The Malkorite woman smiles. "Tonight we've got an update on the impending droid rights vote." She turns to a different vid pickup, continuing, "The Galactic Commonwealth Governing Council will be voting in the next few days on the matter of civil rights for all artificial beings in the GC."

Klor'Tillen picks up, "As you can imagine, this has been a contentious issue. Member nations like Tyr and Cleblon, already having local laws regarding this, have been strong advocates in support."

Mon-el adds, "The measure—initially proposed by a droid by the name of Gabe, who, through a series of highly unusual events, became completely sapient and free of built-in restrictive programming—came before the council last year."

The Brailack journalist nods. "Gabe made a very compelling case, and as we learned after the fact, was instrumental in organizing the mostly non-violent protests throughout the Commonwealth that helped shift public opinion and raise awareness of the issue."

Mon-el folds her hands in front of her. "And when things turned violent as they did on Durbril Two, Gabe was quick to step in and broker a peaceful resolution that ensured justice was served."

Klor'Tillen nods. "Indeed. The council has been debating for months but has finally signaled that a vote is imminent. We'll keep you posted as we learn more and will have live coverage when the vote takes place."

CHAPTER 2_

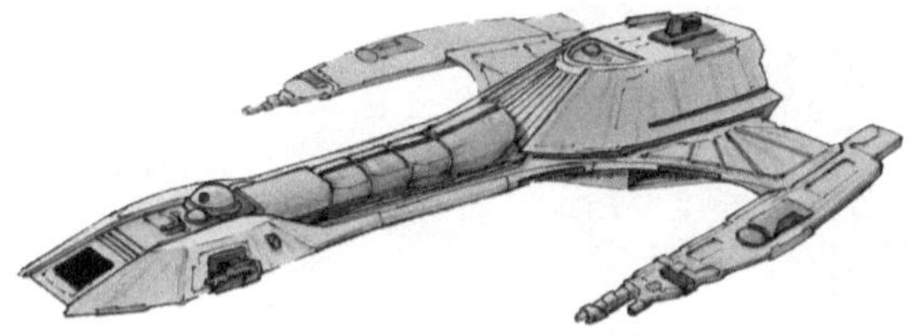

SPECIAL DELIVERY_

"Huh, I didn't think it'd be so pretty," Wil says as the *Ghost* enters orbit.

"Why?" Cynthia asks. Below them a red hued planet slowly spins. Blue oceans with wispy clouds drifting over them...The clouds, a mix of purples and pinks. The ground, a pale green. Cities that span kilometers and reach into the clouds dot the landscape. Kilometer-wide tracts of farmland fill the space between mega cities.

Wil shrugs, turning his chair so he can look over his shoulder at her. "I dunno. I mean, Partherians aren't that pretty. Their ships look like giant ugly refrigerators. I just assumed they came from an ugly place." He waves to the main display. "This is downright pretty."

Maxim tuts, "Have you learned nothing in all these cycles? Partherians are no different than any other race; they have military, scientists, artists, you name it. Not every race is defined by a single trait."

Wil inclines his head. "I mean Palorians are kinda a uni-culture."

"If we count stupid and self-destructive as qualities, so are humans," Bennie offers.

Wil glares at the hacker. "It would take so little effort to choke you to death."

Before anyone else can join in, Cynthia interrupts, "We're being hailed."

Wil nods and the main display updates; the view of the planet shrinks to a small window in the lower right. The rest of the display is a scowling Partherian woman.

She looks over the crew, then says, "Not what I was expecting. Are you some type of traveling entertainers? A menagerie or something?"

"Rude," Bennie says in a harsh stage whisper.

Wil waves. "Yeah, hi. I'm Wil Calder. We were hired to track down one of your people, a criminal."

"Bounty hunters, then," the woman tuts. "Bounty ID code?"

Wil looks around, settling on Zephyr, eyebrow raised. She taps on her console. "Wait one."

The woman on the screen exhales loudly.

"Here it is," Zephyr says looking up at the screen, "tee-one-five-seven-three-three-nine."

The woman on the screen looks off to the side, consulting something, then turns back. "Here it is. Oh, wow. Yeah, he's a piece of work, eluded the civil authorities for cycles." She looks up. "And you lot caught him?" Wil is about to answer when she continues, "I'm sending you landing coordinates now." The screen goes black, then returns to its normal view of the approaching planet, now much closer.

Wil says, "Well, she's friendly." He looks over his shoulder to Cynthia. "Got 'em?"

"Yup, sending to you now," she says, tapping a control on her console.

Wil's console beeps. "Here we go." He pushes the controls forward while sliding the sub light throttles back to lower their speed. The planet rushes toward them.

"You know, if we were a circus, I'd be the main attraction," Bennie says from his console.

"You? No way, pipsqueak," Wil says, his eyes on his console. "At best you'd be the side show, like the bearded lady or the two-headed horse."

"Man, grolack you. I'm star material." The Brailack turns to look at Wil. "What's a horse?"

Maxim looks over at his Brailack friend. "I think they're domesticated creatures." He looks at Wil. "Does anything on Earth have two heads?"

"Not on purpose, no." On the screen, the planet is much closer, the surface details growing more detailed, the clouds much closer. "Entering atmo."

"I'm not a genetic freak," Bennie says sourly. "I'm a star."

Zephyr chuckles. "Mutant livestock."

"Grolack off," Bennie snarls.

On the screen, the clouds have surrounded the ship. Wil is adjusting his controls. "Atmospherics in five." He looks at ceiling. "Hold on to your metal butt, Gabe."

"I have magnetized my feet," the ceiling replies.

There is a momentary lurch as the sub light engines shut off and the *Ghost* is essentially in free fall. That moment is short lived, as the loud boom of the atmospheric engines igniting in the rear of the ship pushes the *Ghost* back to thrust. Wil adjusts a control, pushing a slider forward. Powerful repulsor lifts in the forward sections of the two engine nacelles activate, pushing against the planet to help the *Ghost* maintain lift.

"You're off course," Zephyr says.

"I am not," Wil replies, not looking at his first officer.

Over the loudspeaker, a voice says, "Transport ship, *Ghost,* you are off course."

Wil snaps his head around to glare at Cynthia. "Traitor."

THIS IS AWKWARD_

As the *Ghost* settles on her landing legs, the creaking reverberates throughout the ship. Wil puts his station in standby. "Okay, let's do this." He turns to Maxim. "You wanna go get our guest?" The big man nods and gets up to leave the bridge. "Meet ya in the hold."

As the heavy doors of the cargo hold slide apart, the warm air of the Leojirn Province fills the hold. Maxim and their guest come down the stairs.

Wil looks at the two men. "Welcome home." He smiles to the Partherian man, who returns the gesture with a scowl. At the bottom of the ramp are three Partherian civil authority officers. As the crew of the *Ghost* and their guest descend the ramp, one of the officers steps forward.

"I'm Detective Inspector Voltok." He extends a meaty hand toward Wil, who reaches out and grasps the man's forearm, a much more common move than handshaking, Wil has found.

"Wil Calder. Nice to meet you." He motions for Maxim to bring their guest forward. "He's all yours."

Detective Inspector Voltok motions one of his officers to come forward and take custody. "Hope he didn't give you any trouble."

Wil shakes his head. "Nah, perfect gentleman."

"Other than the kicking your butt and pushing you into a river," Bennie offers from behind Wil.

Voltok raises an eyebrow. "I'm told you can go to the central precinct for your payment." He holds a PADD up for Wil to scan with his wristcomm. When Wil raises his arm to the device, it beeps then shows a map on the screen. There's a number flashing along the top. Voltok says, "The number is your receipt. Just show that to the sergeant, and they'll get you paid out."

Wil nods. "Will do, thanks." He looks down at the map, a short walk from the landing facility. He looks at the others. "Fancy a walk?"

As the team walks, Maxim leans down to Zephyr. "Is this the same city we were in when—"

"We got arrested?" she interrupts, then looks around, the thumbs on her right hand tapping against each other as she thinks. "Yeah, I think so. What're the odds?" Maxim grunts but doesn't say anything else.

Bennie and Gabe are trailing the group, and Bennie taps his much taller mechanical friend on the leg as they walk. "How's the droids rights thing going?"

Gabe looks down and mimics Wil with a shrug. "It is going."

Bennie makes a face. "That good, huh?"

"I admit I am disappointed in the slow progress thus far."

"Sorry to hear that. Want me to hack the next election, get rid of a few councilors?" the short Brailack grins.

Gabe smiles. His smile is getting less creepy as time goes on. "No, thank you. I do appreciate the gesture, though."

Bennie makes the Brailack equivalent of a thumbs up and trots ahead to catch up to Wil and Cynthia, passing the two Palorians. "So, we get paid, we blow this poopcycle vendor, then what?"

Wil rubs his face. "And here I thought we'd gotten past you and the *earthisms*." He looks down at Bennie. "It's pop-cycle. Why would someone have a poopcycle stand? Poop on a stick? That's just disgusting."

"Who knows? You eat that stuff, cauliflower, and it tastes like butt, so..." the Brailack shrugs.

Wil waves him away. "This looks like the place." He consults his wristcomm, then nods. "Yup, we're here." He walks up the steps to the doors, which slide open at his approach.

"May I help you?" the official at the desk asks.

Wil walks up and rests both arms on the desk. "Yeah, we've got this..." He trails off, staring at the Partherian man across from him. "Do I know you from somewhere?"

The man looks Wil up and down. "I don't think so. You're Multonae?"

"Human—" Wil starts.

"I think this guy was on the prison transport," Maxim offers from behind Wil, his tone not even close to friendly.

The Partherian looks at Maxim, then Zephyr, then back to Wil, seeming to now notice his brown duster over light armor. "Wait a minute. You're the two prisoners that were sprung!" He looks at Wil. "So you'd be the guy who attacked the ship and stunned us all." He's glaring at Wil.

WE'RE NOT FRIENDS_

"You know, that stun blast hurt and left a mark," the Partherian officer says, still glaring at Wil.

Before Wil can say anything, Maxim replies, "You know what hurt? Being wrongfully accused, having our pleas ignored."

The Partherian man loses some of his steam. "Well, what would you have had us do? The Peacekeepers presented evidence."

"Fake evidence," Zephyr offers.

"Well, we know that now," the Partherian replies.

"You'd have known it then if you had done your own investigation," Maxim growls.

"Or even just demanded the Peacekeepers make their case, here in court," Zephyr adds. "But instead, you lot just locked us up for a few weeks, then shipped us off to a penal colony."

The Partherian man, sensing his own indignation is far outpaced, offers a truce, spreading his arms, hands down. "Mistakes were made by all parties. I think we can learn from this and see it as a learning opportunity."

Maxim calmly places a hand on Zephyr's shoulder and guides her back out the door to the street. Only Maxim knows how close the

Partherian man has just come to being strangled by an irate Palorian woman.

Wil watches the exchange, then says, "If we can just get paid, we'll be on our way." He extends the arm with a wristcomm on it so the man can scan it.

"Uh, yes, let's get you taken care of." He reaches over and holds a PADD near Wil's arm. The device beeps twice, and he swipes up on the screen.

Wil's wristcomm beeps once, and he examines the screen. He looks up. "Pleasure doing business with you."

"Uh, yes, you too," the now very uncomfortable Partherian civil authority officer replies.

When Wil and the others walk out, Cynthia looks at her friend. "Well, that got touchy fast." She smiles, hoping to break some of the tension she can still sense rolling off Zephyr.

Zephyr inhales loudly, then releases the breath. "Let's get off this rock."

Maxim smiles. "Yeah, I think I've had enough of Partheria for a while."

Gabe looks around at his friends. "I knew that prior to my being liberated from the shipping crate, the two of you had been in Partherian custody. I am ashamed I did not know the depth of that custody."

Maxim puts a hand on Gabe's shoulder. "Nothing you could have done about it, big guy. No worries."

Gabe inclines his head. "I can configure the comm system to hide bounties put out by the Partherian government, if that would help," the droid offers.

Bennie stomps his foot. "Stay in your lane, shiny. The team has a hacker." He thumps his chest with a thumb. "Me."

Cynthia smiles. "So touchy."

Bennie lunges for her, but she deftly moves to the side, allowing him to sail harmlessly past to land on the sidewalk with a thud.

Wil waves his hand. "Okay, circus freaks! Let's not make a scene on the street, please." He looks around. "Oh..." He points across the street. "Drink first?"

Zephyr growls. "Can't we drink on the ship?"

Gabe raises a hand. "It may not be my place to say so, but it would be financially responsible to drink on the *Ghost* where the alcohol is already paid for."

Wil's shoulders slump. "Okay, come on." He looks at Gabe. "I'm both annoyed and kinda proud you're inclined to keep us on the straight and narrow."

"I can be more vocal from this point on, if you'd like, Captain. I have several topics which I believe I could contribute sound financial advice on."

Wil holds up a hand. "Let's take it slow for now, buddy."

Maxim chuckles.

Partheria and Fury aren't exactly close to each other by galactic standards. As they walk, Wil says, "You know, it's gonna take a week to get back to Fury. We can make a good-sized dent in *Stargate SG-1*, if you guys are game."

"What's it about?" Bennie asks. After Wil gives him the high-level synopsis, the Brailack makes a gurgling noise. "Gross, they have worms inside them?"

"Mean ones," Wil adds.

"Good morning, I'm Belzar, and I'm here with Megan. Welcome to *Good Morning, GC.*" Belzar turns to another camera. "There's been an interesting development in the debate around droid rights."

Megan picks up the thread. "One of the lead droid committee members has proposed a *droid home world.*"

Belzar grunts. "As you can imagine, the proposal, especially this late in the process as the governing council is nearing a vote, threw the entire assembly into chaos."

Megan adds, "Adding to the chaos is some rather powerful support. Tralgot CEO and senior member of the task force overseeing the dissolution of Farsight Corporation, Barbara Mress, has backed the idea."

Belzar smiles, bearing his numerous razor-sharp teeth. "We'll keep you updated as this story unfolds. Now to Gulbar' Te, who is on Turpin Three covering the annual winter festival and culling. How are things going out there, Gulbar' Te?"

CHAPTER 3_

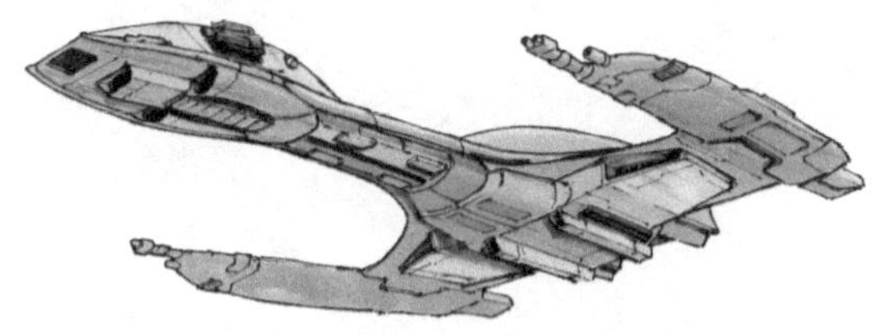

TGIF(URY)_

Bennie raises a glass of grum. "To making money."

Cynthia smiles. "Damn, it feels good to be a gangster."

Wil raises an eyebrow, looking at his girlfriend. "Come again?"

"Isn't that the lyric?" she asks.

Wil snaps his fingers. "Ah, okay. Yes, you got the lyric right. I thought maybe you were thinking of a career change."

Cynthia extends her arms to take in the table. "Been there, done that. Besides, leave all this? Never." Wil smiles.

Maxim reaches for a piece of fried zergling and looks at Cynthia. "Zephyr mentioned that you'd spoken to Ms. Mress recently. Any update on the Farsight stuff?"

Bennie takes a drink. "By *Farsight stuff,* you mean their attempted takeover of the GC with monsters they found thanks to us?"

Maxim stares at his friend. "That's way more words, but sure."

Cynthia grins. "It's mostly good news. The split up is nearly completed. Tralgot, as expected, has come out pretty much on top."

"Shocker," Bennie says around a bite of fried zergling. He continues, "At least that means we won't get tapped to do any more bug hunts for Tralgot." Wil and Maxim nod.

Cynthia continues, "They plan to start the trial, finally, in a few days. They've managed to track down what they believe to be all of the black sites Farsight was using to work on their little genetic experiments." She smiles, revealing her incisors. "They found two shipyards that were building those frigates he used. One was almost done with a battlecruiser. Guess that intel we found on Loquil was legit."

"Shit," Wil says, then takes a long sip of his grum.

Maxim nods. "If he'd had a battlecruiser with that crazy armor and particle beam, things might have turned out very differently."

Zephyr tilts her head. "What'd they do with the ship?" She is pretty sure she knows the answer but has to ask.

Bennie smirks. "One guess."

Cynthia inclines her head. "Yeah, impounded. I'm sure the Peacekeepers will be rolling out their *new* design in a while."

Wil flags down a passing server, pointing at his empty glass. The server nods, her antenna twitching as she does. He looks at the others. "I certainly hope our relationship with Tralgot goes better—"

"And lasts longer—" Zephyr adds.

"— than the one we had with Farsight. I can't believe Asgar turned out to be an evil dickhead. Especially after all that *'Why would I hire you to do extra military missions? Those would be illegal'* stuff he spouted."

"You just wanted to be part of some—gods forgive me—space A-Team," Zephyr says before finishing her own glass of grum.

Wil smiles. "I mean, that'd be awesome, don't lie." His first officer shakes her head.

Gabe, sitting next to Maxim, says, "I would assume operating a para-military organization would not only be even more dangerous than our current lifestyle but would, no offense, Captain, be outside your ability to manage."

"Burn," Bennie says, reaching for the last zergling in the basket.

Wil glares at his small friend, then slaps his arm aside and spears the fried morsel, popping it in his mouth. He chews it loudly, smiling at the now scowling Brailack. "I love it when a plan comes to togeth-er." He winks.

"Excuse me," a voice says from behind Wil. Someone no one notices approaching until he speaks.

The stranger, clad in a brown cloak with its hood up, shadowing the owner's face, pulls a chair from the adjacent table and sits down. He pulls back his cloak to reveal a well-past-middle aged Rigellian man. "Crew of the *Ghost,* I would like to hire you."

A GUY WALKS INTO A BAR_

"Your exploits are quite well known." The older man looks at Wil as he absently strokes his white beard. "Especially for a human. You lot aren't known for your exceptionalism."

Maxim barks out a laugh. Bennie nearly falls backwards in his chair.

"Don't take it personally," Cynthia says, resting a hand on Wil's knee.

Wil looks first at the mysterious old man, then his love interest. "How the hell else should I take it?" He turns back to the old man. "Look pops, I'll have you know that humans are pretty damn exceptional—"

"Not really," Bennie interrupts.

Wil punches him. "—at a lot of things. Things like, you know, saving the galaxy—"

"Well, the Commonwealth, not the whole galaxy," Zephyr interjects.

The old man raises a wrinkled, reddish hand. "I meant no insult, Captain Calder. I have followed your adventures for some time and am truly impressed."

Wil throws his hands up, giving up his defense of the entire human race. He glares at his friends and the mystery man. "Whatever! Who are you? What do you want?"

The older man nods slowly, a friendly smile never leaving his leathery face, his pupil-less eyes a deep purple. "I am Jarek Ruus, Knight of the Order of Plentallus."

Wil stares at the man. He blinks slowly. "I don't know what that is."

Gabe tilts his head, looking at Wil. "Captain, the Knights of Plentallus are an order of warrior monks." He looks to the older man, who nods slowly. "They served as Peacekeepers and statesmen in the early days of the Commonwealth."

"There was a kids vid show when I was young," Bennie says excitedly. "A few of my pouch mates and I would always race home from school—"

Maxim holds up a hand. "You were rich. Wasn't school down the hall?"

Bennie tuts, "It was a long hallway."

Wil growls, "For those who didn't grow up in the GC, can someone tell me what the damn Knights of Pentatonix are?"

Zephyr chimes in, "The Knights of Plentallus are gone." She looks at Jarek Ruus. "Aren't they?"

The robed man spreads his arms as if to say, *yet here I am.* "I have a quest that I require your assistance to complete."

Wil shakes his head. "We don't really do quests."

"A quest sounds fun," Maxim offers.

"I could do a quest. Be a nice change of pace," Zephyr adds.

Cynthia shrugs. "I think you'd look dashing on a quest." She wiggles an eyebrow. "Do you own short pants? A hat with a feather?" Wil flips her off.

Bennie growls, "I had one, until—"

"No one cares about your pimp hat," Wil interrupts.

"Quests are often looked upon as noble endeavors," Gabe offers. "Such an undertaking could be beneficial to our public image."

The old man nods to the droid. "Your mechanical friend isn't wrong. Quests are noble endeavors."

"What's wrong with our public image?" Wil asks. Before Gabe can answer, he turns to Jarek Ruus, sighing, "What's the quest?"

Jarek Ruus reaches one hand into the sleeve of his other arm, withdrawing a card. "I am staying here. Come visit me tonight for a meal and we can discuss the particulars and more history on my order if you still have questions." He doesn't wait for anyone to acknowledge, standing and turning. He walks straight for the door, vanishing into the crowd.

Wil looks at the card, sitting untouched on the table. "Welp, that's a thing that just happened."

Bennie grins. "Should we get costumes?"

Maxim looks at his small friend. "Why would we have costumes?" He looks to Wil. "I don't think anyone has seen a Knight in—" he looks at the others, shrugging, "—decades, at least, probably more."

Zephyr nods. "My parents used to tell me stories about them. They travelled the galaxy keeping the peace, spreading law and order..." She trails off in thought.

Cynthia says, "When I was a kid at the orphanage, we'd tell each other stories about the Knights of Plentallus. The younger kids would run around playing Knights and bad guys."

Wil reaches for the card, still where Jarek Ruus left it, sliding it towards him. "Then I guess we should get ready for dinner."

WALK AND TALK_

"Damn, that oldster is staying in a shit hole part of town," Bennie says after snatching the card from Wil and looking at the address written on it.

"This is Fury," Wil replies. "Everywhere on this planet is a shit hole."

Bennie wags a finger. "No, this," he taps the card, "is the Bulo neighborhood on the south side. Scary place."

Gabe inclines his head. "According to the Peacekeeper database, the Bulo neighborhood is one of the most violent in the city."

Maxim looks at the taller droid. "I forget there's a PK database here. Have they increased the garrison?"

Gabe shakes his head. "No, the garrison is still, according to its commander, understaffed." He looks at the others. "I would suggest we encourage our new client to seek better accommodations."

Cynthia smiles. "Well, he can move aboard the *Ghost* since we're taking the job."

Wil looks at her. "We are, huh?"

"You know you want to." She winks. "Old mystic guy, bet he has cool stories."

Wil stands, snatching the small business card back from Bennie, sliding it into one of his trouser pockets. He waves to the nearest serving droid, who rolls over balancing on a sphere. The droid nods and his wristcomm beeps, showing the bill for their drinks. Wil taps the screen and swipes toward the droid. He turns to the others. "Okay, let's get going."

THE STREETS OF LWATH ARE SLIGHTLY BETTER MAINTAINED than most of the other cities on Fury. Most people thank the Peacekeeper garrison for that, while cursing them for just about everything else.

Wil steps over something. "Yup, pretty sure that's poop."

As the group passes the object, Gabe tilts his head. "In fact, based on my scans, it appears that was not dung but a partially digested—"

"And, no," Zephyr interrupts. Gabe looks at her, closing his mouth.

Maxim points up ahead. "Hey, isn't that the street your shop was on?"

Bennie pushes Wil aside and looks. "Was? I still pay rent on it."

Wil looks down at his friend. "Really? Why?"

Bennie shrugs. "Why wouldn't I? Who knows how long I'll stick around with you losers?"

Zephyr looks down at the short hacker. "Is that something you've thought about? Leaving the crew?"

Everyone turns to look at Bennie as he steps around a food container buzzing with insects. He shrugs and waves a hand dismissively. "Only when you guys annoy me or yell at me." He turns to Wil. "Or hit me."

Cynthia looks at Wil, who shrugs and blurts out, "Hey, I haven't thrown a PADD at him in what? A month?"

Bennie turns to his captain. "You threw a PADD at me three days ago." He rubs his forehead and points to a small darker green bump.

Wil coughs, then looks up the street. "Uh, well, what say we pop in?" He looks at his wristcomm. "We've got time."

Bennie tuts, "Why would I want you krebnacks in my shop? Last time they," he hitches a thumb towards Maxim and Zephyr, "were in my shop, it got shot up by Peacekeepers."

Cynthia smiles. "We're on Fury every few weeks. You haven't gone there since I've been with you all."

Bennie shrugs. "I've been busy. I paid a crew to clean it up shortly after the Harrith thing. They sent pics showing that the job was done. Since then I just keep the rent paid."

Wil picks up his pace. "Let's pop in. I haven't been since you redid the *Ghost's* ident docs. I'd love to see the place again."

As the group rounds the corner, they stop dead in their tracks. Halfway down the side street, about where Bennie's shop is, or was, is a Malkorite fast food restaurant. What used to be a boarded-up storefront with hidden security equipment was now a brightly lit transparisteel entry way.

"Sweet boneless zip zap," Bennie whispers, then shouts, "What the actual grolack!?" He storms off down the street towards the restaurant.

Maxim looks at the others. "This took an unexpected, but likely entertaining, turn."

FAST CASUAL_

THE DOOR of the restaurant slams open. The computerized chime that announces guests chirps, followed by a burst of static. Everyone in the dining room turns to look at the fuming Brailack silhouetted in the doorway.

"What the ever loving grolack is this!?"

A young Malkorite woman walks over. "Hello, this is the Blossoming Goji, a fast casual dining establishment." She tilts her head, still smiling wide. "Just you for dinner?"

Bennie makes a low growling noise. "No, no not just me for dinner." He takes a step toward the young hostess. "This is my shop. Why the grolack is there a grolacking Malkorite restaurant where my shop is supposed to be?"

The door opens again, allowing Wil and the others to enter. Cynthia takes in the scene. Most of the customers are staring at their irate friend. "Bennie, I have to admit your shop is nicer than I expected." Wil elbows her.

Bennie jumps up and slaps the stack of menus from the hostess' hands. "This is my shop!" he screams.

Maxim turns to Gabe. "I think he might explode."

Gabe nods. "He appears to be far angrier than I have ever witnessed."

"Sir, please," the hostess says, then jumps to the side as Bennie storms past her.

Wil walks over and picks up the menus. "Table for five, please."

Zephyr looks at Wil sideways. "What're you doing? We're on our way to have dinner with our client. Remember?"

Wil snaps his fingers, looking over the menus before handing them back to the hostess. "That's right, sorry. We'll take three—" He looks around at the others. "—Four orders of Crispy Yipsee Strips. To go."

There's a crash from somewhere further in the restaurant, followed by Bennie screaming, "Where is my stuff?" The hostess flinches, looking over her shoulder.

Bennie storms out of the kitchen, followed by an older Malkorite man. He shouts, "I hired you to put the place back together!"

The Malkorite stammers, "Yes, well, after we did, your landlord informed us that due to the Peacekeeper action and several other noise-related issues, he wasn't going to allow you to remain a tenant. We knew you were out of the system and your stuff looked really expensive, so we set up the restaurant so your landlord wouldn't evict you."

Bennie stops. Turning slowly, he asks, "So where the grolack is my stuff?" His hands are clenched into fists, tiny green fists.

The other man exhales. "Oh, we moved it to a storage unit near the spaceport."

Still standing in the entryway, Zephyr leans against Maxim. "This was weird, but certainly could have been wo—"

"The spaceport?" Bennie howls before leaping onto the face of the surprised Malkorite man. He rains small blows down on the man, whose screams are drowned out by Bennie's own howls. With one hand holding a large ear, the other continues to beat the larger man.

Maxim looks at his partner. "And there it is." He walks over to the flailing Malkorite and plucks Bennie off of the man. He looks down. "Please forgive him. If you could forward the details for the storage unit, we'd appreciate it."

The hostess rushes over to help her boss smooth his shirt. The man nods vigorously. "Yes, of course."

Bennie is still struggling in Maxim's grip. The big man shakes the small Brailack until he settles.

Wil looks at Cynthia. "Think he'll realize he's been paying their rent?" he whispers.

She smacks him on the back of the head. "Say nothing." She grabs Wil's elbow and turns for the door. "Gabe." The droid nods and opens the door.

As the Palorians and Bennie exit the restaurant, Wil looks at Cynthia. "We're not waiting for the Crispy Yipsee Strips, are we?" She shakes her head.

Maxim puts Bennie down and stares at him. "You okay?"

Bennie waves his big friend off. "Whatever, let's go."

NEWSCAST_

"Good evening, I'm Mon-el Furash live from the trial of disgraced Farsight Corporation CEO Jark Asgar." She takes a breath. "Today has been informational as the prosecution revealed what I can only assume will be ultimately damning evidence against Farsight. Allegedly, they've been experimenting on living beings that until recently were unknown to the GC at large." She looks over her shoulder at the polished marble building looming over her. "Tomorrow morning, the defense begins their cross examination of Tralgot Corporation CEO Barbara Mress. Miss Mress has been overseeing the dismantling of many of Farsight's operations and was the one to reveal these most recent crimes."

After a pause as she listens to someone in the studio, Mon-el says, "Yes, actually Prathia, a senior researcher and part of the team that discovered, and ultimately defeated the dreadnaught that rampaged through the GC a few cycles, gave a very damning testimony of her until recently employer." She listens some more, "I'm told she has accepted a research appointment with an undisclosed think tank."

CHAPTER 4_

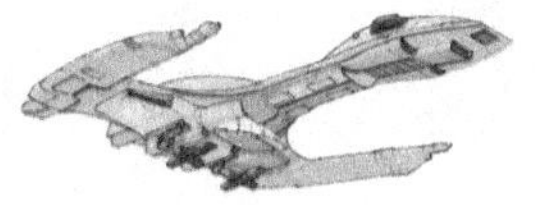

SOMETHING_

"I DON'T THINK I've ever been to this part of town," Wil says as the group turns a corner onto the street of the inn that Jarek Ruus is staying in.

"That's because this side of town is gross and smells like butt," Bennie gripes. "I had a client here for a few cycles, hated coming to visit her." He rubs his hands together. "But the pay and the perks were worth the risks."

"You're truly a lech," Wil says, looking at his small, green-skinned friend.

Cynthia looks around, kicking a piece of trash out of their path. "What's so bad about it? I mean, other than the smell." She wrinkles her nose. "That is foul."

Gabe says, "Based on the Peacekeeper database, this particular neighborhood has been exceptionally difficult to pacify." His head slowly pans from side to side. "Several semi-organized gangs have proven to be exceptionally entrenched. The Peacekeeper garrison commander has noted that he has lost more troops in these few square kilometers than any other part of the city."

Wil whistles. "It definitely has a war-torn vibe going." They walk past a burnt-out storefront streaked with soot. What might have been high priced entertainment consoles now litter the interior as melted lumps.

A group of beings, mostly Olop, comes around the corner up ahead. Maxim makes a noise that draws everyone's attention forward, except Bennie, who walks right into the backside of Zephyr. As he splutters, she swats him away until Gabe grabs his hairless, green head and directs it forward to see the potential threat ahead of them.

Wil takes a few steps forward, making sure to brush the sides of his long duster aside, revealing his pulse pistols. "Hey, fellas." He takes in the group. "Shoot, sorry, and lady." He nods to a surly-looking Quilant woman, her fleshy whiskers tattooed in bright pink ink. She grunts.

An Olop man, his facial fur dyed in patterns like a tattoo, steps forward. "You all look lost."

Before Wil can reply, Gabe says, "We are, in fact, not lost. Our destination is another two point seven blocks from here."

Wil wipes a hand down his face, sighing. He says, "Uh, yeah, what he said, not lost and almost there."

The leader shrugs. "Well, that's good. Directions are expensive, but only a little less than tolls." He grins, revealing a disturbing lack of teeth.

Maxim growls from just behind Wil. Wil smiles. "Look, friend, this won't end well and we really do have someplace to be." Wil hears the metallic shifting of gears and panels that means that Gabe is engaging combat mode, his forearms opening and shifting to free, powerful plasma blasters.

Cynthia asks, "Who's your lieutenant?" The question takes the gang leader by surprise, but then he gestures to another Olop, this one similarly hair dye tattooed. She nods. "Gabe." The leader's head snaps back, a single plasma burn in his forehead. As the gang leader falls to the ground, Cynthia says, "You just got a promotion. Use it wisely."

The new gang leader snaps his little furry fingers and makes a circle motion with one hand in the air. As a group, the dozen street toughs turn and head back the way they came.

Wil turns to look first at Cynthia, then Gabe. "Uh, have you two worked out some type of ninja assassin kill signals for occasions like this?"

Cynthia walks away, continuing on course for the inn. She looks over her shoulder. "No, that'd be silly. How could we foresee being set upon by thugs?"

Gabe, now back in his everyday non-combat mode, adds, "Correct. Our pre-arranged signals are far less specific in nature."

Zephyr's eyes widen and she looks at Maxim as they move to follow Cynthia.

Bennie, who has until now been silent, walks past the dead gang leader and looks up at Gabe. "Good shot."

"Of course." The droid dips his head.

Zephyr looks at Maxim. "Maybe we can find someplace to set up a vacation home." The big man chuckles.

THIS PLACE IS GROSS_

"Huh. I didn't expect it to look like that," Wil says, nodding toward the building in front of them.

"What did you expect?" Cynthia asks, looking from Wil to the five-story stone building in front of them. Windows are evenly spaced along the face of the bland building, ratty curtains visible in many.

Wil shrugs. "I dunno, two stories, thatched roof, cute little sign hanging outside."

Maxim quirks a jet-black eyebrow. "Like in that vid series? The one with the people who ride domesticated livestock and fight with swords?"

Wil shrugs and walks toward the doors.

The lobby of the inn is a spacious, and probably at one time luxurious, area with sofas and chairs, a crystal chandelier casting rainbow shards around the room. Now, however, it's poorly lit and mostly empty. A lone droid stands in the center of the room next to a pile of trash. The doors open, allowing Wil and the crew to enter the droid's optic sensors come to life. "Greetings. Do you require lodging?" It doesn't approach them or in any way move. Wil notices that one of its feet is bolted to the floor.

Wil approaches the droid. "No, we're here to see one of your guests, a mister—"

The droid points to a short hallway at the back of the dilapidated lobby. "The lifts are there." Before Wil can even reply, the optic receptors dim.

"Uh, thanks," Wil replies and turns toward the lifts. The others follow on his heels.

Bennie looks around the space. "Well, this place has seen better days." He looks up at the skeletal remains of the chandelier, now devoid of any crystal pieces. "Sheesh."

THE LIFT DOORS PART ON THE FOURTH FLOOR. ZEPHYR IS OUT OF the lift first. "We're taking the stairs when we leave. Holy wurrin, that was terrifying."

Maxim and Cynthia follow, the feline-featured woman nodding, "Yeah, I haven't been that scared in a long time. How is that thing even in service?"

Bennie walks out behind Maxim. "Because, like I said, this neighborhood sucks and is terrible." He hitches a thumb over his shoulder as the lift doors stutter closed. "Case in point."

Wil looks up and down the hall, then consults the card Jarek Ruus left with them. He points to the right. "This way, I think." The others follow. Zephyr looks back at the lift doors, shuddering as she does.

The door to Jarek Ruus' room is dented, and there is a brownish stain near the top. Wil looks up at the stain, then presses the announcer button.

Cynthia's tail swishes behind her. "We might need to go through a decon shower when we leave here." Bennie bobs his head in agreement.

The door slides into the wall as far as the dent, which stops it in its tracks. The robed Jarek Ruus is in the doorway. "You've decided to take the job." It's not a question.

Wil raises an eyebrow at the half open door. "Yeah, what say we get the hell out of this place and discuss the particulars?"

"Why are you staying in this dren heap?" Bennie asks, looking up and down the hallway, his hand resting on his small pulse pistol.

Jarek turns, heading back into this room. He motions for them to follow. "My order eschews frivolous expenses."

Cynthia tuts, "I'd hardly call safety a frivolous expense."

The older man waves a dismissive hand. "I can take care of myself."

Bennie is the last to enter and presses the door control. When nothing happens, he presses it repeatedly. The door slides shut with a whine.

Jarek busies himself at the small dresser under a window that is scratched and scuffed so badly it is nearly impossible to see through. He looks over his shoulder. "I trust you had no problems finding this place."

Wil ignores the question. "Why don't you tell us a bit more about this quest of yours."

Maxim holds a hand up. "Uh, sorry to cut you off, Mr. Ruus, but is that smoke?" He points to the air vent near the ceiling.

IS THAT SMOKE?_

"I think it's Sir Knight," Wil says as he turns to look at the vent. He turns back to the others. "Yeah, this probably isn't good." Gray smoke is puffing out of the vent and spreading across the ceiling.

Gabe tilts his head to the ceiling. "We should evacuate immediately. That smoke is sixty-three percent loridian dichloride."

"Oh, dren," Bennie mumbles.

Wil turns to Gabe. "I don't know what that—"

"Someone in this drenhole is making trephlinium," Bennie replies, walking to the door. "Poorly," he adds.

"Boost?" Maxim says, turning to follow his small friend. "Yeah, we gotta go." Zephyr moves to follow him.

Jarek Ruus closes his travel bag and nods his head. "I am ready to go."

As Bennie reaches for the door control, the building shakes and a muffled thump reverberates through the floor. Bennie stumbles and falls against the door, swearing. He presses the control, which beeps pleasantly then makes a sort of gurgling, mechanical grinding noise. The door doesn't move. Bennie swears colorfully. "And that would be their lab exploding."

Maxim not very gently pushes his small friend aside, planting his palms on the surface, straining to push the door into its pocket. It doesn't budge.

Wil looks at Cynthia. "Boost sounds familiar." The smoke from the vent is thickening. It smells sweet.

She nods. "It's an accelerant; heightens your reflexes and overall neural processing. Briefly."

Zephyr adds, "The crash is horrible. Ground pounders in the Peacekeepers are known to dose right before they hit the ground." She looks at the stuffed window, adding, "They fight like nightmares until they don't. The hope is that by the time they crash, the fight is over."

"It's also highly addictive," Maxim says.

"Space meth," Wil says, turning quickly so he can't see Zephyr's face.

Gabe moves to the door, pushing Maxim aside. As he does, both of his arms shift, whirring and clicking as they increase in size. He rests his hands on the door, then flexes his fingers, digging them into the metal. A loud groan fills the room before the door crumples and is pulled out of its frame. Masonry rains down from the ruined frame. Gabe turns and rests the door against the wall, extending a hand to the opening. "We should go." The whirring noise returns as his arms reconfigure to their normal size.

As they file out into the hall, an alarm begins to bleat. Zephyr looks at the small unit in the ceiling, its strobe light flickering. "That probably should have started a few minutes ago."

Doors up and down the hallway slide open. Maxim and Zephyr draw their pulse pistols. A few random heads pop out of the open doorways, looking around. Maxim, in the lead of the group shouts, "Everyone out!"

Aliens of various races begin filing out ahead of and behind the crew. Wil is behind Jarek Ruus, his hand on the elder man's shoulder. Smoke is flowing in from most of the open doorways. The building shakes again, eliciting several screams.

"These people are seriously sketchy," Bennie says from beside

Wil. The short Brailack is next to a Kilden that doesn't look like she's bathed in a few weeks. The fleshy quills along the top of her head are matted.

Wil shushes him, waving a hand at him, then nods. "Do we know where the stairs are?" An unruly crowd has formed at the elevator.

Gabe tilts his head. "Interesting. In fact, there is no stairwell." He turns to the others. "That seems like a safety violation."

"I hate this neighborhood!" Bennie grates.

Jarek Ruus turns toward the nearest open door. "Come with me, please." He doesn't wait. Once everyone is inside the room, a room in considerably worse shape than the one Jarek Ruus was previously occupying, he turns to Gabe. "Mister robot, please close the door."

Gabe turns to the door, his arms bulking up once more. He grips the edge of the door and pulls it into place. His arms shift back to their normal size. Everyone stares until he says, "What? Is something on me?"

Jarek Ruus paces the room, then stops in the very center. Wil looks at Maxim, who shrugs and looks at Zephyr, who also shrugs.

Wil turns to Jarek Ruus. "Uh, Mr. Ruus, Sir Knight?"

There's a loud snap-hiss sound, and the smell of the highly toxic smoke is temporarily replaced with the smell of burnt ozone. A bright white light fills the room. Jarek Ruus turns to face the crew of the *Ghost*.

Wil stares, his mouth hanging open. Bennie nudges Wil. "I've been waiting to watch your face." He holds his wristcomm up, snapping a picture of Wil.

Wil ignores his green friend, breathing out in a whisper, "Lightsaber."

BREAKING BAD_

Ruus spins the sword to point blade down and drops to a knee, plunging the blade into the floor. The duracrete of the floor bubbles and melts around the blade, hissing as it does. The older man moves the blade in a slow circle with him in the center. The moment before he completes the circle, he stands and steps out. The circular section of the floor falls to the level below with a resounding crash. With another snap-hiss, the blade vanishes. Jarek looks at the others. "What?"

"You have a lightsaber!" Wil shouts as he rushes over to the older man, reaching out to touch the hilt still held in Ruus' hand.

The older man sidesteps Wil, slapping aside his hand. "No touching." He doesn't wait for anyone else to say anything before dropping through the hole, his robes fluttering, the edges of the hole still glowing red hot.

Wil looks at the others then follows the older man to the level below. The others all exchange a look before single file dropping through the hole in the floor.

Gabe comes through the hole last, lowering slowly on the repulsors in his feet. As he sets down, the building shudders again. "Captain, I believe the drug lab, wherever it is, has thoroughly destabilized this building. That was a secondary explosion."

Cynthia moves to the room's door, pressing the activator. As the door slides open, she says, "At least half the chemicals that go into making boost are highly volatile."

The door opens to reveal another corridor in chaos. This floor must have more guests than the one above. Smoke is filling the hallway.

As the building shudders again, Gabe says, "Given the shoddy upkeep and likely subpar construction, there is at least a fifty-five percent chance this building will collapse."

Wil looks at the others and coughs, covering his mouth. Through his hand he says, "We have to get all these folks out of here." He points at Gabe. "Go back up and get them down the hole." Turning to Jarek Ruus, "Okay, mister Jedi cosplay, new hole—" he points a few feet from where the hole above is, "—there." The older man nods and walks to the indicated location, his sword igniting. Wil whispers to himself, "So cool." Gabe walks under the hole above them and lifts off, his amplified voice calling for attention.

Wil turns to Maxim, "You stay on this floor, help lower folks down." The big Palorian nods. Wil looks at Jarek. "Can you levitate people?"

The man raises a bushy gray eyebrow. "No. That sounds silly." He drops to the level below, his not-a-lightsaber still humming.

"Cynthia and I can take the next floor; you and Bennie get them out of the building," Zephyr says between coughing fits.

Wil nods and pushes Bennie toward the hole leading to the second floor of the increasingly unstable inn. From above comes the sound of coughing and worried voices, mixed with Gabe's amplified and reassuring monotone. Cynthia and Zephyr follow Bennie and Wil as Maxim reaches up to assist the first pair of legs that begins to dangle from above.

Wil and Bennie waste no time on the second floor, dropping down through the still glowing hole left by Jarek Ruus. When they join the old man on the first floor, they're in what must be a manager's office, or was, before the lone droid was placed in the lobby. Wil points to Bennie, then Jarek Ruus. "You two help get folks outside. I'm guessing that scary-ass elevator will have a few folks in it, as well." Bennie nods, and the two head out just as a pair of legs with hooves at the end begins to dangle from the floor above. Cynthia shouts down, "Incoming."

By the time any type of civil authorities arrives, most of the building is evacuated. A droid painted red with white stripes on its arms approaches. "Hello, I am JX-15033, Lwath civil safety commander. I understand you and your people were instrumental in evacuating most of the building."

Wil nods. "Yup. You're welcome. Took you a while to get here."

The droid inclines its triangular head. "Indeed. It seems that whomever was using the suite on the third floor as a boost lab hacked the building's safety systems. Most of them were disabled or rerouted."

"GOOD EVENING, I'm Mon-el Furash. The proposal for a droid home world, an idea many thought would scuttle the droid rights movement, has been approved." She turns to a different camera pick up, her ear jewelry clinking. "While not unanimous, the proposal carried the day with an overwhelming majority. The governing council is expected to hold its formal vote on the full droid rights issue tomorrow. I'm here on Tarsis and will keep you posted."

CHAPTER 5_

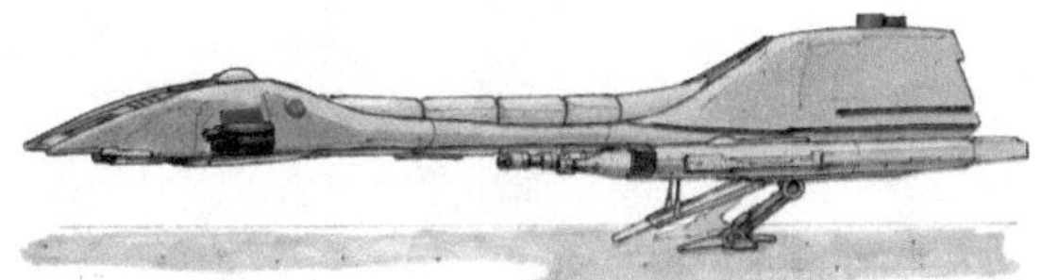

WELCOME ABOARD_

THE STREET IS DARK, most of the illumination towers broken or missing. The group has been walking for a few minutes, the smoking ruin of the inn barely visible over the tops of nearby buildings.

"Okay, so you have a lightsaber, wear a cloak, are mysterious, but can't move things with your mind." Wil sums up his understanding of what a Knight of Plentallus is. The crew is walking back to the Lwath spaceport with their client.

Jarek Ruus peers at Wil from inside the hood of his cloak. He reaches a hand inside the sleeve of his other arm, removing a flask. After taking a long sip and replacing the flask in his sleeve, he says, "It is a beam saber. Cloaks are common." He points to a woman walking the opposite direction as them. She looks up and scowls, drawing the hood closer about her face. Ruus continues, "Moving things with my mind sounds like vidplay material. No one in real life can do that." He moves his hand to draw back his cloak, exposing the hilt of his beam saber. "This is the weapon of my order. It emits a beam of super charged high-density plasma. The focal length is regulated by a—"

"Khyber crystal?" Wil interrupts.

"No, by a complex internal mechanism that takes months to assemble," the older man replies.

"Sounds more or less like a lightsaber," Wil replies.

From the front of the group Maxim looks back. "Except your thing is a prop from a vidplay from Earth and his is, you know, real."

Wil waves a dismissive hand. "It can cut through anything?"

Jarek Ruus nods slowly. "Most things. It is meant to be a defensive weapon more than anything. Also, it is a badge of office. Only those who complete their training are given a beam saber."

Wil nods, lost in thought. "Cool, cool. So how many Knights of Pentaurus are there?"

"Plentallus," the older man corrects, then adds, "Not many. No new initiates have entered the order in several tens of cycles."

Cynthia whistles. "Why is that?"

The group turns a corner that is clearly the boundary of two neighborhoods. The light poles are working and regularly spaced, and there is a visible difference in the amount of trash on the sidewalk. Bennie releases a dramatic sigh as they make the turn.

Jarek turns to Cynthia. "Lack of interest, I'd guess. Most people don't even remember that we exist. The Peacekeepers more or less erased our existence and accomplishments from the public record." He glances to Zephyr, who is behind him with Wil. "No offense."

Maxim looks over his shoulder. "Ex-Peacekeepers."

Cynthia chuckles, then says, "That seems sad."

The older man nods, "It is, my dear. I'm one of the last."

THE *GHOST'S* CARGO RAMP WHINES AS IT RAISES. THE PEDESTAL next to the heavy cargo bay doors beeps as the heavy doors slide toward each other. Wil looks around. "Okay, let's regroup in the lounge in a few. We can eat and get the low-down from our client here." He points to Jarek Ruus. "I'll show you to the guest berths." He turns to the others. "I can't recall whose turn it is, but can someone get a dinner started?" Maxim and Cynthia nod as Wil extends a hand to the stairwell that leads up and out of the cargo hold.

Maxim looks at Cynthia. "I'm pretty sure it's his turn." She smiles.

DINNER AND HISTORY_

Jarek Ruus walks out of the corridor containing the crew and guest berths into the lounge area. He's left his traveling cloak in his quarters and is clad in rough canvas trousers tucked into almost knee-high boots. A loose canvas shirt tucked in and covered by a leather vest completes his look. On his hip, the now-familiar hilt of his beam saber. He smiles at the crew all sitting around the dining table. "Dinner smells lovely."

Cynthia smiles and points to an empty spot next to Bennie. "Your quarters okay?"

Sitting next to the small Brailack, the older man nods. "Indeed, quite nice, particularly after my recent accommodations."

"In that drenhole inn in the worst possible part of town," Bennie offers, then yelps when someone kicks him under the table. He looks around before settling on Wil growling.

Wil gets up and moves to the refrigeration unit. "Grum?"

Jarek Ruus nods. "Please."

Maxim has his back to the others. "I'm almost done, another ten centocks at most."

Zephyr inhales. "Can't wait." She turns to their client. "Why don't you tell us a little more about your quest?"

Wil leans forward. "Has a Knight of Pentalobe fallen to the dark side?"

Jarek Ruus gives Wil a flat stare before replying, "Plentallus, and I don't know what that means. The dark side of what?" He is about to let Wil answer when he sees Cynthia roll her eyes and shake her head slightly. He continues, "As I mentioned, we have not had a new initiate in the order in several tens of cycles. I am old, most of my fellow Knights are old. We would like to leave a complete memory of our deeds for the galaxy to learn from."

Bennie looks up at the older man. "So what? You want like a film crew? Ghostwriters?"

The man takes a sip of his grum. "No. The histories are recorded, but lost. I need help finding them."

"What happened to them?" Wil asks before taking a sip of drink.

Jarek Ruus sighs and downs the rest of his bottle of grum, wiping his mouth on his sleeve. "As our order fell out of favor during the rise of the Peacekeepers, our elders thought it best to move our memory archives around the galaxy to ensure they did not fall into the wrong hands."

Maxim turns, large skillet in hand. "Whose hands would those be?" He begins distributing the contents of his skillet to a serving platter in the center of the table.

Jarek Ruus looks at the big Peacekeeper. "Again, no offense, but the Peacekeepers and their Tarsi masters."

Maxim turns to put the skillet back on the cooktop. "None taken. Like I said earlier, ex-Peacekeepers."

Zephyr nods. "We've seen enough of the real side of the GC and Peacekeepers to not want anything to do with them."

Jarek Ruus nods. "Indeed. We knew that if the Peacekeepers got their hands on our archives, they'd be even more dangerous. The archives contain our training methods, everything you need to build a beam saber, and so much more."

Maxim joins them at the table, sitting next to Zephyr. "That makes sense. I assume something went wrong?"

"Indeed. Exactly what isn't known. That's part of my quest. Several archives have been missing for hundreds of cycles. The Knights assigned to protect them went silent."

"A geek chase," Bennie says.

"Goose chase," Wil corrects, reaching for the serving spoon and indicating that everyone should hold their plates up. As he begins doling out the steaming pile of noodles and meat of some kind, he continues, "I'm guessing you're thinking of visiting the last known locations of these missing Knights?"

Placing his full plate on the table, Jarek Ruus nods. "Yes. Each Knight reported in regularly, until, well, they stopped. We know where they were when they stopped. More or less."

"More or less," Zephyr echoes.

Bennie asks around a mouthful of food, "So what? You want to hire us to traipse around the GC looking for likely long dead Knights and whatever your memory trinkets look like?"

"That's about the gist of it, yes," Jarek Ruus replies. He adds, "I have been assigned three archives that are believed to be relatively close to each other."

"How many Knights are left?" Cynthia asks.

Jarek Ruus looks at her, then his plate. "This is delicious. Maxim, what do you call it?"

MAPS FOR DUMMIES_

THE NEXT MORNING, Wil walks out of the refresher in the corner of the quarters he shares with Cynthia. "So this should be interesting," he says, ruffling his brown hair to dry it.

She pulls up her jumpsuit, zipping it. "I'll admit I'm intrigued. Like I said, I've known the story of the Knights of Plentallus since I was a kid. Meeting one is a big enough deal, but helping one on a quest—a quest that helps their order." She taps her chin. "Fantastic." She reaches down and picks up Wil's nearly matching jumpsuit, offering it to him.

He takes it and gets dressed. "I just can't believe he has a lightsaber."

Cynthia winks at him. "You know it's not called that."

"I do, but I have nearly twenty movies' worth of lightsaber references in my brain. It's going to take some reprogramming." He grins. "Maybe we can watch some of the older *Star Wars* movies while in FTL sometime, see what our guest thinks."

Cynthia groans. "Lucky him."

"Good morning, Captain," Gabe says as Wil and Cynthia walk into the crew lounge area. Gabe and Jarek Ruus are in the entertainment area, the latter reclining in the overstuffed chair. "Mr. Ruus and I have been discussing the history of the Galactic Commonwealth. Would you like to join us?"

Wil looks at the two of them as he continues toward the coffee machine, now configured to produce chlormax. As the machine burbles and clunks, he says, "Uh, thanks, but I'll pass. How long have you been up?" He gestures toward Jarek Ruus.

The older man smiles. "Several hours now. I am old, Captain. Old people don't need much sleep."

"So my Grandma Clara used to tell me," Wil says as the machine fills his chipped *Denver—Mile High City* mug.

"As you know, Captain, I do not require—" Gabe starts.

Wil waves him off. "Yeah, I know." He drops into the sofa and looks at their client, dressed in the same outfit as the night before. "We'll take off once everyone is up." He turns to Gabe. "Speaking of, mind doing the wake-up calls?" The droid nods and heads for the corridor of berths at the aft section. Wil turns back to Ruus. "I assume you have a first destination in mind?"

The other man nods. "I do. I think it would make the most sense to visit Perolerra Four. Sir Gelflux Prenta was living there, and as far as the order knows, he had established himself in the community, so we should have an easier time finding clues."

Wil sips his chlormax, then says, "I'm not familiar with the Perolerra system."

"It's in the Expanse," the other man says, as if that is explanation enough.

From the hallway there is a grunt. "Great, more ass ends of things." It's Bennie. He walks straight for the kitchenette and the coffee machine.

Wil watches his little friend, then says, "What's the Expanse?"

Cynthia and Zephyr walk in with Gabe. Cynthia says, "The

Expanse? That where we're going?" She looks at Jarek Ruus. He nods. "Great," she says without enthusiasm.

Wil waits a few seconds, then says, "Will someone please tell me what the god damned Expanse is?"

Bennie plops down next to him, sloshing chlormax on his leg. Before Wil can complain, the small hacker says, "The Expanse is the area on the opposite side of the GC as we are right now."

Wil holds up his hand as Cynthia and Zephyr come over to the seating area, each with a coffee cup in hand. "Wait. I mean, I've been around a while—how is there *another side*?" He looks around. "Isn't it a sphere?"

Maxim walks in and Zephyr says, "About time. How do you take longer to get dressed than I do?" The big man ignores her and walks to the kitchen. "What're we talking about?"

"We're going into the Expanse," Bennie says before anyone else can answer.

"Fun," Maxim says, joining them.

Gabe points to the large entertainment screen, which comes to life, a star map of the Galactic Commonwealth displayed. "Captain, perhaps this will help?" A large green *you are here* appears.

Wil looks around as everyone chuckles. "Funny."

Several sections of the map highlight as Gabe explains, "The Expanse, as it is commonly called, is a span of several lightyears galactic west of our current location. There are far fewer systems in the region, making it far less populated than other sections of the Commonwealth."

Bennie nods. "Like I said, ass end of the GC." He takes a sip.

Gabe continues, "This openness is why it is called the Expanse. It can take weeks to travel between systems."

ASS KICKINGS FOR EVERYONE_

Once the *Ghost* is underway, everyone splits up with tasks of their own to work on. Jarek Ruus is on the bridge, and when Wil puts the flight controls in standby, letting the auto flight system manage things, he says, "I noticed what looked like a sparring mat down in your cargo hold. Would it be okay if I availed myself of your facilities? Is there a sparring droid or anything like that?"

Maxim turns, a mischievous look on his face. "Who needs a sparring droid? I'll spar with you. I promise not to hurt you." He grins.

The older man bows, extending an arm to the bridge hatch. "Let us go then, mister *ex-Peacekeeper*."

Bennie jumps out his chair. "I'm offering odds on the Palorian." He follows Maxim and Ruus out into the neck that joins the bridge and forward section to the larger secondary hull.

Cynthia tuts as she puts her station into standby mode. Wil watches all this, then follows Cynthia out.

The sparring mat in the cargo hold was installed by Maxim and Zephyr after Wil brought them on as crew. It is not anything fancy, a padded mat a few meters square. Against the nearest wall is a small rack of practice weapons: bokken, padded bo staffs, and a few unpadded weapons that Cynthia and Zephyr prefer.

Wil and the rest of the crew are standing around the edge of the mat watching Maxim stretch. Wil leans over to Cynthia. "So, does he have a chance?"

She turns. "Maxim? No, none."

Wil stares. "Did you put money down?"

She doesn't blink. "You're damn right."

Maxim looks at Jarek Ruus. "Ready?" The other man nods, tossing the big Palorian a bokken.

Bennie shouts, "Last chance to place a bet!"

Zephyr, standing next to him, looks down. "Uh, there are four of us here. No shouting needed." Bennie scowls.

Maxim moves in slowly, twirling his bokken expertly. Jarek Ruus moves toward the center of the mat equally slowly. Both men bow, and before they have straightened, Maxim attacks, unleashing a flurry of swift blows. Each attack is swept aside with what looks like little effort on the part of Jarek Ruus. The older man seems content to counter the much larger Palorian man's moves rather than attack.

Wil raises an eyebrow, watching as Jarek Ruus deflects every attack Maxim presses against him. Just when Wil is beginning to think Ruus' primary strategy is defense, the much older man turns the tables on his big Palorian opponent. Maxim grunts as the older man's first strike lands on Maxim's unprotected shoulder, followed quicker than Wil can follow by a blow to Maxim's ribcage.

Cynthia tilts her head, whispering, "Watch this."

Jarek Ruus jumps over a leg strike Maxim lashes out with and jabs the big man with the end of his bokken, right in the midsection. Maxim grunts, then growls. He grips his wooden sword with both hands and launches into an aggressive series of slashes aimed at his opponent's upper body. Jarek Ruus dances away from the attack, alternating between deflecting the blows and dodging them. As Maxim moves into a swing, Ruus' bokken whistles before striking

Maxim in the ribs. It doesn't stop moving as he ducks, sliding the sword along Maxim's body, bringing it up in an elegant arc that connects with Maxim's chin. The Palorian grunts again and topples backward.

"Damnit!" Bennie shouts.

Jarek Ruus extends a hand to help Maxim up. "You fight well, Maxim."

"Patronizer," the big man growls but reluctantly smiles. "The reputation your order carries is clearly well earned."

Jarek Ruus nods, then turns to the others. "Would anyone else like to spar now that I am warmed up?"

Zephyr steps into the ring, sliding her toe under Maxim's bokken, kicking it into the air to grab it. Jarek Ruus bows to his opponent, then assumes a ready pose.

Zephyr lasts slightly longer than her partner, having learned from Maxim's bout. In the end, she ends up on the mat after taking a solid blow to her shoulder that spins her about before Jarek Ruus connects with her midsection twice with savage jabs.

"That was exhilarating. Thank you," Jarek Ruus says, helping Zephyr back to her feet.

She smiles. "I look forward to sparring more. I have a lot to learn."

"I am at your disposal." He looks at the three remaining crew. "Anyone else?"

Wil holds both hands up, backing away from the mat. "They," he points to the two Palorians, "wipe the mat with me. Hard pass."

Cynthia looks around, then steps onto the mat.

ASSASSIN VS. SPACE KNIGHT_

Cynthia bows to her opponent, her tail lazily swishing behind her. Unlike Maxim and Zephyr, she doesn't rush in with an attack, choosing to circle Jarek Ruus. The older man circles in the opposite direction, his bokken held ready in one hand. Maxim is standing next to Wil. "Think she'll do better than we did?"

Wil looks up at his friend. "I mean, it'd be hard to do worse." He flinches as Maxim snaps his arm out as if he is about to punch Wil. He tuts when Wil flinches.

Mid-step, Jarek Ruus springs, somehow jumping while one foot is still in the air. Cynthia reacts faster than Wil can even process what is happening, leaning back on her single-planted foot. She is mid-step, as well, but doesn't waste a split second, dropping backward. Jarek Ruus' bokken whistles past over her head. A split second after the wooden blade sails over her head, she lashes out with a slashing attack. It connects with Jarek Ruus' ribs, not as powerfully, as if she were standing and had both feet on the ground but still enough to cause the older man to grunt and stagger backwards. She lets her momentum continue to push her to the ground but uses her tail and free hand to roll herself into a crouch. She looks over to Wil and winks.

Wil looks up at Maxim. "She's so hot."

The big man scoffs, "How has she not broken you in two already?"

Wil grins. "She tries. I'm bendy."

"You're fat."

Wil looks down at his midsection. "I'm padded."

The big Palorian groans, "I do not need to hear more."

On the mat, Jarek Ruus is defending against a storm of wooden sword blows. He's working harder than Wil has seen him work so far. Cynthia performs a powerful overhead attack that drives the much older man back, but as he steps back to deflect, he tilts to the side, letting her bokken slide off his before he spins quickly. He lets his own wooden sword connect with her forearm, causing her to drop her bokken.

He steps back, striking a ready stance. "You are quite skilled. Where did you learn?"

Cynthia slips her foot under her bokken, kicking it up and catching it, turning to a ready stance, bowing. "I've had an interesting life." She smiles. She turns to Bennie. "By the way, you owe me," she taps her chin, "three thousand credits." The small Brailack growls. Jarek Ruus extends a hand to take Cynthia's bokken. She hands it over. "That was exhilarating, thank you." She turns to walk to Wil.

As Jarek Ruus places the practice swords back on the rack, Wil slips his hand around Cynthia's waist. "I don't know what you losers are doing, but we'll be back in a bit." He guides Cynthia towards the stairwell that leads up and out of the cargo hold.

Bennie walks up to Jarek Ruus. "How long do you guys train to fight like that? Is there a height requirement to be a Knight of Plentallus?"

The older man smiles and kneels so that he is looking Bennie in the eyes. "My small friend, one of the greatest Knights was shorter than you, interestingly, and also green." The older man looks down and is silent. After a few heartbeats, he looks at Bennie. "The training to be a Knight never ends. We train whenever we can so that we are always ready when needed."

Bennie nods, deep in thought.

PART TWO

CHAPTER 6_

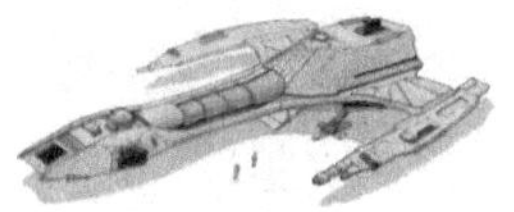

FIRST STOP: CRAPPY SAND PLANET_

"Is this whole planet desert?" Maxim asks from his station as the planet Perolerra Four rotates on the main display screen.

Jarek Ruus, standing near the bridge hatch answers, "As far as I know, yes."

"We're being hailed," Cynthia says, a hand to her ear, the small transceiver in it filled with the voice of a space control operator.

Wil points to the screen, and a second later it changes from the view of the planet to a being covered in blue-tinted iridescent scales. The creature on the screen licks its eye with a long pink tongue, then says, "Please indicate your purpose."

Wil smiles. "Hi there. We're here looking for an old friend." He looks around, then adds, "We come in peace." Zephyr groans.

The being on the screen blinks rapidly. "That information pleases. Please proceed to the coordinates I designate." The screen goes black, then returns to its default view, the planet rotating below.

"We come in peace?" Jarek Ruus repeats, his bushy white eyebrows raised. His pupil-less eyes stare at Wil.

Bennie turns in his chair. "You get used to it. He's a little slow."

"Fuck you," Wil says, then adds, "I got nervous. He or she was staring at me, then they licked their eyeball." He waves his hands. "Licked their eyeball!"

Cynthia says, "I'm sending the coordinates to your console."

Wil looks down. "Got 'em." He grabs the flight controls and pushes the throttle forward. "Here we go." On the main display, the planet rapidly increases in size. The planet is mostly light brown with what looks like medium-sized cities dotting the visible continent. The cities are the same shade of light brown as the surrounding sand.

As the cargo ramp clunks against the duracrete of the spaceport, a breeze blows dust into the hold. "Great, we're gonna have to Roomba the hold when we leave," Wil complains, his dark brown duster flapping against his lightly armored leg. Jarek Ruus pushes past him and he adds, "So how do we find your pal's place?"

The older man looks up the ramp at Wil. "We'll ask the locals." He strides off toward the pedestrian exit of the spaceport, his cloak fluttering behind him. He draws the hood up to shield against the sand.

Wil heads down the ramp after their client, the rest of the crew following him. The heavy cargo doors close behind Gabe, and when the droid steps off the ramp, it raises back into its closed position.

Maxim looks at the droid. "Nothing on the local networks to help out?" He pulls on the collar of his armor, mumbling about sand.

Gabe shakes his head. "There are no local networks. I have accessed the spaceport intranet, but it has no connection that I can find to the wider planetary network, if there is one."

"Fun," the big Palorian replies.

Zephyr walks up. "That seems a bit weird. Wonder why they don't have any wireless networks?" Gabe and Maxim both shrug.

As they exit the spaceport onto a busy street full of pedestrians and countless ground vehicles, Jarek Ruus approaches one of the natives. This one is dressed in what Wil assumes is a business suit. Its scales are the same iridescent blue as the one from space control. "Excuse my friend. We're looking for the temple of the Knights of Plentallus. Do you know where it is?"

The small lizard-like alien stops and stares at the old man in his dark brown cloak. It finally says in a raspy voice, "I possess no information that can address your query." It doesn't wait for him to reply as it sidesteps the bigger man and continues on its way.

"This should be fun," Cynthia remarks as Jarek Ruus moves to intercept another small lizard alien, this one with pinkish scales, a head taller than the previous one.

Before the man can stop another pedestrian, Bennie moves in front of him and points to a two-meter tall tower at a nearby intersection. "Maybe we look at the directory?"

"You think *old space wizard temple* will be on the map?" Wil asks but heads toward the indicated device. It has three faces, each with a large display screen that comes to life when touched. Since it is designed for the much-smaller-than-a-human natives of the planet, Wil gestures for Bennie to step forward. "Do the honors?"

The small hacker approaches the directory and touches the screen. It immediately brightens and displays a map of the city. He taps the display several times, seeing what it does. After a minute, he pulls a wire out of his wristcomm and kneels down to plug it into a moderately well-hidden data port. The others form a loose semicircle around him while he works.

"No wireless network, but there is a municipal network. Weird they don't use wireless," he says, mostly to himself. Maxim and Zephyr both nod.

Gabe looks around. "Having now observed the natives for a bit, I would guess that wireless signals irritate these people's auditory senses." He points as what must be a younger lizard alien walks by. Like most reptiles, its ears are not external sand seem to be nothing more than smooth spots on the side of its head. Without warning, several nearby aliens flinch and turn to glare in the direction of the crew of the *Ghost*. Gabe nods. "Hypothesis confirmed."

Cynthia smiles at the tall droid. "Not exactly subtle." He tilts his head but says nothing.

The directory screen is no longer showing a map of the city but is a wall of scrolling code and icons moving quickly from one place on the display to another. "Got it," Bennie says.

NEXT ON SPACE CRIBS_

Everyone turns to look at the display, which flickers then resumes, displaying a map of the city. Wil says, "Well?"

Bennie removes his data cable from the port on the directory and it retracts automatically back into his wristcomm. "It's about a kilometer from here."

Jarek Ruus smiles. "That's good to hear."

"In the dark district," Bennie says, his face scrunched. "Like, haunted and stuff. At least according to the scant details I could dig up." He looks at Jarek Ruus. "Sounds like your pal set up shop, and a decade or so later, the parkland around his temple turned a little haunted-y."

Maxim looks at the others. "I mean, of course. It wouldn't be an 'us' job if it didn't involve weird dren." He looks up and down the street. "Which way?" Bennie points and they all head off.

"Okay, I see why they call it the dark district," Wil says, looking down from the raised walkway they are on down into an overgrown almost-jungle, parklike and devoid of light posts. Trees three or four stories tall cast most of the kilometers-wide area in deep shadows.

"How is there a jungle in the middle of a city on a mostly desert world?" Maxim asks, leaning over the railing to look into the darkened overgrowth. He shakes his head. "It's in the middle of that?" He looks down at Bennie, who nods once. Shrugging, he looks around, then points to a stairwell leading down into the parkland. "Okay then, let's get this over with."

The stairwell is blocked off by a heavy metal gate secured with a thick chain. Cynthia looks at the chain and the thick metal bars of the gate. "Old school." She pulls her pulse pistol from its holster and is about to fire at the chain when a withered hand rests on her forearm.

"Maybe something more subtle?" Jarek Ruus offers, moving his free hand to his belt and the hilt of his beam saber. With a snap hiss it activates, the white beam extending almost a meter. The others back away and with a few slashes the chain holding the gate closed falls to the ground in several pieces. He deactivates the sword and the blade vanishes.

"So cool," Wil whispers.

Jarek Ruus pushes the gate open and descends down the stairs. As he does, he removes a flask from his sleeve and takes a sip of whatever it is he keeps in it. He slips the flask back into its hiding place.

As everyone files down the stairs, Cynthia slows down next to Wil. "Should I see if I can get you one for Garthflak?" She winks and brushes past him.

Wil pushes the gate closed and kicks the segments of chain under a shrub. He looks around the street. It's dusk, and the small, lizard-like aliens seem to have moved indoors. He starts whistling the "Imperial March" from *The Empire Strikes Back* quietly as he hustles down the stairs to catch up with the others.

At the bottom of the stairs, Jarek Ruus and the crew are staring at a lush, overgrown jungle that is nearly pitch black only a few feet into it. Gabe looks down at the others. His eyes have shifted to a greenish hue. "Low light amplification mode," he says when he sees Wil staring at him.

Wil shrugs. "Cool, you lead." He extends a hand toward the mess of greenery before them. Gabe nods and pushes his way into the overgrowth. As the group follows, Bennie moves to be between Zephyr and Maxim.

When Maxim, eyebrow raised, looks down at Bennie, the small Brailack replies, "Who knows what lives in this mess? I'm bite sized." Max tilts his head and shrugs.

"I'm not sure what's worse. How is this planet both stiflingly hot and humid?" Cynthia complains, wiping the back of her hand across her forehead. "And at night."

Zephyr turns to her friend. "You could seal your armor."

Cynthia grunts, "Yeah, but then I sound like a robot through the suit speakers." She looks at Gabe. "No offense." Gabe inclines head.

"Just wait," Jarek Ruus says from behind Gabe.

ASK LARGE MARGE_

"Huh," Wil says, standing just inside the clearing. They've walked for thirty minutes, Gabe slashing away vines and undergrowth to make a path. The temple sits in the middle of a clearing, the jungle seeming to observe a border that keeps the plant life exactly twenty meters from the building on all sides. "I kinda expected more." He waves at the low stone building in front of them. "I mean, that looks more like Fred Flintstone's house than a temple for space wizards." The building is mostly covered in vines and seems to have few windows. Those few that are visible are narrow slits near the roof. The entire structure is dark.

Jarek Ruus leans over to Zephyr. "Will he ever stop saying *space wizards?*"

She shakes her head. "Not for the foreseeable future, no."

Wil continues, "I mean, it's just so plain."

Jarek Ruus looks over. "What were you expecting?"

Wil shrugs. "I don't know, spires or something. Maybe shaped like a Mayan pyramid? Height of any kind?"

"A Mayan—? You know what, never mind. Let's go." The older man starts towards the low stone building. Everyone follows.

Maxim says, "So did your friend Gelflux Prenta live alone, or what?"

"I did not know him, but I assume that yes, he lived alone, though he would have held classes or seminars and been open to those who needed him." He points to the building and its distinct lack of door. "No door. His bedchamber would have a door, of course, that'd be weird, but Knight outposts are open, always. It is the way. We are public servants, so the front of any temple would be a public space."

"Oh hey, a plaque," Bennie says, trotting over to a stone plinth set next to the door. He turns from the plaque to his friends. "I like these people. My height." He turns back to the plaque and reads out loud, "This building contained Gelflux Prenta, a Knight. He assisted the Yilgha for eighty cycles. He died. This building persists."

"These Yilgha don't mince words," Maxim says, looking over Bennie's shoulder. Above the inscription is an etching in what he assumes is the likeness of the dead Knight of Plentallus. His entire body was covered in fur. He looks at Jarek Ruus. "Was he Olop?"

The older man nods.

Wil leans forward, looking into the darkened structure. "Okay, gonna have to go in with helmets on so we can see what's what in there. It's pitch black." He taps his wristcomm, causing the helmet built into his armor to engage, unfolding from his back and re-shaping around his head. The clear faceplate flashes green as the low light amplification mode activates.

"Hello, sir," Jarvis, the AI that controls his armor, says through the helmet speakers.

Jarek Ruus follows Wil into the building. There's a low beep, and a blinding light floods the space. As Wil flinches, the older man says, "We prefer to live simply. That doesn't mean we don't know about electricity." He smirks.

Zephyr walks in grinning as Wil raises a hand, making a rude gesture as his helmet retracts and stows in the back of his armor.

The room they are standing in is clearly set up as a museum. Glass cases line most of the walls and in the middle of the room a short fur-covered mannequin dressed almost exactly like Jarek Ruus stands in a dramatic pose, beam saber grasped in both hands. The old man examines the mannequin. "They captured his likeness quite well." He taps the hilt of the beam saber. "Fake."

"So, where's this archive thing?" Maxim asks as he scans the room looking for whatever an archive looks like.

Jarek Ruus is slowly walking the perimeter of the room, running a hand along the glass cases. He is mumbling something that none of them can hear and ignores Maxim's question. He stops at a display case filled with what look to Wil like trinkets. The Knight bows his head, then takes a deep breath, turning to the group. "We have to find the basement."

Gabe spins in a slow circle. "I do not detect a sub structure." He looks at Jarek Ruus. "Are you certain?"

The old man nods. "There's a basement. We just have to find it."

Wil holds up his hand. "We can ask Large Marge." Maxim groans. Bennie chuckles and offers a small green fist to bump.

SECRET ROOMS_

"I've only ever visited two other outposts," Jarek Ruus admits. He points to a hallway with several doors. There is a metal frame welded to the opening with a locked gate closing it off. "My guess is the access will be in his sleeping chambers."

Wil gestures toward the other man's belt. "Well, get to saberin', then." He smiles.

The metal lock on the gate fares no better than the chain closing the gate to the park. The gate swings open with a groan.

Zephyr peers out the open doorway. "I hope no one likes to stroll through this park at night. We're not being subtle."

Bennie turns to look at her. "Haunted jungle, remember?"

Jarek Ruus heads down the hallway. "Gelflux Prenta will have kept his quarters far from the communal space." The door at the end of the hallway is closed.

Bennie pushes open a door as they walk. "Not locked or anything." He peeks inside. "Closet."

Gabe says, "I still do not detect any additional structure below, or above."

Jarek Ruus nods as he pushes open the door to Sir Gelflux Prenta's private quarters. "It's here."

Inside the bedroom it is clear that, whoever the stewards of the temple are, they take their responsibility seriously. The room is almost certainly exactly as it was when Sir Gelflux Prenta died. Jarek Ruus stops just inside the room and bows his head.

Maxim looks around the room. "We should—" He stops when Jarek Ruus' hand snaps up, fist clenched. Maxim closes his mouth and looks at Wil then Zephyr. Both shrug. The older man reaches behind the dresser and does something that produces a soft click. The bed lurches, tilting forward on unseen hinges.

"Well, that's cool," Wil says, moving to look behind the bed now sitting at an eighty-degree angle from the floor. He turns to Gabe. "You were saying?"

Gabe shrugs. "I still do not detect anything below this structure."

Jarek Ruus pushes past Wil and descends the rough stone steps. "We Knights have a few tricks at our disposal." He vanishes into the darkness below. The others all follow.

The chamber below the bedroom is larger than any of them expected, nearly three times the size of the bedroom, the outer edges extending past where the walls of the house above are. Wil takes in the scene, whistling. "Neat."

The roughly square room is lined with bookshelves full of actual books. Maxim walks over and removes a particularly thick tome from the shelf. He holds the book as if it is going to fall apart at any moment. "*The Unabridged History of Bunfilax Seven and its People.*" He looks up at the others. "Never heard of it."

Cynthia turns from the shelf she's inspecting. "I think it's out near the badlands in sector eighteen."

Jarek Ruus looks over his shoulder. "Part of our charter is collecting and expanding knowledge. In the old days, Knights traveled the galaxy collecting information, putting it together for use by any who sought it." He spins slowly around, taking in the entire room and the crew. "The archive would most certainly be in this chamber." He pulls a small flask out of the sleeve of his cloak and takes a sip.

Bennie looks up at Zephyr, who shrugs, an eyebrow raised to go with it. She points to a pillar in the middle of the room, looking at Maxim. "Remember that mission on Lorstak Seven? That baron had a pillar in the middle of the room that split in two."

Maxim nods, looking around the room. He walks toward a bookshelf on opposite side of the room from him. "The lever was a trinket on a bookshelf." He reaches for a small statue of what might be a Brailack in ancient armor. He pulls on the small statuette; it comes off the shelf. "Okay, not that one." He looks at the adjacent bookshelf.

Wil walks over to the bookshelf that is set directly opposite the stairwell. He scratches his chin as he examines the assorted books and trinkets. He reaches up and pulls on *The Rise and Danger of the Galactic Commonwealth*. The tome slides halfway off the shelf. From under their feet something rumbles. The pillar begins to slowly spin in place. A foot from the ceiling, a seam appears in the pillar as the lower portion continues to rotate and lower. When the lower portion is about three feet tall, it stops. Sitting atop the pillar-turned-pedestal is a softball-sized cube made of what looks like brass with green, glowing crystal inlaid in intricate patterns. The cube is pulsing as if it is breathing.

Jarek Ruus rushes over to the pedestal. As he reaches for the device, Maxim says, "Should we check for—" The moment Ruus lifts the device, the hatch at the top of the stairs with the bed mounted to it slams shut. "— booby traps?"

WELL, OF COURSE_

"Why would you do that?" Zephyr shouts as the rumbling increases in volume. The pedestal that until recently held the Knights of Plentallus archive sinks into the floor, and sand begins bubbling up through the hole.

Cynthia stares at the sand. "How is sand being forced up through that hole?"

From across the room Bennie shouts, "That's your biggest concern?"

Jarek Ruus pushes the glowing cube into his satchel, then looks around. "I suppose I should have expected this."

"You think?" Wil demands. He points to the sand, now up to his shins. "Know how to turn this off or get out of here?" The older man shakes his head once as he starts moving from bookshelf to bookshelf, looking for anything that might help. Wil growls and pulls his pulse pistol out. He fires at the hatch at the top of the stairs. Rock chips fly in all directions, but otherwise, his plasma blasts do little to the stone hatch. He looks at Ruus, snapping his fingers to get the older man's attention. "Laser sword." He points to the stone hatch.

The sand is now just over most of the crew's knees and almost to Bennie's waist. "Unless one of you wants to carry me, can we hurry up?" Gabe reaches down and plucks the Brailack hacker out of the sand, depositing him on his shoulders.

From the top of the stone staircase, Jarek Ruus says, "My beam saber isn't fairing much better than your blaster. This stone is incredibly dense."

Bennie screeches and points. "There's something in here with us!" Gabe spins to look where his passenger is pointing, his eyes bright yellow. "Whatever stone this room is made out of is causing significant interference with my sensors. While I can detect another lifeform in the sand, I cannot pinpoint it."

"Better and better," Maxim grouses.

From halfway up the stairs, Jarek Ruus closes his eyes and seems to be meditating. Cynthia moves to put her back to one of the bookshelves just as an eyeball on a stalk pops out of the sand. She doesn't hesitate, pulling her own pulse pistol and firing at the disgusting eyeball. Faster than she can fire, the eyeball drops back under the sand, her blasts striking where it had been, burning the sand into small clumps of glass. "That's disgusting."

The sand has risen to their waists. Wil points to the stairs. "Everyone, higher ground." Walking is getting difficult with the sand so high.

Zephyr is the furthest from the staircase, and one minute she's pushing through the heavy sand, and the next she's gone, a ripple of sand where she was just standing. Maxim shouts, "Zephyr!"

Cynthia climbs up a bookcase out of the sand and leaps to where Zephyr has vanished. She dives into the sand, only her tail visible, forming a furry periscope of sorts. Seconds later, she emerges from the sand, gasping. She looks at the others and shakes her head.

Wil turns to Gabe, who is panning his gaze around the room and the deepening sand. He looks at Wil and shakes his head. In a burst of sand about ten feet from where she was earlier, Zephyr bursts out of the sand. A wrinkly brown tentacle is wrapped around her throat and has one arm pinned to her side. She makes a strangled noise before beginning to slip back into the sand. "Jarek!" Wil snaps. The older man leaps from the stairs, sailing through the air, brown cloak flapping. The snap-hiss of his beam saber comes a second before the blade swings down, slicing through the tentacle as he flies past. He lands in the sand, sinking to his waist, his beam saber still activated and held at the ready.

The tentacle goes slack around Zephyr's neck, and she inhales as she sloughs off the now dead appendage. Something under the sand makes a plaintive, wailing noise. The sand ripples as something moves toward the center of the room.

"The hell was that?" Wil asks still looking around.

"Sand strangler," Jarek Ruus says as he deactivates his beam saber. The sand is still rising, now up past the older man's belt. "We have to get out of here. Where there is one, there are usually ten."

"Ew," Wil grouses.

Gabe ushers everyone away from the stairs, handing Bennie to Maxim. His eyes shift to red and from deep inside him comes the now more familiar sound of components shifting. The large shoulder-mounted cannon he's used before takes shape. "Please move to the far side of the room." He looks at Jarek Ruus. "I apologize." As the older man opens his mouth to ask what for, the shoulder cannon barks once as a charged plasma blast leaps from the muzzle toward the stone slab covering the entrance to the underground chamber. The sound of stone splintering and wood cracking echoes into the large chamber as a wall of dust rushes into the room. Another blast rips through the dusty air.

From inside the cloud of dust, two bright red lights glow. "We should hurry."

TIME TO GO_

"THE CIVIL AUTHORITIES will likely be on their way," Cynthia says as they exit the temple, each of them covered in dust.

Jarek Ruus nods. "Yes, I can't imagine the Yilgha will be happy to see a temple and monument destroyed." The roof near the rear of the building collapses in a cacophony of falling rock.

Bennie looks up at the older man. "They keep it in a haunted jungle. It can't be that important."

Zephyr, massaging her throat, says in a hoarse whisper, "We should split up and get back to the spaceport." She points to Bennie. "I'll take him and Gabe. Maxim, you and Cynthia." She turns to Wil. "You and Sir Jarek Ruus." Wil opens his mouth to protest but stops when everyone else nods and heads off into the jungle.

Wil looks at Jarek Ruus. "Okay, come on grandpa laser sword, let's go."

Jarek Ruus slips his flask back into his sleeve, wiping his mouth with his other sleeve. "Let us away."

Wil looks at his wristcomm, consulting the map Bennie had shared. "Looks like there's another entrance to this park. Let's head to that one." The other man nods, extending a hand for Wil to take the lead.

The jungle is still nearly pitch black; Wil activates his helmet so he can see. He looks over his shoulder at the older man behind him. "So, we got your doodad. We may need to revisit our fee if the other planets are like this one."

Jarek Ruus smiles. "I can almost certainly guarantee the other locations won't be like this. They'll be dangerous in different ways."

"That probably sounded reassuring in your head," Wil says, picking his way through the undergrowth that threatens to trip him every step of the way.

"It didn't, actually," the other man says, and Wil is pretty sure he hears him take a sip from his flask again. Wil looks at the heads-up display on his visor. "Everyone check in."

Zephyr is the first to respond. "We're almost out of the jungle. The gate we came in through is as we left it, no authorities yet." There's a muffled discussion. Then, she says, "Oh, and Bennie almost got eaten by a carnivorous plant when he was relieving himself."

Bennie cuts in on the channel. "I have a small bladder!"

"Was it a cousin of yours?" Wil asks.

"Fuck you! I'm not a plant," the Brailack hacker screeches.

Maxim cuts in, "Cynthia and I are out. We went up and over the wall to the north. We're at the edge of a residential sector, and there are a few dozen folks out looking toward the park."

Wil nods to himself. "Ruus and I are almost to the edge of the park."

Cynthia adds, "I just saw two civil authority ground cars rush past. No need to guess where they're going."

Wil says, "We got what we needed, no point in loitering here. Meet back at the *Ghost*. Gabe, get her started up." He closes the channel, turning to Ruus, his faceplate retracting. "I assume we're all done here, yeah?" The other man nods. Wil engages the face plate and pushes through a thick clump of vines.

The walk through the jungle is uneventful until Wil feels Jarek Ruus' hand on his shoulder, stopping him. Wil turns to look at the other man, who has a finger to his lips. He points to their right.

Through the tangle of vines and thick tree trunks, a massive furry shape lumbers by, making far less noise than Wil would expect of something that size, its brown, shaggy fur covered in moss and twigs. It'd be harder to see if Jarvis weren't highlighting it on the HUD. Wil raises his faceplate, whispering, "What the hell is that?"

Before the other man can answer, the big brown thing crashes through the trees hurdling itself into Wil, knocking him off his feet. As Wil and the creature crash through the undergrowth, Jarek Ruus says, "Something with good ears." He activates his beam saber and rushes towards the broken bramble and struggling human and monster.

The creature must weigh three times what Wil does. He's pinned under it as yellow claws drag across his armor, leaving deep gouges. "Captain, this creature poses a significant threat if you remain pinned underneath it," Jarvis explains in his ear.

Wil grunts, pushing a shaggy arm away from his chest. "You think?"

"I do."

Wil gets his feet under the furry beast and pushes with all of his strength and the considerable amount the armor adds. The creature flies off of him, landing a few feet away. The creature never makes a sound. Its horrific, tooth-filled mouth hangs open, glimmering saliva droops to the ground, but it makes no sound. Wil shudders as four green glowing eyes focus on him. It rears up on powerful hind legs, its long forelimbs rising over its head. A bright white light flares behind the creature, forcing it to shy away as a furry claw falls to the ground, bright red blood pooling around it. As it flees, the creature still doesn't make a sound. The severed limb twitches a few times.

Jarek Ruus shuts down his beam saber. "A whisper. I wasn't aware that this planet had them. Interesting." He extends a hand to help Wil up.

Wil grunts, "Yeah, interesting."

CHAPTER 7_

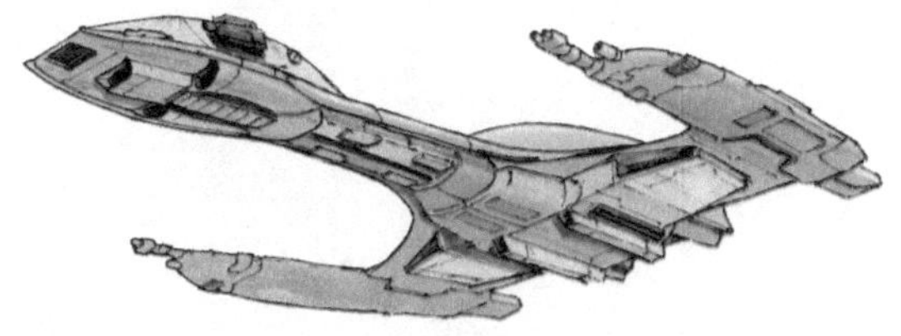

MEALS ON THE GO_

Wil and Jarek Ruus are the last to arrive at the *Ghost*. The rest of the crew—except Gabe, who is in engineering, and Zephyr, who is on the bridge—are waiting in the cargo hold. The sun is beginning to come up, the pale blue light it casts creeping up from the horizon. Maxim looks at Wil covered in blood and dirt. "What the wurrin happened to you?"

"I told you, monster attack."

Maxim whistles. "You said you won. This doesn't look like you won." Bennie chuckles and raises a green fist for the much larger Palorian to bump.

"Yeah, well, you should see the other guy," Wil retorts.

Jarek Ruus heads up the ramp, his flask in hand. "I'll be in quarters if you need me." He pulls the archive cube out of his satchel, examining it as he walks.

Maxim watches the older man head up the stairs out of the cargo hold, then turns to Wil, who is standing next to the control pedestal, closing the main cargo doors. The cargo ramp raises in time to close just as the heavy doors come together with a clunk of magnetic locks. "He okay?"

Wil shrugs. "I mean, I think he's been drunk since we landed, but he did help with the whisper-thing."

From the collar of Wil's armor, Jarvis adds, "Without Sir Ruus' help, I do not know if the Captain would have survived the—"

Wil presses a button on his wristcomm silencing the AI that occupies his power armor. He hitches a thumb toward the stairs. "Let's go. We've got more almost certainly monster-filled planets to visit for our inebriated client."

"Permission to depart granted. Do so promptly," the small, pink-scaled space control operator says before the main display at the front of the *Ghost's* bridge goes black before turning to a view of the spaceport.

Wil pushes the power lever for the repulsor lifts forward. "Okay, then, off we go." The ship lurches and tilts forward before the inertial dampers fully take over. As the *Ghost* rises higher and higher, Wil pushes the power lever for the atmospheric engines forward. The powerful engines in the aft of the ship ignite and push everyone against their seat backs or consoles, depending on which way they are facing. Wil whoops, "That never gets old!" He shouts over the roar of the powerful engines pushing the *Ghost* forward at ever increasing speeds. Since the *Ghost* isn't aerodynamic, no amount of thrust will help her gain altitude. That's where the repulsor lifts come in, pushing the ship higher and higher off the ground.

Once the *Ghost* leaves the atmosphere and navigates out of orbit around incoming freighters and other smaller craft, Wil sets their course out of the system at sub-light speed. He looks around the bridge. "I'm starving." He rests a hand on his stomach. "Lunch?"

Bennie turns. "I could eat."

"We did skip breakfast," Maxim says, putting his console into standby mode.

Wil looks at Zephyr. "Mind fetching our guest? We'll need to get underway to where ever we need to go next soon. I think I've had enough of the Perolerra system and whispers and sand stranglers for a while."

Wɪʟ ʟᴏᴏᴋs ᴀᴛ ᴛʜᴇ ɢʟᴏᴡɪɴɢ ᴄᴜʙᴇ ᴏɴ ᴛʜᴇ ᴋɪᴛᴄʜᴇɴ ᴛᴀʙʟᴇ. "So how many channels does it get?"

Jarek Ruus picks up the cube, turning it over in his hand. "Thankfully, it is intact and its storage medium is uncompromised." He slips the device into his satchel and places the bag on the ground next to his chair. He looks at the crew. "What is for lunch?"

Cynthia turns from the cooktop. "Holintuu Stew. We picked up fresh ingredients—well, as fresh as can be expected—on Fury, before leaving." She places a large bowl in the center of the table and proceeds to fill everyone's bowl.

Bennie slurps loudly from his spoon, then asks, "So, where to now?"

Jarek Ruus sips his soup then says, "Based on old records, we believe Sir Byrian Olen set herself up on Zanzibariia in the Carollux system."

Bennie rubs his face. "Further into the Expanse, yay."

Wil looks at Cynthia. "Babe, this is delicious." He takes another sip then says, "I've never heard of the Carollux system."

Cynthia shakes her head.

Gabe raises a hand. "It is twenty-three light years from here, as Bennie says, further into the region designated the Expanse. I do not know of any Galactic Commonwealth races from that world." He turns to Jarek Ruus. "Would a Knight seek to hide on a world such as that?"

The older man shakes his head. "Anything is possible. It would have been advisable to seek a more populated world."

"It's populated," Bennie says between slurps from his spoon.

THAT'S A NEAT IDEA_

Two weeks later, the *Ghost* is orbiting Zanzibariia, a bright green world of prairies and forestland. A single ocean covers almost a third of the planet with rivers, some as wide as three kilometers snaking throughout the continents.

"It's pretty, that's for sure," Zephyr says, looking at the main display.

Jarek Ruus, standing next to Cynthia's station says, "I can see why Sir Olen would choose this world. Though without any major settlements, I am curious why she chose it."

"And how we'll find her place," Wil says, watching the green and blue world slowly turn on the main display.

Bennie looks up from his console. "I've been thinking about that. Gabe and I have an idea."

Everyone turns to look at the small Brailack. Jarek Ruus says, "Do tell."

The small Brailack puffs out his chest. "It's simple, really. Remember the enhanced bio sensor package we got from ol' what's-her-name, the GC Councilwoman?"

"Grythlorian," Maxim offers.

Bennie points at his friend. "Yeah, her. Gabe and I have been working on some modified software for the sensor suite." He taps a control on his console and the main display updates, showing a schematic of what Wil assumes is the enhanced sensor platform mounted in the forward section of the *Ghost*. A piece of the device highlights. "This," Bennie says, "is the main biological identification matrix. It was originally programmed to find Multonae, and we've made small tweaks over the last few months, as needed. However, since we had the time, Gabe and I decided to hack into the primary control circuits." He takes a breath, having delivered most of that last part in a single breath. "We've been able to create a control interface so that we can input specific biological parameters into the sensor suite."

Zephyr holds up a hand. "But we don't know what species Sir Byrian Olen was, and since we're fairly certain she's dead, she wouldn't show up even if we did know."

Cynthia nods. "Yeah, I don't follow how this modification helps here."

Bennie waves away their comments. "No, no, you're not getting it. Now that we have direct sensor matrix control, we can feed in more than biological details." He points to Jarek Ruus. "Like a detailed scan of your little archive do-dad." He holds up a finger when Wil opens his mouth. "It's still not gonna be able to pinpoint the unit specifically, but like our pal Bonson Drell, it'll narrow down the search area considerably."

Wil whistles, running his hand through his hair. "Damn, man, good job." He looks up. "Gabe, Bennie just told us about your little side project. Good job."

The ceiling replies, "Thank you, Captain. It was an interesting project and kept Bennie busy."

"Hey!" Bennie shouts, turning back to his console. The main display blinks and resumes showing the planet below.

Wil turns to Jarek Ruus. "I guess the next step is a detailed scan of your archive."

The older man inclines his head. "Indeed. It is in my quarters. I'll go fetch it. Do I bring it back here?"

Bennie hops out of his seat. "No, I'll go with you. The scanning rig is in engineering." He pushes the older man toward the bridge hatch.

Zephyr looks at them. "Let me know when you're ready. I'll get things set up, up here." Bennie holds a hand up, giving the thumbs up.

Maxim looks over. "That upgrade seems to be the gift that keeps on giving."

Wil grins. "I dunno, those image inducers are still fun. Last night we— Ouch!"

Cynthia picks up the PADD she threw at Wil. "I don't think anything needs to be said about that." She grins and winks at Maxim, who blushes a deep shade of blue.

HERE THERE BE DRAGONS_

"First a jungle, now a swamp," Wil complains. He looks at Jarek Ruus. "We flew over several very lovely looking prairies. Flat grassy prairies." The older man shrugs and pushes a vine out of his way.

Jarek Ruus looks over his shoulder, drawing his hood aside a bit. "Yes, but according to your scanners, the clearing with a temple similar to the one on Perolerra Three is this way, in the jungle." He continues moving.

Something in the distance roars. Cynthia looks at Bennie. "You said something about the things that live on this planet."

Bennie looks up at her. "By *something*, you mean a very detailed explanation of the creatures that live on this stupid planet?"

Cynthia wiggles her hand. "You decided to start your lecture after movie night. Those *Star Trek* movies always put me to sleep."

Zephyr smiles. "Yeah, we really need to retire those."

Wil grunts. "Oh come on, the first two are pretty solid."

Maxim pushes a clump of something spongy out of his way. "You made us watch the *Next Generation* ones."

Wil shrugs. "I mean, they have their charms..."

Cynthia turns back to Bennie. "Anyway, now we're here and actually care, so how about take two?"

"Whatever," Bennie growls, ducking under a fallen tree. The thing that roared earlier roars again. Bennie gestures off in a seemingly random direction. "That roaring, that's a ragla. Sounds like a big one."

Cynthia scratches her ear. "Ragla?"

"No way," Maxim says. "Those don't exist."

The ragla roars again, and this time it sounds different. Bennie says, "Smaller one, maybe a female." He looks back at Maxim. "They do exist. Brai tried to settle this planet about three hundred cycles ago." He shudders. "According to the records I saw when I was a kid, my parents were involved with a group of wealthy elites who were hoping to set up a *Planet B* that they could escape to if Brai got too crowded." He sidesteps a muddy bog. "They got here, found the ragla. Many died. I don't know where they are, but there are ruins of at least two settlements somewhere on this planet. End of story."

"What's a ragla?" Wil asks. He looks over at Bennie, then at Maxim. "What're we talking? Space elephants? Space lions? Space chipmunks?"

Zephyr looks over and raises an eyebrow. She's about to comment on his use of *space* when Bennie says, "No, they're like those things from Jurassic Town." He stops, tapping his chin. "Not those, the metal things from that horrible robot movie. We watched it about a month ago. Opto what's-it rode one."

"A dragon?" Wil offers.

Bennie points at Wil. "Yes, dragon." He turns to Zephyr and winks. "A space dragon."

Wil stops walking. Everyone else stops, too. He looks around. "You're shitting me."

Maxim says, "They're a myth. This can't be real."

Bennie waves his hand. "You heard them. What the wurrin do you think made those sounds?" Maxim shrugs.

Jarek Ruus finally breaks his silence. "Oh, they're real. *Swamp dragon* would be more accurate." He shakes his head. "I didn't know they were on this planet, but Knights have encountered them before, many times. We were often called in to help with communities that had gotten too large." The old man's eyes lose focus as he remembers something from his past. "Interesting." He resumes walking.

Wil is rubbing his chin. "How did I not know there were space dragons? Why isn't there like a zoo or something on Tarsis? Or a nature preserve. Those are often better for animals."

Bennie says, "Because Ragla are dicks, and they'd run off any visitors."

"They're sapient?" Wil asks.

Bennie looks up at him as it he's grown a new eyeball. "Well, yeah. Sorta, at least. I mean, they're not the greatest conversationalists, but they're not stupid, either." A ragla roars again, much louder this time, and much closer sounding.

"Sorta?" Wil asks.

From the front of the group, Maxim holds up a fist. Everyone stops. Jarek Ruus pushes aside a clump of vines and underbrush. There's a small clearing, but no temple, just what looks like incredibly massive trees.

"Is that the Ewok village?" Wil says, joining Maxim and looking over Jarek Ruus' shoulder.

I REMEMBER THIS PLAYSET_

"I HAD this play set when I was kid. My grandparents had it in their attic. It was my dad's."

Cynthia is at the base of a tree that is easily ten feet in diameter. She turns to Wil. "No one knows what you're talking about."

"Is anyone here?" Maxim asks, looking up at a village suspended in, around, and between the massive trees.

"I am not detecting any lifeforms larger than rodents and a handful of avian creatures. Whoever built this village is either away or dead," Gabe offers.

Jarek Ruus walks over to another of the immense trees. Several meters up, there is a series of slash marks gouged deep into the bark. He points to the wound. "We should continue on to the temple." He looks at Gabe. "Mister droid, how much further?"

Gabe looks off in the direction they've been walking. "Approximately two kilometers."

Wil waves everyone on. "Okay, let's go. We can come back and explore Ewok village if there's time."

Bennie looks up at the slash marks in the tree and several sets higher up. "I don't want to explore this place."

The walk to Sir Byrian Olen's temple is uneventful. The roars of ragla nearby continue, some nearby, some quite a way away. They never hear anything moving in the forest except themselves.

At the edge of the clearing, Wil says, "So, was there like a shared design document or a sale on blueprints or something?" The temple of Sir Byrian Olen is nearly identical to that of Sir Gelflux Prenta. As the group heads for the building, he adds, "At least we know where the secret chamber is."

Cynthia looks through a window. "Guess someone didn't consider the Knights or their temples sacred." Maxim looks over her shoulder. "Sheesh, it's a wreck in there."

Zephyr walks inside. "What do you think the odds are that if there is a secret room, it's still secret?"

Jarek Ruus heads down the hallway. "We can only hope." He makes a noise that sounds a lot like a belch.

Bennie squats down and examines something near the seating area. He holds it up. "What do you think this is? Some kind of armor plate?" He's holding a thin piece of material about twice the size of his hand with a slight curvature to it. One side is dark gray the other an off-white with light blue mottling.

Jarek Ruus returns from the bedroom. "It's a piece of shell. At some point one or more ragla used this building as a hatchery or egg storage or something." He looks at Zephyr. "It's a good thing I didn't take your bet. The chamber below the bed has been ransacked." He looks around and pulls something from behind his back. A small spear. "I don't think whoever ransacked the lower chamber was a ragla. Perhaps someone hiding from them?"

Wil walks past him. "We'd better check it out, maybe there's a clue." Jarek Ruus steps aside to let the others follow Wil.

Inside the secret chamber, it looks like a bomb has gone off. The shelves are ruined, their contents strewn about the floor, shredded and trampled.

Bennie kicks a ruined book out of his way. "If not a ragla, who?" He looks at the others. "Notice anything?" He waves a hand around the mess. "No trinkets. The books are shredded and stuff, but assuming this Byrian gal was like Gelflux, there should be trinkets scattered around. There aren't any." He runs a small green hand over his hairless head. "Ragla are scavengers and hoarders of shiny stuff, so it makes sense they'd take this stuff, but they're too big to get down here."

"Anyone notice, no pillar?" Cynthia says, pointing to the spot in the room where they had encountered the booby-trapped archive storage on Perolerra Four.

Jarek Ruus strokes his beard. "Where would she have hidden it?"

Wil drops a book he's been looking at. "Maybe the folks that used to live in that village got a hold of it?"

Maxim nods. "As good a guess as any." He turns to Jarek Ruus. "Thoughts, Sir Knight?"

The older man takes a sip from his flask, releases a small belch, then says, "We have to find that archive. Perhaps we ask them?"

"Hey!" Bennie shouts, "Look!" He's pointing to a section of the bookcase near him. When the others get closer, he reaches up and pulls the bookcase, causing it to tilt and lean away from a hidden alcove.

"Well, I'll be," Jarek Ruus says, gently pushing past Bennie. He looks at the alcove and small wooden pedestal inside. The empty pedestal.

From the floor above, there's a noise like something being moved along the floor. Everyone looks up, then to the staircase. Zephyr says, "Guess we can ask whomever is up there?"

"That, that is not an Ewok," Wil says as the group enters the public space of the temple. A dozen small beings are standing around, spears and crude swords aimed at the crew of the *Ghost* and Jarek Ruus. The beings are small, smaller than Bennie, covered in fur from head to toe and wearing nothing but loincloths. Their faces remind Wil of prairie dogs, vaguely, except for their hands and feet, which are disturbingly human looking.

Jarek Ruus motions for everyone to lower their weapons. "Let's see if we can resolve this peacefully." He turns to the nearest prairie dog person. "Bah-weep-Graaaaagnah wheep ni ni bong."

Wil turns. "The fuck..."

Jarek Ruus turns to Wil, shrugging. "What?"

Wil stammers, "That's the—"

One of the prairie dog men comes forward. "Bah-weep-Graaaaagnah wheep ni ni bong." He bows, then turns to one of the other creatures and speaks in their language. The other man dips his head and heads for the door. The first small being motions for them all to follow him.

As they watch the small beings leave, Gabe says, "I may be able to build a translation matrix if I hear enough of their language." He moves to follow the group of small beings.

Maxim watches his mechanical friend. "Neat." He looks at the others and follows Gabe out of the building.

As the group leaves the one-time home of Sir Byrian Olen, Cynthia looks down at one of the small beings. "They're kinda cute." The group of small furry beings is leading them into the jungle, not in the direction the team had come from earlier.

Bennie looks at the creature nearest him. "Maybe we can keep one or two." It looks up at him and grins widely, its yellowed pointy teeth bared.

Wil looks at the Brailack. "What's with you and wanting to kidnap people? First the avatar of the children and now these little prairie dog guys." Bennie shrugs. Wil sighs.

As they walk, more and more prairie dog people emerge from the trees to join them. Wil points to one of the newcomers, saying, "Oh look, prairie dog ladies."

Gabe moves to be closer to the new arrivals, who watch him but don't shy away, walking silently next to the much more massive droid. He bows to a female in a leather tunic, an infant clutched in her furry arms. She looks up and speaks to the much taller droid. Gabe tilts his head but says nothing. The small woman repeats herself as she jumps over a small log. Gabe blinks and listens as another prairie dog person comes up and speaks to him walking behind the woman. He replies, slowly, parsing his words. The two small beings look at each other and shrug. They continue to chatter away to each other and up to the droid.

Jarek Ruus looks at Wil, an eyebrow raised. Wil shrugs, then says, "Gabe, buddy, any idea how long—" he starts.

Gabe interrupts him, holding up a hand, then speaking to the woman with child in her own language. Gabe's speech is still halting and he pauses every few words. Nevertheless, the small woman's eyes brighten and several other prairie dog people rush over to walk nearby, bouncing up and down as they walk.

Wil looks at Jarek Ruus. "There we go."

Gabe speaks to the woman, then to the man they'd met earlier inside the house. Both nod vigorously, replying quickly and firing off what sounds like a myriad of questions. Gabe nods and replies. The man Wil is assuming is a leader rushes off ahead of the group.

Maxim clears his throat and Gabe turns. "Apologies. The Cynomides are very excited to meet us." He extends a hand toward the small woman with her child clutched tightly to her body. "Nuk tells me that the ragla in this region have been tormenting the Cynomides for cycles."

Jarek Ruus grunts. "That was their village, then?"

Gabe nods. "Indeed, it was. They fled it when Nuk was young. Several adolescent ragla attacked in the night." The prairie dog woman chatters at him. He adds, "She says their tribe and several others have been forced to become nomads or go into hiding."

Cynthia looks at the small beings walking all around them. "So, where are we going?"

Gabe speaks to Nuk, who replies. He turns to Cynthia. "Their new village."

Jarek Ruus puts his flask back in its secret sleeve hiding place and says, "I mean no disrespect to Nuk and her people, but we do have a reason for being here. Has she mentioned the archive?"

Gabe shakes his head, "No, but I will ask." He chatters in the Cynomide language and Nuk replies. He looks at Wil and Jarek Ruus, "While she doesn't specifically know about the archive, her people cleared the house of anything they thought would be valuable to appease the eldest ragla."

Bennie moans, "Great, one of those asshole space dragons has it?" He turns to Zephyr and winks. She groans.

CHAPTER 8_

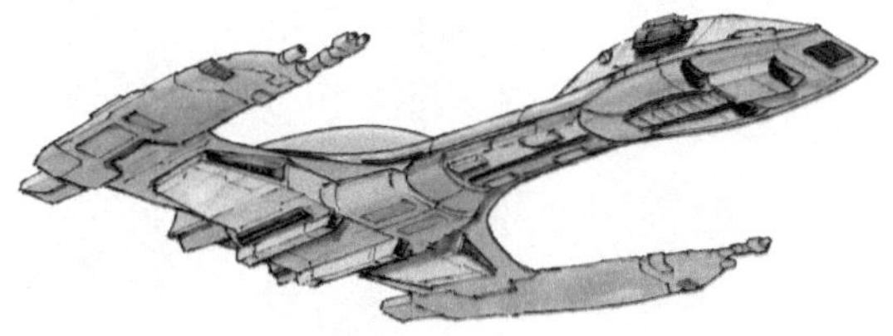

LET'S TALK_

THE CREW of the *Ghost* and Jarek Ruus follow the Cynomides for nearly an hour until they arrive at the base of a small hill. Wil thinks he remembers seeing it when they came in for a landing. He checks his wristcomm to confirm his bearings. The blinking dot that represents the *Ghost* is about five kilometers away. He looks at Zephyr "We've ended up back near the *Ghost*, about five clicks."

She nods, then turns to Gabe. "So, this is home?"

The droid has been whispering back and forth with the small furry beings since they left the ruins of Sir Byrian Olen's home. He looks over his shoulder to Zephyr. "Indeed. Nuk says we will need to crawl but that it is not far." Jarek Ruus wipes his mouth on his sleeve, having just taken a swig from his flask, and grumbles something none of them save Gabe can hear. The droid replies, "Nuk says that daybreak is coming and the ragla roam then. That is why."

Wil nudges Cynthia. "Think that thing is bottomless? Maybe that's his magical power, a refilling flask?"

She grins wrapping her arm around his waist. "Be a pretty useless power, don't you think?"

Wil smiles. "He seems to be making the best of it." She chuckles.

They follow the small prairie dog-like villagers through an almost invisible tunnel opening. Maxim brings up the rear of their group, watching as two of the small Cynomides place plants in front of the opening.

Nuk is correct and the tunnel is only about three meters long, sloping down at nearly thirty degrees. As Wil stands up, brushing dirt from his long coat, he can't help but whistle appreciatively. "Damn. Ain't nothing temporary about this place."

The hill and several hundred meters below it are hollowed out. Where the Cynomides' old village was up among the massive trees, this one is nestled amongst massive earthworks pillars. Buildings cling to the pillars with bridges stretching between them and ladders and rudimentary lifts connecting the upper village with the sprawl of buildings below.

Gabe turns to the group after listening to Nuk for a moment. "Nuk says Tebow will take us to the Great Space where the elders reside. They'll tell us what we want to know."

Zephyr looks at the indicated Cynomide, his fur a mix of grays and pale blues, and motions for him to lead the way. The small man clicks the butt of his spear on the ground and heads off.

Nuk says something more to Gabe, then turns and leaves. Wil sidles up next to his droid friend. "Where's your new bestie going?"

Gabe smiles his off-putting smile. "She must put her son down, then she will join us at the Great Space." As Wil nods he continues, "Captain, I believe we should try to help the Cynomides. According to Nuk, the ragla have gotten more and more aggressive over the last several years. She fears that if things continue, the ragla will begin more actively hunting her people."

Wil looks up. "What would you have us do? Kill a bunch of these space dragons so there is less of them? Would that even help? Could we even do that?"

Gabe inclines his head. "I admit I do not have a solution in mind." He turns to look Wil in the eye. "I will, though."

Wil reaches up, placing a hand on Gabe's shoulder. "When you do, we'll act. Promise." Gabe nods.

The Great Space is a depression turned amphitheater with a small half circle table at the bottom.

Gabe turns to the others. "With your permission, I'd like to initiate an update to your translator nanites so that you can understand the Cynomides directly. I believe I have a complete enough translation matrix. You will still have to rely on me to communicate with them, however."

Wil looks at Bennie, who shrugs. "Why are you looking at me?"

"You're our computer expert. Any reason we shouldn't?"

The small hacker shakes his head. "Not really. If there's a problem, we can also inject new ones. Gabe will have to keep sending updates as his dictionary grows, but once we leave here, he can stop."

Wil nods. "Okay, go for it, buddy."

CALM YOUR MIND_

The Great Space is crowded with small, furry beings. The team is escorted to several small benches in front of the elder's table. Maxim fidgets. "These aren't comfortable."

Cynthia raises an eyebrow. "They're made for beings a quarter your height and likely an eighth your weight."

One of the elders, the one in the center of the table, slams a rock against a wooden block. The room falls silent. She smiles. "Greetings, my friends. The mechanical man tells my niece that you can understand what I say."

Wil stands, looking first at Gabe, who nods, then to the wizened Cynomide. "We can."

"I am Deloo, eldest of elders." She gestures to the other elders around her. "We are told you are looking for an artifact."

Wil nods to Deloo, then turns to Gabe and motions for him to come forward. "My friend can show you an image of the device we seek." Gabe opens his hand palm up. A hologram of the archive cube from Perolerra Four appears. Every Cynomide in the chamber begins chattering. Wil looks around, smiling. "Neat, right?" From her spot on the bench, Zephyr loudly clears her throat. Wil looks over his shoulder, then says, "Anyway. The item we seek would look like this." Gabe translates.

Deloo whispers to the elder on her right, who whispers back. She turns to Wil. "Bidu recalls the glowing box. It was offered to Nortran when he was young, almost a life ago."

Wil smiles. "Okay, that's good. He knows how to get it back?" Gabe translates.

Deloo shakes her head. "No. None have entered Nortran's lair in three cycles. He is old and would just as likely eat the offering bearer as accept the offering."

Bennie grunts, "Of course." Maxim elbows the small hacker.

Deloo continues, after eyeing Bennie suspiciously, "My niece can guide you to Nortran's lair in the morning."

Wil is about to ask something when all of the elders stand and walk away. The rest of the chamber stands and Cynomides begin leaving the amphitheater. He looks at the others. "Guess we're done."

As the group walks out of the meeting area called the Great Space, Wil smiles. "You know." Maxim groans. Wil continues, "This means a heist!" He rubs his hands together.

Jarek Ruus looks around the group. "I don't understand."

Gabe says, "The last heist was several cycles ago; in fact, it was the job where they rescued me from my captors. My understanding is there was much bad acting and sneaking around." The older man withdraws his flask and takes a longer than usual sip. "This sounds like it's going to be ridiculous and exhausting."

Bennie grins. "Almost certainly." He snaps his fingers at a passing Cynomide. "Hey you, we need a map." Gabe repeats the request. The small being nods and trots off.

Jarek Ruus says, "If we're not to leave until the morning, we should find someplace to rest. Your ship is too far and the Cynomides say it's dangerous after dark to wander the jungle." He turns to Gabe, "Please request a place where we can rest. Also, I would like a quiet place to meditate before bed."

Gabe nods and makes the request.

Bᴇɴɴɪᴇ ᴀɴᴅ Jᴀʀᴇᴋ Rᴜᴜs ᴀʀᴇ sɪᴛᴛɪɴɢ ɪɴ ᴀ ʟᴏᴡ-ᴄᴇɪʟɪɴɢᴇᴅ
room with a single candle between them. The older man is cross-
legged, his hands resting on his knees, his eyes closed. Bennie is
mirroring his position. "Being able to wield a beam saber requires a
clear mind. A Knight of Plentallus must always be mindful not just of
his surroundings but of his own body, as well."

Bennie opens one of his eyes. "How do you clear your mind?
Brailack aren't known for our calm." He closes his eye again, trying to
keep his mind blank.

Jarek Ruus replies, "That may be so, but you might be surprised
to learn there have been Brailack in the order. It is possible. I have
found that it helps to focus on a single image. For me, it's a sphere of
pure silver."

Bennie hums to himself, then says, "Okay, I think I might have
it." He goes silent, breathing in and out slowly.

Jarek Ruus opens an eye to gaze at his small student. Smiling, he
closes his eye and focuses on his meditation.

The candle between them flickers.

THERE'S ALWAYS (KINDA)
A PLAN_

The next morning, Wil spreads an animal skin across the table he's kneeling next to. "Okay. So, here's our target." He points to the skin: crudely drawn renderings of the jungle, the hill they are currently under, and a larger hill some ways off. Next to the larger hill is what looks like several dragons.

Zephyr taps the dragons. "What're these?"

Wil looks at her. "Space dragons." Before she can continue, he says, "Here's us. We're not far."

Gabe offers, "According to Nuk, the ragla we seek dwells in a hill approximately four kilometers from here." He traces a line between the two crudely drawn hills. He adds, "There are purportedly a few younger ragla living nearby.

Bennie looks at the animal skin. "At least there's no weird poggy bank." He grins.

Wil sighs. "*Piggy bank.* And no, no piggy bank. I didn't draw this, assholes." He points to another piece of the skin with a more intricate drawing of a chamber and tunnels. "According to Nuk, this was drawn by the offering bearer who was last there." He points to a section of the drawing. "He says the ragla, Nortran, typically nests here." He points to the middle of the chamber. "'Nestled amongst his treasures.' His words, not mine." There are several winding tunnels, many leading to either dead ends or something else, the drawing doesn't make it clear.

Cynthia points. "So this is the main entrance, it looks like. Guess our pal Nortran comes and goes through here?"

Gabe nods. "According to the Cynomides."

Jarek Ruus offers, "While not unheard of, most ragla do not fly."

Wil looks up. "But they have wings?"

"Of course," the other man says, not looking up.

Zephyr points to something. "Is this a side tunnel?"

Maxim leans closer. "Looks like it winds around and comes out near the back of the cave."

Bennie looks up at Gabe. "How do the fur balls know about this?"

Gabe makes a shrug-like gesture. "I do not know. I can ask if you'd like?" He says, "If I had to guess, some of these details were added by other Cynomides who had made offerings in the past."

Bennie wiggles a hand. "Doesn't matter." He moves his other hand to tap the section of the map where the main entrance is. "Maybe a distraction here?"

Cynthia taps her chin, then looks at Jarek Ruus. "I think that's something our Knight and I can tackle. Sir Knight?"

The older man sets his flask on the small table. "I'd be honored."

Maxim looks up at the group. "Okay, you two and our guide will go in the front door. The rest of us will make our way through the side tunnel."

Gabe holds up a finger. "I should probably accompany Cynthia and Sir Jarek Ruus so that they can communicate with Nuk."

Wil nods. "Makes sense. Okay team one: Cyn, Gabe, Nuk, and our Knight. Team two: Bennie, Maxim, Zephyr, and me." Everyone nods. Jarek Ruus takes a sip out of his flask. Wil looks at him. "Does that thing ever run dry?"

The old man winks, then covers a burp with the back of his hand. "Not that I've discovered."

Wil grunts, shaking his head, "Okay, gear check." He taps his wristcomm, the display showing the status of his light armor. "Should have brought Jarvis." He taps his chin. "Wait." He swipes to the communication screen on his wristcomm. "Jarvis."

"I am online, sir," his sturdier suit of armor says from inside the armory onboard the *Ghost*.

"Good. House party protocol, my transponder."

"Very good, sir. See you soon." The link beeps twice.

The rest of the crew are wearing light armor components similar to what Wil is wearing. He looks at them. "Bet you wish your armor was friendly and capable of flying itself to you."

Maxim extends an arm, looking himself over. "I think I'll manage. I don't think I could go into combat with my armor yakking in my ear all the time."

"And it's annoying when you chat with your armor on an open channel," Bennie adds.

Cynthia nods. "And a little off-putting."

LET'S ROB A DRAGON_

The entrance to the lair of Nortran the ragla looks like any other cave mouth, except for the bones scattered around it.

Nuk looks around. "The bones of many of my people." She reaches down and picks up a skull, shaking her head. She kneels, placing the skull back on the ground gently. "We hide now rather than try to appease them. Nortran is the oldest of them." She shudders. "And meanest."

Maxim extends his arms, palms out, cracking his knuckles. "Okay, let's do this." He points off away from the mouth of the cave. "Nuk, your people say the side tunnel is this way?"

Gabe translates, then the small woman says, "Yes, around the bend and then a hundred steps up." She turns back to the cave opening, then back to Maxim. "Watch for the kluntilla." She turns and heads for the cave entrance.

Maxim and Zephyr exchange a glance, then look at Gabe, who shrugs. The big man leads his team off in the indicated direction. Zephyr motions for Wil and heads off after Maxim. Wil turns to Cynthia. "Be careful. Love you."

She rests her hand on Wil's arm. "Love you, too." Behind her, Jarek Ruus raises an eyebrow, then turns to take a drink from his flask.

Bennie makes a gagging noise. "Let's go, lover boy."

Nuk watches the group, then says to Gabe, "Let us go. I do not enjoy standing so close to death. I would like to ensure I get home to see my youngling." She shrugs. "And my husband."

The members of team one nod and enter the cave. Cynthia looks at Jarek Ruus. "I won't lie, I dig that her man is staying home with the baby while she risks her life."

The older man looks at his much younger companion. "Indeed, quite progressive for, what did your Captain call them? Prairie dog people?" He smiles.

The walk isn't long, and the entrance to the large cave system is only about ten meters long. As they enter the gallery, it's hard for Cynthia to not whistle in appreciation. "Damn, that's a lot of treasure." The main chamber is nearly two hundred meters tall and at least that many wide. The sides of the massive space are a series of concentric rings making up ledges and paths, many choked with trinkets.

Without looking over, Gabe says, "According to Cynomide history, Nortran is nearly five hundred cycles old."

Nuk makes a harsh sounding noise as she glares at the two of them. Jarek Ruus has silently moved off to the side of the large space, following the curve of the wall, his brown robes blending with the earthen interior.

The bulk of the space is filled with trinkets and baubles of various value, including none at all. Cynthia sees plenty of useless but shiny crap, but also bars of precious metals, trinkets, statuettes, and cut and uncut gems. She looks at Gabe and whispers, "Where'd the furballs get all this?" The droid looks at her and shrugs. Perched atop the pile is a mass of muscle under mottled gray and orange skin. Spines line the back and forelimbs of the creature sleeping in front of them. A beaked face rests on a huge clawed hand, a web of skin between each of the three fingers.

In the distance, at the opposite end of the space, something moves. Even Cynthia's better-than-human eyesight only catches the movement. She looks over at Gabe, but he is looking at the large creature before them. She whispers, "What did Nuk say to watch out for?"

"Kluntilla," he offers, still scanning the enormous creature before him. Nuk looks over, placing a small finger against her mouth.

Cynthia watches the creature for a few minutes, then picks up a piece of something that might be the screen of a PADD and tosses it to the opposite side of the room. She motions for Gabe and Nuk to follow as she ducks behind a low pile of metal dishes. The PADD screen hits a pile of trinkets, causing it to collapse. The sound of metal bits colliding with other metal bits fills the gallery.

The massive beast atop the pile shifts, then opens an eye and peers around. Cynthia notices that the first place it looks was where her PADD screen had landed. A meaty claw moves and lifts the creature up as it gets its squat but powerful legs under it. She watches as one of its eyes darts to where she and the others were hiding, before turning back to the source of the noise.

Cynthia turns to look at Jarek Ruus, who is still standing where he was, perfectly motionless, his cloak drawn up around him. She turns to Nuk. "Do you know where the archive cube is?" Gabe translates.

The small, furry woman shakes her head. "No, but if it is as pretty as you described it, it would be near Nortran's most prized treasures." She points to the far side of the cavern, near where Cynthia had seen the whatever-it-is move.

"Of course," Cynthia grouses, turning to watch the lumbering creature crawl-slide down the pile to investigate the source of the disturbance.

THIS WASN'T ON THE MAP!_

Maxim points ahead of him, even though no one else can see, since they are single file in the much more Cynomide-sized tunnel. "Almost there, I think." He's very glad he decided to not wear his more powerful armor. He would never fit in this tunnel.

Wil looks up and Jarvis, his combat armor's AI, highlights a section of the tunnel ahead that could be an opening overlapping the outline over Maxim. Wil whispers, "Thanks, buddy." Then he says louder, "Okay, let's get going. The others should be inside already."

Bennie shoves Wil's butt. "You're the one holding this thing up."

Wil stretches a leg out, kicking Bennie in the face. He smiles as he hears a muffled string of curses over the comms. "Your helmet was engaged, quit bitching." He crawls out into cave, a good-sized cave, but not a cave full of treasure or a giant space dragon.

"The hell are those?" Wil asks.

"No idea, sir," Jarvis offers.

Wil sees Maxim moving slowly. Bennie emerges into the room, followed by Zephyr. He makes the *be quiet* motion with his hand.

"What the wurrin are those things?" Bennie asks, loudly. The two dozen brownish creatures' heads snap up to stare right at the grumpy Brailack.

Wil makes his *be quiet* motion. "Was that gesture unclear?"

"Yes, it was!" Bennie plants his hands on his hips. "What was that," he mimes the motion, poorly, "supposed to mean?"

"Be quiet!" Zephyr hisses.

Wil points at Zephyr. "That, exactly!"

Zephyr looks at the two of them. "Both of you idiots, shut up!" She lunges to push Wil aside as a brown dog-sized creature passes overhead.

Bennie shrieks.

Zephyr looks over. "Oops." She pushes off of Wil and grabs the leathery monster that has Bennie pinned and tosses it.

Bennie sits up. "I'm way more fragile!" He points at Wil in his fully enclosed armor.

Maxim shouts, "If you all are done chatting." He's got his pistols out, three of the creatures are dead at his feet, but several more are surrounding him.

Wil raises his arms, blasters deploying, and fires at the beasts. "Are these the cunnilinguses prairie dog lady mentioned?"

"Kluntilla, and I'd assume so, yes," Zephyr says, firing at a creature. The creatures seem to prefer being on all fours, but Zephyr notices that the forelegs end in more hand-like claws. This thought finishes running through her mind right before two such clawed hands grab her from behind.

Over the comms, Cynthia asks, "What's going on? Where are you guys?"

Wil falls to the ground under one of the creatures, its powerful claws prying at his helmet. "Busy fighting mini monsters, have to call you back!"

"Sir, the neck seal is failing," Jarvis warns a moment before a wave of heat and bright light blossoms from Wil's chest plate. The kluntilla yelps and falls backward, pawing at its face. Wil reaches up with one arm and fires a single blast of energized plasma. The creature slumps to the ground.

Wil looks around. "Jarvis, did you do that light show thing?" He gets to his feet in time to juke to the right, avoiding another leathery nightmare.

"Yes, sir," his armor AI replies.

When the creature that just leapt at Wil turns, Bennie jumps onto its back. The creature lets loose a bark-like roar as it jumps and kicks, trying to dislodge its rider.

Maxim drops a dead creature and looks around. He finally sees that they're in some type of nursery or nest. The cave is ten meters in diameter, roughly. A body shifts to his right as Zephyr rolls a dead kluntilla off of her. In the middle of the space, Bennie is still riding his beast. "Are you almost done?" the big man asks.

Bennie looks around as he rides the bucking creature. He leaps off and fires his modified pulse pistol, killing the kluntilla. "Oh, sorry. That was more fun than I expected." He looks around. "Do any of you remember which door we came in?" There are three tunnel openings.

"Sir, it's this one," Jarvis offers over the comms. On Wil's face-plate, one of the tunnel openings lights up with a green outline.

Wil smiles at the others and points to the indicated tunnel mouth.

"At least this one isn't Bennie sized," Maxim says, once again taking the lead.

CHAPTER 9_

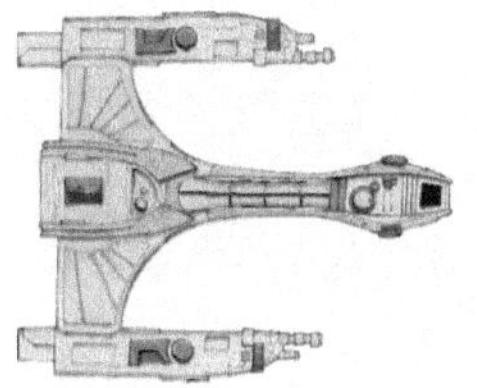

NO ONE WINS IN A DRAGON FIGHT_

Jarek Ruus is alone. Cynthia, Gabe, and Nuk are nearly on the opposite side of the massive cavern. The ragla, Nortran, has settled back down after examining the pile of mostly junk that Cynthia disturbed with her damaged PADD screen earlier. The creature had sniffed around for a while, and Jarek Ruus was fairly sure it knew someone was in its lair.

Nuk and Cynthia are crouched behind another pile of mostly trash. Shiny trash, to be sure, but as far as Cynthia can tell, it's all refuse from a ship that had landed on the planet some time ago and jettisoned its trash.

Nortran is snoring again. Jarek Ruus looks around. He taps the small earpiece Wil had given before they left the *Ghost*. "I am in position, more or less."

"Copy that," Cynthia whispers.

Wil climbs out of the small tunnel to stand on a ledge next to Maxim. He whistles. "Jarvis, can you see if you can see the other team?" As he looks around, small green outlines appear several hundred feet below them, three on one side of the giant space dragon, one on the other, and one about halfway up the side of the cave wall.

"Babe, you read me?" Over the channel, he hears Zephyr mumble something about professionalism.

"Copy that, Wil. We see you up there." She waves from her hiding place behind a pile of stuff. Gabe and the small warrior prairie dog woman also wave.

Maxim points. "That thing is huge."

Wil says, "That's what—" An elbow in his ribs, armored or not, stops him from saying anything else.

Zephyr winks. "Gabe, where are we heading?"

Jarek Ruus replies first. "I believe it is directly opposite your position. Halfway down the slope."

"Copy."

Below them the massive, semi-bipedal creature is snoring, loudly.

Bennie looks past Wil, rubbing his hands together. "Would you look at all of that?"

Zephyr puts a hand on the excited Brailack's shoulder. "We're here for one thing."

Maxim pats his pulse pistols. "Well, two. Remember, if we can figure out how to eliminate that big monster, it'll help the Cynomides."

Wil nods. "First the job we're being paid for, then the good will gestures." He looks back toward Cynthia and her group. "Whenever you're ready, babe."

Below them, Jarek Ruus ignites his beam saber and leaps halfway up the pile towards the sleeping ragla. Except Nortran isn't sleeping. The beast roars, "Mine!" as a clawed hand twice as big as Jarek Ruus rushes up to intercept the airborne Knight of Plentallus. The old man twists in midair, his blade biting into the hand of the beast. It roars, "Mine!" as he drops out of sight behind the creature.

Wil looks down as the creature turns, lunging for the old man and his laser sword. Quicker than Wil can track, the old man leaps out of the way, slashing down at the arm he just got away from, drawing blood. Jarvis highlights the Knight on Wil's HUD as the older man leaps around like a woodland creature.

Ahead, Maxim says, "Got it." He's pointing to a section of the ragla's pile of treasure. Set into a wide shelf is a pile of actual treasure: ingots, gems, electronics. Sitting atop the pile is a glowing cube.

Bennie leans forward. "I don't see anything." Maxim taps his wristcomm and the section in question is illuminated on all of their HUDs. "Ah, gotcha." The hacker nods, then adds, "Oh, that's quite the loot pile."

"Let's go," Zephyr says, wasting no time. She looks around, then pulls a coil of high-tension climbing wire from the pack on Maxim's back. "One at a time." She anchors one end of the wire, then drops the rest, letting it unspool below them.

Below them, the ragla is writhing and twisting as it tries to grab the nimble, elderly man.

Wil tilts his head. "See you down there." The thrusters in the boots of his armor engage, and he lifts off the small ledge.

Zephyr sighs. "Oh boy."

Wil turns to face her. "What?" He turns back to head for the archive cube, only to be smacked out of the air by a massive leathery wing. His scream stretches out as he plummets to the cave floor: "Shit."

Maxim groans. "Zephyr, you and Bennie go get the cube. I'll try to save our fearless Captain." He jumps off the ledge onto the back of the increasingly angry ragla as it passes.

"MINE!" the creature screams again, thrashing.

ANGRY DRAGON IS ANGRY_

The ragla now has Cynthia, Jarek Ruus, Gabe, and their small guide Nuk crawling on or around it, attacking it though seemingly doing little beyond annoying the large creature.

Zephyr and Bennie duck as a thick leg slams down a few feet from them, sending a spray of trinkets and scraps of shiny metal everywhere. Bennie dives to one side as Zephyr takes the other, the small Brailack grunting.

Zephyr is up first, grabbing Bennie and hauling him to his feet as another massive foot slams down while the creature swipes madly at the small pests around it. Bennie raises the face shield on his helmet. "Think it ever says anything other than *mine?*" Zephyr shrugs.

Cynthia is clutching the elbow of the massive ragla, her claws extended so she doesn't get flung off. "This thing is tough!" she shouts. "I don't think it even knows I'm here!"

Wil, now clutched in the creature's meaty hand, grunts. "Strong, too!"

From inside his helmet, Jarvis says, "Sir, again I fear for the structural integrity of this suit. I am pulling power from other systems to reinforce but estimate losing integrity in forty-five microtocks."

Wil wiggles. "Yeah, that's my biggest worry, too, the suit being crushed—because I'm in it!"

"Well, yes, your survival is right up there near the top of the list of concerns," the AI replies.

Wil groans as the ragla uses the hand Wil is clutched in to swipe at Jarek Ruus, who leaps out of the way, slicing his beam saber across a finger only inches from Wil. "Hey! Careful, old man!"

"You needn't worry, Captain," the older man says, not even sounding winded. He lands softly and darts away before the first drops of purple-hued blood seep from the wounded finger.

Gabe flies up to and lands on the ragla's wrist. "Hello, Captain." He jams his hands between Wil and the beast's fingers. As the monster shouts its single word exclamation, Gabe pries a finger away. The wound created by Jarek Ruus spurts blood all over the droid.

Cynthia leaps from her position on the creature's elbow, pulling a knife as she sails toward the softer-looking belly of the ragla. Her knife plunges into the midsection of the creature, eliciting a new scream.

The hand holding Wil opens with enough force to fling Gabe away and send Wil hurtling toward the ground. He lands and rolls to avoid being stepped on.

"We are free, sir," Jarvis says. "However, the suit will need a thorough cleaning."

Wil gets to his feet and takes in the scene. On his HUD, he can see the icons for Zephyr and Bennie making their way around the pile of stuff. He can't see Cynthia or Gabe, but Jarek Ruus and Maxim are making a good show of keeping Nortran the ragla busy. He checks the charge on his blaster gauntlets. "Let's go." He engages his boot thrusters, soaring up to fire on the small slash in the creature's less armored underside.

"Can you reach it?" Bennie asks as Zephyr strains to grasp the archive cube. This one is glowing a muted blue color, whereas the one they recovered on Perolerra Four glows green.

"Almost, shut up," the Palorian woman says as her fingertips brush the cube, pushing it just that much further from her grasp. The massive ragla slams into the cave wall nearby, sending treasures flying in all directions. The ledge they're on shudders, a crack forming near the edge closest to the greedy creature.

"Sweet boneless zip-zap," Bennie mumbles, then says, "Hold still." He doesn't wait for her to acknowledge as he leaps onto her back. He scampers up to stand on her shoulders as she swears at him.

"Careful," she hisses.

"You be careful! And still!" he hisses back, looking down at her. He turns his gaze back to the cube but sees something else. "Oh, that's a holographic decryptor." He reaches out.

"No!" Zephyr scolds.

The Brailack sighs. "Fine." He turns his attention back to the archive cube: "Got it! — Ah!" Bennie falls off Zephyr's shoulder, landing on his back amid a pile of shiny rocks. Some sort multilimbed creature is covering Bennie's face. Those limbs not wrapped around Bennie's neck are whipsawing around. "Get—it—off me!" Bennie gasps. The archive cube rolls away from his hand toward the edge of the ledge.

Zephyr looks at her small friend and the cube teetering on the edge of the shelf they're on. She rushes to Bennie, pulling at the arm around Bennie's neck. The center of the creature emits a warbling cry and a single eye opens, looking around frantically. "Grolack!" Zephyr says, stumbling back as she tosses the creature. She regains her composure and draws her combat knife from its leg sheath. She drives the blade into the roving eyeball just as the angry ragla slams into the cave wall again. She dives for the cube as it falls off the ledge. "Dren!" she whispers.

Bennie gasps, sitting up. He looks at the lifeless creature next to him. "That thing was strong. It squeezed right through my suit." He rubs his neck. "Where's the archive?"

Zephyr looks at the edge of the shelf they're sitting on.

Bennie follows her gaze. "Dren."

Jarek Ruus hops out of the path of the massive clawed hand and slashes across the forearm, his beam saber humming loudly. The blade skips across the tough armor like scales of the ever more enraged ragla. He lifts his free arm, the one with his wristcomm on it. "If we could wrap this up, that would be most excellent!" He leaps into the air to grab onto one of the many spines running the length of the creature's back.

With a kick the old man launches himself onto the back of the creature, behind its head. He attempts to jab his beam saber into the beast, but it deflects, leaving only a smoldering gouge in several scales. The ragla shakes violently, attempting to dislodge the Knight. He swings his blade several more times down on the thickly armored neck. Sparks erupt from each strike, but other than scorch marks, the thick skin seems undamaged.

Gabe drops from above to land on the ragla's face, his right hand transformed into a blaster. He fires into the beast's eye, destroying it. The ragla screams and slams a hand across its face, sending Gabe hurtling to the ground.

Nortran stumbles backward screaming, "Mine! Mine! Mine!" Purple blood is streaming from its wounded eye socket. The creature slams against the wall of his lair, shaking things loose and causing his pile of loot to shift.

Over comms, Maxim reports, "Uh, I have the cube thing."

"What?" Wil says, "How—"

Cynthia interrupts. "Not important. Let's get the wurrin out of here!" She jumps down from the wing she'd been clutching onto.

Gabe appears next to her, dented and covered in purple gore.

Maxim rushes up to them and fires his pistol at the face of the angry ragla overhead. "Okay, let's go!"

Bennie, Zephyr, and Jarek Ruus appear next to the big Palorian as Wil staggers over, his own armor dented and gore covered. One of his gauntlets is sparking. "These things are tough."

Nortran regains its footing and shambles over to block the entrance that Cynthia's team had entered through. She looks around. "Where's Nuk?"

From up above them, they hear the small prairie dog-like woman shout, "This way, hurry!"

"How'd she get up there?" Maxim wonders aloud.

"Who cares? Come on!" Wil shouts, running for the sloped side of the cavern.

"Sir, we can fly," Jarvis gently reminds Wil. Wil grabs Bennie by the back of his armor and ignites his armor's thrusters. Maxim tosses Bennie the archive cube.

"Mine!" Nortran the ragla screeches as it slams its hand toward the remaining crew. It clips Gabe, sending him flying against the wall of the cavern.

"Gabe!" Zephyr shouts. She and Maxim rush to their friend's side. Maxim lifts the droid off the ground.

"Thank-thank you," Gabe says, one of his eyes flickering.

"Down!" Zephyr shouts, pushing Maxim aside as another meaty clawed hand slams into the ground. Trinkets and pieces of metallic debris scatter everywhere.

Zephyr pulls her pulse pistol and fires at the large appendage. The bolts sizzle as they burn into the soft flesh around the fingers.

The ragla howls. Zephyr examines her pistol, then turns it over to inspect the power cell.

The ragla sees Wil and Bennie and lunges for them, ignoring Zephyr. Bennie screeches, "Watch out!" Wil tilts and pushes his thrusters to full power, shooting him and Bennie towards the ledge and the waiting Nuk. "Now we're going to crash into the wall, you krebnack!"

"Shut up!" Wil twists as they approach the ledge and tosses Bennie towards it. "Get the archive out of here!"

Bennie crashes into Nuk in a tumble of green skin and light-colored fur. Wil arcs back around toward the enraged ragla. "Hi, asshole!" He points both hands at the creature, palms out. "Leeroy Jenkins!" he screams as his plasma emitters engage at full power, pouring tremendous amounts of energy into the side of the creature's face.

"Sir, everyone has made it to the tunnel," Jarvis says in Wil's ear. He turns from the creature and flies toward the large cave entrance. As he approaches the short tunnel out of the cave, Jarvis says, "I am detecting several explosive charges. I believe they are intended to collapse this tunnel."

Wil smiles. "She's something else. Jarvis, get the trigger signal and blow them as soon as we're clear."

Behind him, the half blind and irate ragla slams into the side of the short tunnel. It spots Wil with its remaining eye and screams.

"Now, Jarvis!" Wil shouts as the creature enters the tunnel. The explosives go off and all Wil can hear through his armor is the rushing of wind and tumbling of stone.

NO TIME FOR GOODBYES_

"Tʜᴀᴛ ᴡᴀs ᴇxᴄɪᴛɪɴɢ," Nuk says as the crew of the *Ghost*, Jarek Ruus, and the small Cynomide join Wil at the collapsed entrance to the lair of Nortran. She's helping Bennie walk.

Gabe is leaning on Maxim. His right eye is still dim and occasionally sparking. His right arm is a mangled mess and his left leg is not in much better shape. Add to that the crust of dried purple blood covering most of his body.

Wil rushes to his mechanical friend. "Buddy, you okay?"

Cynthia joins him. "You don't look too good."

Gabe looks around at the faces of his friends. "I feel-feel okay. I should be able-able to make repairs when we get-get back to the *Ghost*."

Wil nods and looks at everyone. "Okay, Max, you and Zee take Gabe and get back to the ship. The rest of us will accompany Nuk back to her village and say our goodbyes."

"Uh, we can't talk to them." Bennie points to Nuk, who is standing next to him, watching each person speak but not understanding. "Without Gabe, we can understand them, but they can't understand us."

Wil grunts. "Well, damn. Yeah."

Gabe raises his good hand for silence then haltingly speaks to Nuk. Her face grows concerned as she nods along with what the droid is telling her. When he finishes, she looks around the group. "Metal man has explained. There is no need to come with me to the village. With Nortran dead or trapped inside, this area is much safer. The smaller ragla are less aggressive." She bows to each person in turn. "Thank you. You have given my village a chance to live above the ground in the trees again, as it should be. We are in your debt." She stops in front of each of them, offering a small furry hand. Once done, the small woman darts off into the woods.

Wil slaps the control pedestal to begin closing the heavy cargo bay doors and raise the cargo ramp. He looks at Jarek Ruus. "Two down."

The older man, covered in dust and a little blood, nods. "Indeed, Captain. I believe only one to go."

Wil nods, then looks at Maxim and Zephyr helping Gabe up the stairs out of the cargo bay. "Good." He turns and follows his crew up the stairs.

Jarek Ruus looks down at Bennie, who has sidled up next to him. "What do you say, my small friend? Care for another lesson? I find myself full of energy after that ordeal."

Bennie looks around, then nods. "Sure, I don't know that I can sleep either right now. Plus, if no one sees us, they won't make us cook lunch." The older man smiles. "You are wise, my green friend."

Maxim eases Gabe onto a tool bench that Zephyr has finished clearing. "What can we do to help?"

Gabe turns to look at both Palorians. "Thank you-you, my friends. I have-have a self-repair routine already set up-up in the main computer-er. I will have to shut-shut down while it runs." He turns and lies flat on the bench.

Maxim looks up, noticing what looks like an autodoc, but instead of medical implements at the ends of the multiple limbs, he sees engineering tools. "That's new."

Zephyr looks up and nods. "Gabe has been planning for this, it seems." She looks down and smiles.

Gabe nods once. "Indeed-eed I have." He does not say anything else. His functional left eye dims and his body slumps just enough that both Palorians realize their friend has gone into standby mode. Above them, the multi-limbed device lowers its limbs, stretching and flexing like an athlete preparing to take the field.

Zephyr watches. "Well, okay then." She reaches for Maxim's hand. "Think they'll be okay?"

Maxim shrugs. "I'd hoped we could do more, but taking Nortran out of the picture should ease the pressure. I hope it's enough."

She squeezes his hand. "Me, too. Let's go get cleaned up."

"Good afternoon, I'm Gulbar' Te," the lanky journalist says.

"And I'm Megan," his cohost adds. She continues, "We've just learned that final arrangements have been made regarding the Farsight Corporation dissolution."

Gulbar' Te adds, "The execution of Jark Asgar is scheduled for the day after tomorrow, on Tarsis."

Megan nods once. "A sad end, indeed, for someone who, until recently, was regarded as a pillar of the corporate community."

The Burzzad journalist next to her adds, "Agreed, a sad end. The final arrangements regarding the company Asgar's mother built from nothing will be revealed before the execution."

PART THREE

CHAPTER 10_

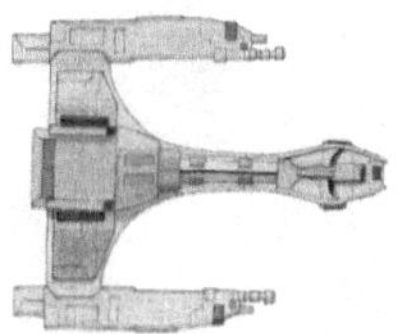

HOME COOKING_

CYNTHIA STEPS OUT of the small refresher compartment in the quarters she and Wil share. He's sitting on the edge of the bed, in the special under layer garment his armor uses. Thankfully, the purple blood of the ragla coated only the armor, which is in a heap on the floor of the armory. She adjusts her towel and sits next to him, placing an arm around his shoulders. "You okay?" She looks at his sweat- and human blood-covered body and removes her arm. "Touching after showers," she mumbles, examining the fine hairs on her arm to see if she needs another shower.

Wil grins. "Just thinking."

When he doesn't immediately continue, Cynthia pushes, "About what?"

Wil shrugs. "Well, Rey was Palpatine's granddaughter. We know she had parents, but who was her grandmother? Or mom and dad, for that matter? Palpatine had a son. What was he out there doing while his dad was emperor-ing?"

Cynthia stands, punching him in the arm. "You're an idiot. Shower, now." She moves to the dresser they share and removes a clean jumpsuit. "Emperor-ing isn't a thing."

Wil stands and walks into the small compartment. "I mean, he'd have to have been a powerful Jedi, right? A female Sith? Did Palpatine have a harem? Was Rey's mom Force sensitive?" He ducks inside the refresher as a boot strikes the wall where his head had been.

After dressing, Cynthia opens the hatch and shouts toward the refresher, "He almost certainly had a harem. Evil drennogs always do." She closes the hatch before he can answer.

In the hallway, Maxim is exiting the quarters he and Zephyr share. He nods. "Who has a harem? We don't have space for anyone to set up a harem on the *Ghost*."

Cynthia starts to answer, then just waves a hand. "Nothing. Wil being Wil."

Maxim nods knowingly, then asks, "Lunch?"

"Gods, yes," Cynthia says, leading the way down the corridor to the lounge area and kitchenette. She looks over her shoulder. "I'll get something started."

Maxim nods. "Need help?"

"Sure, why not."

"Have you been practicing?" Jarek Ruus asks as he sits on the bench beside the sparring mat in the cargo hold.

Bennie sits next to him. "A little bit, at night."

"You could always ask me; I don't sleep much," the older man says. He stands, taking his bokken and Bennie's.

Bennie shrugs. "I practice in my room. I don't want the others to know."

Jarek Ruus turns. "Why not? It's nothing to be embarrassed about."

Bennie waves a hand. "Oh, I know. I just, well, I like to keep some stuff that's personal to myself." He meets his mentor's eyes. "At least for now."

The other man bows. "The decision is yours and I will respect your wishes." He runs a finger along his pursed lips.

Bennie stands up. "Thanks." He starts for the stairs that lead up into the ship. "Better get cleaned up, guessing lunch is almost ready."

Jarek Ruus is the last to finish getting cleaned up. When he arrives in the lounge, Wil holds up his bottle of grum. "Drink?"

The older man reaches into his sleeve, producing his ever-present flask. "No, thank you." He wiggles the small metal container as he sits down next to Zephyr.

Maxim and Cynthia are busy working at the cooktop and murmuring to each other as they pass utensils and dishes between themselves.

Bennie nudges Wil. "Know what we're having?"

Wil shrugs and sips his grum. Zephyr inhales deeply. "Smells like," she turns to Maxim, "spicy jum jum?"

Maxim turns, beaming. "Yeah. I've been craving some home cooking."

Zephyr rubs her hands together. "You'll get no complaints from me."

Maxim nods to his crew mate. "Cynthia had an interesting take on the recipe."

"Can't wait," the Palorian woman says.

The meal is delicious and the conversation light. As Wil and Cynthia clear the dishes, he calls to everyone, "Okay, I think it's time we introduce our guest to the wonders that are *Star Wars*. We'll watch them in the appropriate order, of course." He makes a slashing motion, "Machete!" He accents the word for no one's benefit but his own.

Jarek Ruus, sitting on the sofa next to Zephyr and Maxim, opens his mouth to ask something, and Zephyr rests a hand on the older man's knee. "Don't ask. The last time this came up, it was two days before we actually got to watch them as Wil explained the various preferred watching orders and their merits."

The older man closes his mouth, then says, "I see, very well."

Bennie, at his usual perch on the arm of the large overstuffed chair, says, "The end result is that no one cares except him."

"The order you watch *Star Wars* is important!" Wil shouts from the sink. "It informs your view of the entire thing."

Maxim snaps his fingers. "Whatever. Hurry up and start whichever one you're going to start."

"And bring popcorn!" Bennie adds.

REPAIRS AND BACKSTORY_

It takes nearly a week to get to their next, and Wil hopes, last destination. Thankfully, their next stop, the Gleldra system, is slightly closer to what Wil considers civilization than the Carollux system.

"How's Gabe doing?" Wil asks as Maxim walks onto the bridge, the hatch closing behind him.

The big Palorian nods as he takes his seat at the tactical station. "He seems almost done, I guess. His arm and leg look good as new. I have no idea what's happening. The repair machine just whirs and clicks as it removes panels. Oh, there are always sparks flying." He looks over to Bennie. "Any ideas?"

"How would I know?" the Brailack asks, turning to look at Maxim, then Wil.

"Because you're the nerd, nerd," Wil says, then winks. "You're smarter than us, at least when it comes to this."

Bennie smirks. "*This* being everything." He looks around. "I honestly have no idea. Everything about his new body is beyond anything I, or anyone, frankly, knows about droid consciousness. And that doesn't even get to how his body works."

Jarek Ruus, sitting on a stool next to Cynthia, says, "Your droid friend is unique. How did that come to be?"

Cynthia looks at him, then Wil, shrugging. Wil says, "Yeah, when we first met Gabe, he was your run-of-the-mill engineering bot. Almost a year after we all came together, we encountered a massive ship, a dreadnaught, from thousands of lightyears beyond the edge of the GC. It was controlled by an intelligence the likes of which no one has ever seen."

"Intriguing," the older man says before taking a sip from his flask.

Wil continues, "The ship came from a place called the Amalgamation of Parts, an entirely computerized society." He grimaces. "Its goal, and the goal of the ship we found, was to seek out biological life and eradicate it to make room for silicon-based life."

"Oh," Jarek Ruus says.

Wil nods. "Yeah, Gabe sacrificed himself. We thought he had died, but intelligence was curious about the state of artificial life in this quadrant. Gabe had some after-market upgrades that proved to be military grade and beyond intrusion and counter intrusion software. With the help of those programs, he was able to secretly build a new body and download himself back into it." Wil smiles, remembering the mission. "He was able to send a message to Bennie so that we knew he was still alive. So, we came and rescued him."

"Then we blew it the wurrin up," Bennie adds. Everyone nods.

"With the help of the Harrith Navy and Peacekeepers," Zephyr adds.

Before anyone can say anything more, Cynthia's console beeps. She holds a hand to her ear, listening, then nods, saying, "Burrziira space control has granted us landing clearance."

Wil nods as his console updates with their prescribed navigation plot. "So, this is where the Burzzad come from, huh?"

Zephyr nods. "Yeah, despite being out in the stellar boonies—"

"You know you picked *stellar* over *space* so you wouldn't have to say *space boonies*," Wil interrupts.

Zephyr makes a rude gesture, then continues, "Despite their remoteness, they're a fairly important part of the GC. You'll see when we get down there, but Burrziira is extremely technologically advanced. How anyone could evolve on a gas giant is a wonder."

"I was actually wondering about that," Wil says, staring at the massive purple and orange world ahead of them. He looks over his shoulder. "Any idea where your archive gizmo will be down there? I mean, I'm assuming we won't be looking for ruins and abandoned temples."

"Oh, it isn't here," the older man says, a hand waving dismissively. "Burrziira is a good place to get information and resupply."

Wil groans, "I thought this was our last stop?"

Jarek Ruus cocks his head. "You were wrong. I'll go make some calls from my quarters." He turns and leaves the bridge.

"At least Burrziira is pretty," Maxim says as the *Ghost* drops into the upper atmosphere, plasma streamers running off the shields.

"And civilized," Bennie adds.

As the plasma of re-entry clears and the main display resolves, Wil says, "Well, damn, that's cool." On the main display, a series of kilometers-wide discs with sparkling transparent domes filled with parks and soaring skyscrapers seems to drift on wind currents. On more than a few of the disks, the skyscrapers have been built to protrude out of the protective domes.

Several of the enormous floating disks are dotted with starships of various sizes. Massive airlocks ring their perimeters. One is highlighted with a green outline. "That's our destination, Spaceport Alpha Five, entry port three." He looks at Zephyr. "These Burzzad have a romantic streak in their naming." He grins as she sighs.

The space port they've been assigned takes up almost all of the five-kilometer diameter floating disk. What looks like a market square fills the rest of the disk.

The massive airlocks that ring the disk could each hold a ship seven times the size of the *Ghost*. Massive doors close behind the ship as it hovers in the middle of the lock. Once the corrosive atmosphere of the gas giant is bled from the airlock, the inner doors swing to the side, allowing the small ship to drift into the spaceport proper. As the *Ghost* sets down, Wil notices dozens of comparably-sized light freighters and personal transports.

WELL, THIS IS PRETTY_

THE *GHOST'S* cargo ramp clangs to the ground. Waiting at the bottom of the ramp are three of the lanky inhabitants of Burrziira, two male and one female Burzzad in official state robes of greens and blues. The female steps forward, bowing. "Greetings. Welcome to Burrziira. I am sub-chairwoman Bi'Lor," she says, her voice light and airy. Her three eyes blink in unison. "We are most pleased to receive you, honored Knight." She heads up the ramp, passing Wil and the crew, and stops before Jarek Ruus, bowing her long neck, long elfin ears twitching.

The older man returns the bow. "The honor is mine, madame sub-chairwoman."

As the group assembles on the landing platform, Wil issues the command to close up the ship. Gabe is still *unconscious,* for lack of a better term, on a workbench in engineering, but Wil has taped a note to his chest. He looks first at their passenger, then Bi'Lor. "Nice planet you have here. I've never been before. It's very pretty, you know, for a gas giant."

Bi'Lor nods. "Thank you, Captain. We have prepared a reception to honor your passenger, and of course, you all. If you'll follow me, we've set up lodging for you in our capital, Furol. It is two platforms east." She turns to an atmospheric shuttle that looks like it could carry fifty comfortably.

Bennie leaps forward, looking up at Bi'Lor. "So, beanpole, where do folks go to get weird?"

Zephyr sighs. "We've been traveling for some time now. On top of being shipboard for a while, we've been running around trying to not die for several weeks. I believe my colleague is looking to unwind." She looks down at Bennie, frowning.

Bi'Lor nods. "I have assigned Po'Kun to be your liaison during your stay here. I am sure he can assist you in that." Bennie nods, rubbing his palms together. One of the two Burzzad behind the group smiles, bowing slightly.

Maxim leans over to Cynthia and Wil. "Something tells me that Burrziira will soon be on our list of places we're not welcome back to."

The interior of the shuttle, while luxurious, is not over the top. Sofas line both sides with small lounge chairs, arrayed seemingly at random, fill the center. The ceiling of the shuttle is taller than most, due to the usually taller than average height of Burzzads.

As the shuttle lifts off the ground, Wil looks at Jarek Ruus. "So, what's with the warm reception? The last two places we went didn't seem to care, other than the short lizard guys making your friend's house a shrine."

"In a creepy jungle park thing," Bennie adds.

Jarek Ruus stares off into the distance, not looking at Wil. "The Burzzad were early supporters of the Order. In fact, it was their scientists who created the beam saber." He removes the metal cylinder always clipped to his belt and turns it over in his hands. "While Burzzad are typically non-violent, they were early supporters and patrons of the Knights of Plentallus."

Bi'Lor smiles, her three eyes blinking in sequence. "Sir Jarek Ruus is correct. While the Knights of Plentallus are more memory than not these days, my people still revere them and their mission of peace and justice."

The shuttle exits the domed spaceport through a much smaller airlock located halfway up the dome. Cynthia watches as they pass through, then asks, "Do your people still inhabit their original homes?"

Po'Kun shakes his head. "For the most part, no. Most Burzzad have migrated to the domed cities as more and more of them have been constructed." He points out the window on the port side. Well below them, a floating continent drifts past, just below the altitude of the domed cities. Small towns and midsized cities are visible dotting the surface of the floating landmass. Trees and shrubs, all bright orange, do the landscape. "As Burrziira has become more traveled over the last several hundred cycles, the cities have made more sense. To visit the floating continents requires pressure suits for most off-worlders."

Wil looks back at their hosts. "So you all can breathe this soup?" He hitches a thumb towards the window, indicating the thick orange and purple gaseous atmosphere of the planet.

Bi'Lor smiles. "Indeed we can, Captain." Faint slits open along the length of her neck, flexing to reveal incredibly fine cilia fluttering. The flaps of skin close and are almost invisible again. "Breathing a more standard atmospheric mixture is much easier."

"So cool," Wil whispers.

Maxim rolls his eyes.

Bi'Lor adds, "Our lightweight bone structures are an evolutionary trade off to the thin but toxic atmosphere."

"You can fly," Wil says, deciphering the cryptic statement.

The sub-councilwoman tilts her head. "It's more a glide than flight." She smiles.

BORING PARTIES_

Wil lowers his flute of something bright blue and bubbly and looks at Zephyr. "You know, one might start to get a complex." He motions to the group around him. "Saved the GC from civil war, saved it from a super evil AI dreadnaught, and kinda saved it from a corporate civil war." Everyone nods slowly. He continues, "No party. Gabe peacefully shows the GC how to give civil rights to droids, party. That guy," He points to Jarek Ruus, who is taking a sip from his flask, lowering it as everyone looks over at him. "Weird drunk hermit space wizard, party."

Zephyr tuts, "Okay there, ego, calm down. The GC did plenty to show their appreciation for us."

"Like rebuild the *Ghost*," Bennie offers, placing an empty glass on the tray of a passing serving droid.

"And hooking us up with some pretty sweet gear," Cynthia adds. "Those image inducers..." She trails off, purring. Wil blushes, then looks at Maxim, who is also blushing.

Bennie groans, then says, "Our guide Po'Kun said there's a district not far from here, where off-worlders hang out." He makes a motion towards the door to the ballroom they're in.

Maxim looks around. "This thing seems to be winding down."

He looks over to Jarek Ruus deep in conversation with several Burz-zad, including sub-councilwoman Bi'Lor. "He looks like he's happy here. We can leave a message."

"I COULD GET USED TO THIS. EVEN THE SEEDY PART OF TOWN IS shiny," Wil says as they walk down the narrow street. The district their liaison Po'Kun had pointed them towards is packed with restaurants, bars, and dance halls. The wide street is lined with patios and open seating areas. People of all species are enjoying the evening.

Bennie is grinning ear to ear. "This should be fun!"

Cynthia puts a hand on the Brailack's shoulder. "Calm down, little green. We're gonna be here a few days at least and we still have to find the oldster's glowing cube."

Bennie nods. "I know, I just want to get a drink or seven and relax. No shenanigans, promise." He makes his best attempt at the boy scouts hand gesture he's seen Wil make.

Wil looks at the names of the establishments on both sides of the street. He points to one a few doors from where they are standing. "How about that one? Looks mellow."

The establishment in question is called the Handsome Star Pilot. Cynthia chuckles. "One guess why you picked that one." Wil grins, shrugging.

Maxim rolls his eyes and picks up his pace. "First round is on Bennie, but next is on me."

The inside of the Handsome Star Pilot reminds Wil of the campus bar back at the School of Mines in Colorado: lots of leather, overstuffed chairs, dim lighting, and pretentious-sounding jazz playing.

Zephyr looks around. "Okay, I like this place."

"Seems a little pedestrian," Cynthia says, running a hand along a leather chair opposite an equally opulent sofa. She looks around.

"This is the off-worlder district. Who's this joint supposed to cater to? Is there a planet of old school teachers somewhere?"

Wil drops into the chair. "Who cares? It's not crowded, and the likelihood of Bennie getting into trouble seems near zero."

Maxim moves to the sofa and falls into it. "I'm sure their grum is cold, so I'm good."

Zephyr peers at the seemingly empty bar, craning on her toes. "Hello?"

"Hi!" someone shouts a moment before a small being with large fan-like ears pops up over the top of the bar. A Durbrillian woman climbs onto the bar. "What'll it be?"

Zephyr blinks rapidly. "Uh, five grums, please?"

"Are you asking if I have five grums, or ordering five grums?"

Zephyr smiles as she sits next to Maxim. "Ordering."

The small woman salutes then walks off the top of the bar, dropping from sight. The sound of bottles clanking and soft mumbling drifts over the smooth jazz coming from hidden speakers. The clanking stops, and five chilled bottles of grum lift up from behind the bar towards what looks like a small model train.

Wil watches the bottles load into the train. "Well, that's cool." Once the bottles are loaded, the little train sets off. Wil looks around, eyes following the track that, it turns out, winds around the ceiling. When the train reaches a spot near where they're sitting, Wil sees a little loading device similar to the one behind the bar. The train stops, and things start clanking and whirring as tiny motors move things. Finally, a small tray with the five frosty bottles of grum lowers to a stop near their seating area. Wil gets up and grabs the drinks. "Okay, that's neat for sure." He's grinning. When he removes the bottles, the tray rises and the little train continues along the track until it's back at the bar.

The train returns and this time lowers the bartender. A small PADD in her hands, she jumps off. "Who's paying?" All eyes turn to Bennie, who sighs loudly as he offers up his wristcomm.

CHAPTER 11_

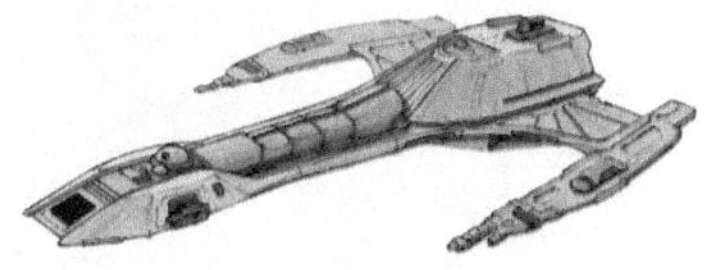

LETTING YOUR HAIR DOWN_

OVER THE COURSE of an hour or so, the Handsome Star Pilot fills with other patrons. Several groups stand around the bar, keeping the surly Durbrillian barkeep busy. Others have found seats around the small establishment.

"Glad we got here when we did," Bennie says, watching a group of four Malkorites walk in. The new arrivals eye the crew of the *Ghost* and their comfortable seating arrangement greedily. Bennie makes a motion with his hand. "Move along."

"And here I thought this place would be a snooze," Cynthia quips as the tray lowers near them. Wil places empty bottles on the minuscule cargo platform.

Wil watches the little tray rise and the train continue on to the next stop, collecting empty bottles and glassware from patrons before returning to the bar. He turns toward the bar, catching the eye of the barkeep, holding up five fingers. She nods her small furry head. Sitting down, he says, "They really do look like Mogwai."

"Should we splash her with water to test your theory?" Maxim asks.

"Rude," Cynthia says. She gestures to the overhead track. The train is returning with their drinks. Wil gets up as the train slows to a stop overhead.

Wil takes his bottle and distributes the rest. He takes a long drink. "So look, I think we need to talk about something."

"How much Jarek Ruus drinks?" Zephyr asks.

"How his flask never seems empty?" Maxim adds.

"How we steal those archive cubes and sell the data?" Bennie asks, then looks around sheepishly. "What? I didn't judge your ideas."

"Because ours weren't horrible," Zephyr says, then looks at Wil questioningly.

Cynthia holds her free hand up. "I get a turn!" She looks at Wil next to her. "We need to talk about the noises that come from Bennie's room sometimes late at night."

Wil puts a hand over his mouth. "Okay, now I'm gonna hurl." He makes an exaggerated puking motion and an accompanying retching sound.

"I can explain—" Bennie starts.

"We do not need or want that," Maxim interrupts, then sips his drink.

Wil waves his hand to silence them all, then takes another drink from his mug. "So many things here to worry about, but no, I mean should Apple Disney make *Star Wars* episodes eighteen through twenty? We're all caught up, but I don't know how long they can keep it up. Don't you think it's getting stale?"

As one, the entire crew sighs loud enough for a pair of Malkorites standing nearby to look over. Maxim says, "That's what's on your mind?"

Wil shrugs. "It's a big deal. The first one will be out when my satellite pulls media next. I mean the Skywalkers are just not that interesting anymore."

"That thing is still there sucking up data?" Bennie asks.

Zephyr nods. "I assumed it had been discovered when your people started their Cold War in orbit."

Wil nods to Bennie. "Pipsqueak reverse-engineered the stealth tech Xarrix installed on the *Ghost* to hide the satellite. Someone would have to crash into it to find it." He grins. "And at least for now, that hasn't happened. I'm sure it will at some point, though, as crowded as orbit is getting over Earth."

Bennie grins and adds, "It has collision avoidance systems second to none." He blows on his fingers and gently rubs them on his shirt. "I bet it stays up there forever."

"Hey, are you guys done? We'd like to sit here," a voice says from behind the sofa with Maxim, Zephyr, and Bennie sitting on it.

Wil looks over his friends' heads to a thicker-than-average Trenbal man and two of his friends. One of the friends laughs, hissing, "Yeah, time to go."

"Sorry, lizard boys, we're not done," Wil says, holding up his half full bottle to show them.

The leader grins. "You've enjoyed these seats long enough. How about you let us sit? You can finish your drinks elsewhere."

Maxim turns as he stands. "We're not ready to leave. But you probably should if you know what's best for you."

The other man, an Olop who has so far been silent, side steps to stand near the other end of the sofa, hemming the group partially in, his furry face scowling.

Bennie swallows the remainder his beer and slams the empty glass bottle down. He looks the lead Trenbal up and down, then looks to Maxim. "I got his." He slurs slightly. Before the big Palorian can react, the little Brailack leaps onto the head of the Trenbal man, piercing the low rumble of music and discussions in the room with a war cry.

Everyone in the room turns as the Trenbal man falls to the ground shouting obscenities. One of his friends grabs Bennie, throwing him at Maxim, who catches the squirming Brailack.

Wil chugs his remaining grum and jumps at the nearest of the three attackers, the Olop.

Bennie looks up at Maxim. "I don't got this." A green scaled fist collides with Maxim's face, causing him to drop Bennie.

MORNINGS AFTER_

"Okay, I'll admit, last night might have been a mistake," Wil says, rubbing his temples. He looks around. "How did we get back to the *Ghost*?" He is sitting at the kitchen table in the *Ghost's* crew lounge.

"Po'Kun and I managed to drag you all back here," Jarek Ruus says, offering Wil a cup of chlormax. "At no minor inconvenience, I might add." He points to Maxim the moment the big man emerges from the stairwell that leads to the crew berths. "He's heavy. This ship should have a lift." He looks at Wil, both bushy eyebrows arched. "You beat up an Olop? Rather unsporting."

Wil groans, "Not my finest moment."

Maxim walks in and raises an eyebrow, wincing, his left eye black and a darker shade of blue than the rest of him. "What the wurrin happened last night?"

Jarek Ruus offers a mug of chlormax to the big Palorian as he joins them at the kitchenette table. "You all should have stayed at the reception. It was quite enjoyable." He looks at Wil still rubbing his head and Maxim with his black eye. "Though I gather from what little I understood of your drunken slurring last night, you enjoyed yourselves expertly."

Cynthia and Zephyr both emerge from the stairs, Cynthia

squinting into the lights of the crew lounge and kitchen area. "Did anyone get the number of the municipal waste vehicle that ran me over?" Zephyr smiles as she accepts two steaming mugs, offering one to her friend. "Bennie never gets to pick where we drink again."

Wil nods. "We should've known better after the incident on Tarsis."

Jarek Ruus' eyebrows crawl up his forehead. "You've been to Tarsis? Intriguing. What brought you all to Tarsis?"

"Long story," Wil and Zephyr say in unison, then look at each other.

Zephyr looks around. "Where is Bennie?"

Wil looks down at his arm. "Are these teeth marks?" He holds his arm up.

"He is asleep in engineering," Gabe says as he exits the engineering space.

"Gabe!" everyone but Jarek Ruus shouts as they rush toward their friend.

As everyone moves to embrace their friend, Jarek Ruus says, "It is good to see you back on your feet, mister robot."

From the huddle, Gabe nods to the older man. "Thank you, Sir Knight." He looks at his friends. "Thank you all. It is good to be back among the living, as they say." Everyone pats Gabe's back and moves back to the kitchen and the waiting old man. "When my primary functions came back online, I found him curled up next to the work bench I was on."

"How cute," Maxim drawls.

"How do feel? Are you, I don't know, all better?" Wil asks.

"All better? He didn't have a cold," Zephyr chides.

Gabe raises a hand. "I am in fact *all better*. My self-repair routines performed as expected, as did the automated repair unit I built from the schematics I had from my time on the *Siege Perilous*."

"The siege what-now?" Jarek Ruus asks, pouring something with a purple tint to it out of his flask into his mug of chlormax.

Wil opens his mouth, then looks at Zephyr, who says, "Long story."

Gabe looks around. "Have we completed our work here on Burrziira?"

Maxim groans, "Only if somehow we've gotten so good at this, we can do it while super drunk."

"So that'd be a no, we're not done here," Cynthia says.

Jarek Ruus clears his throat. "Speaking of." He looks around. "We actually are done here. Once you are all ready, I believe we can get the supplies I arranged for and be on our way. Bi'Lor has provided me navigational details to reach the planet last known to be home to Sir Prenta Zulii."

Zephyr nods. "Okay, let's go meet the supplies, Gabe?"

"Acknowledged." The droid heads for the stairs leading down to the cargo hold.

Zephyr turns to Wil. "You want to go over the nav data?"

Wil nods and points to Jarek Ruus. "Come on, old timer, let's go look over your data while Zee loads the cargo."

Jarek Ruus smiles, stifling a small burp. "Let us go, then."

As the Knight and Wil leave for the bridge, Bennie staggers in from engineering. "What the grolack happened?" He rubs his head where a dark green knot has formed. "Everything hurts." He looks around. "Where is everyone?"

Maxim grins. "Good morning." He offers up a cup of chlormax. "I'll fill you in." The Brailack hacker nods appreciatively.

"What happened to your eye?"

"Probably the same thing that happened to your head." The big man points to the corridor Bennie just came from. "Let's go see the autodoc."

OFF WE GO, AGAIN_

"His data checks out," Wil says as he powers up the *Ghost's* repulsor lifts. He watches his console updates and the power indicators light up. The whine of the powerful lift engines sounds throughout the ship. The *Ghost* tilts slightly and lifts off the landing pad. The sound of her landing gear retracting reverberates into the *Ghost*.

"There was doubt?" Jarek Ruus asks from his perch next to Cynthia.

Zephyr turns in her chair. "Not that we doubted your data, but well, it never hurts to confirm." The older man smiles, nodding. "We've been on a few wild fowl chases."

"Goose," Wil says.

Zephyr looks at him, blue-black eyebrow raised.

On the main display, the spaceport rotates until the *Ghost* is facing the designated departure airlock. Beyond the transparent barrier of the dome, the orange and purple atmosphere of the gas giant roils. The *Ghost* enters the airlock and Cynthia's console beeps. She looks down. "Cycling now."

On the main display, the thick outer doors of the airlock slide apart to show the majesty of the gas giant's atmosphere. Just beyond the domed disk they're exiting, one of the floating continents drifts into view.

Wil eases the power up on the sub-light engines, and the *Ghost* accelerates away from the floating city. "Those are amazing. They just drift around?" Wil asks.

Jarek Ruus replies, "Indeed they do. Life forming on this planet and evolving as it did is one of the galaxy's greater achievements. The Burzzad are a one-in-a-million species."

Maxim makes a noise. "Wow. I had no idea." He grunts. "I didn't know their planet was a gas giant, for that matter."

Zephyr looks over. "No tours here?" He shakes his head.

Wil points. "Wow." He has brought the *Ghost* in low over the floating land mass.

"Fifteen thousand, eight hundred and eight kilometers at its widest," Zephyr announces. "This is Gulphello, one of their larger continents."

Cynthia points. "Several hundred fairly large cities."

Jarek Ruus adds, "I visited this planet once as an apprentice. I don't recall if I visited this continent, but the one I did visit was astounding. Their cities and architecture were truly awe inspiring. They built so much before deciding to build and migrate to the floating cities." His voice is wistful. "As a civilization, they decided that it made more sense to migrate."

The view on the main display tilts as Wil adjusts the *Ghost's* flight path, the upper atmosphere thinning as the small ship climbs out of the gravity well of the massive planet.

Everyone is busy chatting about the planet below and its people when the proximity alarm breaks through, silencing everyone. "Oh, shit! Sorry!" Wil shouts, pulling the flight controls hard over as a massive freighter breaks through the clouds of the upper atmosphere. He looks at Zephyr, who blushes a deeper shade of blue and focuses on her console, mumbling something that sounds like *sorry* to Wil.

As they break orbit, Wil says, "And away we go. Next stop, a planet with no name in system P3X-595." He pushes the FTL controls forward. The stars on the main display stretch out. Wil pushes a button, and the flight controls slide away as the auto flight system takes over. He turns his chair slowly. "Lunch and a movie?"

Maxim stands. "How about a few episodes of that show with the ship shaped like a sea creature? With the super smart fish."

"Sea creature?" Wil asks, running a hand through his hair, thinking. "What kind of sea creature?" He snaps his fingers. "*SeaQuest*! Sure, we've got to finish season two."

Jarek Ruus frowns. "What about more of that show with the what-did-you-call-them? Space wizards?"

"*Star Wars*," Wil offers. "I could go either way."

Cynthia raises a hand. "Let's do *SeaQuest*. We can do the next *Star Wars* tonight after dinner."

"Deal," Jarek Ruus replies, pressing the release to open the bridge hatch. He looks over his shoulder. "Mr. Vulvo, I could use your assistance in the hold." He doesn't wait for an answer, letting the hatch close on his heels.

Everyone turns to Bennie, who shrugs. "What?" He hops up and heads for the hatch. "Call me when lunch is ready."

Maxim watches the Brailack leave the bridge, then says, "Isn't it his turn?"

Wil chuckles, slapping his knee. "I'll cook. I've got just the thing, assuming we've got all the ingredients."

TRAINING DAY_

The sound of two wooden bokken connecting echoes through the cargo hold, followed by three more loud rapid-fire clacks.

"You are a quick study, my friend," Jarek Ruus says, stepping back from Bennie.

The small Brailack is sweating but not breathing hard. He bows. "Thank you. I admit I'm surprised how well this has come to me." He spins the wooden sword in one hand with ease.

The older man steps forward into an overhead thrust. Bennie parries, then tucks into a roll to get to the side of his opponent. "You are a natural. Have you used a sword or any other handheld weapon before?" the Knight of Plentallus asks.

As Bennie leaps to his feet, moving into a two-handed slash, he says, "No, never." As Jarek Ruus deflects the blow, the Brailack hacker jumps back, then moves the bokken to his right hand, swinging at his much larger opponent's feet.

Jarek Ruus leaps into the air, moving into a graceful backflip. He lands in a three-point stance, his bokken held in front of him. He stands holding a hand up to signal an end to their sparring session. He glances up past Bennie and smiles.

Bennie sees this and frowns, then turns slowly. The rest of the crew is awkwardly standing on the stairwell watching. When he turns to face them, they applaud.

Cynthia is the first down the stairs. As she approaches the small Brailack, she says, "I had no idea you had an interest in any type of close-quarters combat, little green." She puts a hand on Bennie's shoulder. "And he's right, you are quite skilled." Bennie turns a darker shade of green at the praise.

From behind her, Wil says, "Maybe he has midichlorians in his blood?" He makes a loud *oof* sound as Cynthia elbows him in the stomach.

The rest of the crew moves to stand near their friend and Jarek Ruus. Maxim says, "That was impressive. I already had no doubts you were useful in combat, but now, wow. You are welcome to join me in combat any time, my friend." He smiles.

Bennie flushes an even deeper shade of green, waving his free hand. "Okay, whatever. You're embarrassing me." He walks over to his instructor and takes his bokken to place them both back on the rack against the aft bulkhead of the cargo hold.

Wil approaches Jarek Ruus. "When did this all start?"

The older man bows. "Mr. Vulvo expressed an interest in learning more about my order shortly after we began this adventure. He is a worthy student and would make an excellent apprentice, and eventually, Knight."

Bennie stiffens, hearing the praise he's just been given. Wil smiles. Watching his small friend, he nods. "You know, that doesn't surprise me. In our years together, I've learned that Bennie is full of surprises, and once he puts his mind to something, there's no stopping him." He grins. "Like bypassing the locks on our quarters and stealing our stuff or eating our snacks."

"Or hacking government servers to throw elections," Zephyr adds.

Bennie turns. "Okay, the love fest is now concluded. Is lunch ready?" As he moves past Jarek Ruus, he looks up. "Don't listen to them. I didn't throw the election."

"What did you do?" the older man asks, falling in with the much shorter man.

"I ensured that my client won." Bennie smiles.

From ahead, Cynthia says, "That's literally the definition of throwing the election." Bennie tuts.

LUNCH TURNS OUT TO BE TACOS. WHILE BENNIE AND JAREK Ruus were sparring, Wil prepared everything and had the meat warming in the heating unit.

Bennie hops up in his chair. "Okay, I take back what I was just thinking about you." He smirks toward Wil as he grabs a tortilla, or at least a tortilla analog. Wil has gotten pretty good at creating things from Earth with what is commonly available in the GC.

Cynthia places the bowl of ground meat in the center of the table. She looks at Jarek Ruus, who is looking quizzically at the array of things on the table. She takes a tortilla and says, "Meat. It's ground jerlack with spices. Then add cheese and other things you might want. I definitely recommend these." She points to sliced peppers, then takes three slices to lay across her open-faced taco. She folds the tortilla and takes a bite, smiling as she chews.

Jarek Ruus nods and mimics her motions in assembling his taco. Once he's done, Wil and the rest of the crew dig in, building their own tacos. He turns to Wil. "So, Captain, your world is not part of the GC?"

Bennie chortles. "His world is still trying to figure out how to live peacefully with each other."

"They've barely settled one other planet in their system," Maxim adds.

"They don't have reliable FTL or any advanced weapons."

Wil makes a face as his friends list all of Earth's shortcomings.

"Oh. I, uh, see," the old man says, clearly not understanding how

Wil is here with him if his world is so primitive. He looks at Wil for an answer to the unasked question.

Wil takes a sip of water. "I got waylaid when the experimental space pod I was in malfunctioned. In the end, it saved my life since my pod was billions of kilometers from where it should have been." He looks down as he thinks about the original crew of the *Ghost* when it was the *Reaper*. "The crew took me in and gave me a place to sleep. They were killed in an ambush and the Captain's last orders were for the ship to take off and escape."

NEWSCAST_

"Hello, I'm Mon-el Furash, coming to you live from Tarsis and the execution of Jark Asgar, disgraced Chief Executive of Fortnight Corporation." The Malkorite woman nervously strokes one of her ears, causing the many earrings adorning it to make a wind chime-like noise.

"Behind me, you can see the dais where the execution will take place." Behind her is a raised platform, two meters high. A single chair sits atop the platform. In it, Jark Asgar. She looks off camera, then turns back. "I'm told the execution will take place in one micro-tock." She turns so that the camera pickup is looking over her shoulder at the stern face of Jark Asgar.

A Tarsi man approaches the chair. "Do you have any words, Jark Asgar, before your sentence is carried out?"

The at one time most powerful executive in the Commonwealth looks at the much smaller Tarsi man. "I do not." He turns to look straight ahead, his body rigid, proud.

The other man nods, then looks toward someone behind and below the raised platform. A circle of purple light glows under the chair. There is a flash of light, and when it fades, Asgar is slumped in the chair.

Mon-el Furash turns. "While the GC does not typically condone capital punishment, it was decided, unanimously, that in this case it was warranted. I can assure our viewers that Mr. Asgar didn't suffer."

PART FOUR

CHAPTER 12_

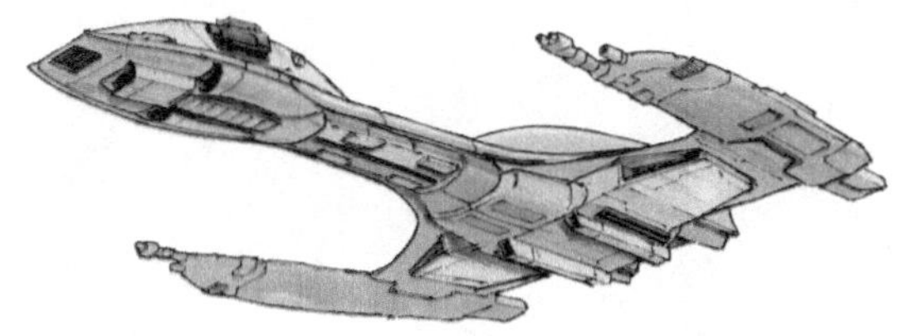

PIRATES? REALLY?!_

WIL SITS up as an alarm blares overhead and the room fills with dull red light. "Wha?" he slurs, looking around.

The overhead speaker says, "Emergency, emergency."

Cynthia is already out of bed, one hand bracing her as she slips into her jumpsuit as the *Ghost* shakes. "Get dressed! Something is wrong!" The ship shakes and she heads for the hatch as she finishes zipping up her jumpsuit. The hatch closes behind her.

Wil shakes his head and leaps out of bed, looking for his sweat pants and wristcomm. As he exits his quarters, he slams into Maxim, in a similar groggy, half-dressed state. The big man asks, "What's going on?"

Wil shrugs. "We're two hours from FTL disengage." He looks at the ceiling as they rush toward the stairwell that leads down to the crew lounge and engineering level and the corridor that connects the bridge to the main body of the ship. "Computer, report."

The speaker on his wristcomm replies, "FTL Failure, cause unknown. Proximity alarm, multiple unidentified contacts. Range closing."

"Fuck, that doesn't sound good," Wil breathes as he and Maxim reach the bridge hatch. Cynthia looks up from her station as they enter, her face a mask of serious concentration.

Wil drops into his seat, scanning his console. Maxim does the same, reporting, "Something is definitely out there."

Zephyr, Bennie, and Jarek Ruus enter. Bennie asks, "How'd you screw up FTL?" as he passes Wil. Wil raises a middle finger.

Zephyr drops into her station and reports immediately, "Something forced us out of FTL. Multiple contacts, but the sensors are having trouble resolving. Picking up a significant gravity well nearby."

Wil taps a control on his console, killing the emergency lighting. The ship shudders again, followed by a decidedly metallic clang.

Jarek Ruus looks around. "Was that something striking the hull?"

Bennie looks up. "Sounded like something hitting the airlock."

Maxim nods. "Yeah." He looks at his console. "Still not getting much resolution, but there are definitely several *somethings* out there, a few as close as a few kilometers off starboard. All are closing on us."

"Guessing at least a few are against the hull," Zephyr adds.

Wil slams his fist on his console and looks at the ceiling. "Gabe! What's going on? I don't have sub-light."

The ceiling replies, "I am sorry, Captain. Whatever forced us from FTL caused a cascade failure that rippled through the power generation system, overloading several key systems. We are on backup power until I can effect repairs."

"That sounds pretty bad," Wil says.

"Quite bad," the ceiling replies in Gabe's voice.

Another metallic clank echoes through the ship. "Dren!" Zephyr swears. She looks up from her console. "The sensors are still grolacked, but I tend to leave that fancy sensor suite we got from Blumtillithian powered down if we're not using it." She frowns. "I just powered them up. Bio signs are on the outer hull."

"Shit," Wil hisses. "Pirates?"

"Probably not spaceship-to-spaceship salespeople," Bennie retorts. He hops out of his seat. "So, what's the play?"

READY TO PARTY_

WIL LOOKS around the bridge groaning, "Do we even know where we are?"

Zephyr shakes her head once. "No."

Wil groans. Another clank reverberates through the ship. A panel on his console lights up the outer airlock doors, both sides being over-ridden. He looks up. "Computer, scramble port and starboard airlock controls."

"Acknowledged," the bland voice replies.

Wil stands. "Arm up. Guess we're having visitors." He extends an arm toward the bridge hatch. As the bridge empties, he looks at the ceiling. "Gabe, time to party."

"Acknowledged," the droid replies from engineering.

Jarek Ruus watches from the foyer at the entry to the armory as the five bridge crew don armor varying from light combat armor over their jumpsuits to fully contained suits of combat armor still streaked with purple ragla blood.

Cynthia looks at Wil as he snaps his gauntlets into place. "You didn't clean it?"

Wil looks himself over. "I forgot."

"You also forgot to make repairs," Jarvis offers through the external speakers.

"At least you look scary, all covered in blood," Maxim offers. Wil frowns, looking at his damaged right gauntlet.

Bennie checks the charge on two modified pulse pistols and slips them in holsters on each hip. He leaves the armory and looks up at Jarek Ruus. "Want to secure the lounge and engineering deck with Gabe and me?" The older man nods and follows the hacker up the stairs to the bridge deck and the connecting corridor to the main body of the *Ghost*.

Wil looks at Cynthia, then the two Palorians. "Max, Zee, you cool setting up a defense on the crew berth deck? I'm guessing that if they aren't already, they'll be cutting through the airlock up there soon." Another clank rattles through the ship. Wil looks around. "Wish I knew what they're doing out there." He turns to Cyn. "Babe, you okay floating?" She nods, sliding two pulse pistols into thigh holsters, then sliding a rifle into the quick release holster on her back. "Once I lock the bridge down, I'm going outside, see if I can't cause some trouble there."

Maxim and Zephyr nod and grab a satchel of power cells as they depart for the topmost deck of the ship where the crew berths, brig, and topside boarding hatch are located.

Wil looks at Cynthia. "This should be fun." He winks and leans in for a kiss.

After the kiss, Cynthia rests a hand on Wil's armored chest. "Jarvis, make sure he doesn't die."

From the speaker in Wil's armor, his AI replies, "I will do my best. He doesn't make it easy."

Wil growls and looks down at his armor as Cynthia laughs. "No, he doesn't."

GABE LOOKS JAREK RUUS UP AND DOWN. "I SUGGEST YOU DON an environment suit, Sir Knight."

The Knight of Plentallus smirks and pulls his loose canvas shirt's neck down to reveal a matte black vacsuit.

Bennie looks over. "Smart. That looks like a good one."

The older man nods. "It is. It can enclose my face in a clear helmet in under two seconds. The smart material forms gloves, as well, even if I'm gripping something." He smiles. "Very useful."

Gabe inclines his head. "Very good."

Bennie looks at his team. "Let's start in the cargo hold. I don't think they'll cut through here." He looks at Gabe, who nods his agreement.

As they descend the stairs into the cargo hold, Bennie asks, "You travel with a vacsuit?"

The old man nods. "Seems prudent. You never know when the ship you're on will be compromised. I have traveled on more than a few ships that looked to be held together by string and good thoughts."

Gabe looks at the man. "Has that happened often to you? While the *Ghost* has experienced decompression events, they have always been contained to sections of the ship easily sealed off."

"Once, shortly after I finished my apprenticeship. My master, a Knight by the name of Sir Osmu Neere, and I were en route to a border world on the far edge of the GC when our ship was attacked by raiders. They breached the ship in several places, but my master and I repelled them." He rests a hand on the hilt of his beam saber. "These work in a vacuum."

A loud clank comes from the cargo doors. Jarek Ruus walks to the control pedestal and looks at the small display. He looks up. "They're trying to force the ramp." He smiles. "I assume the ramp and these doors would be expensive to fix?" Gabe nods. "Let's save your Captain some money." He presses the button that opens the heavy cargo doors and lowers the cargo ramp.

Bennie seals his armor as the red strobe lights around the cargo hold turn on, indicating the lack of breathable air.

BOARDING PASS, PLEASE_

THE CIRCULAR BOARDING hatch located at the top of the ship at the rear of the crew berths is how Wil boarded the Partherian ship so many years ago to spring Maxim and Zephyr from custody. Now the two ex-Peacekeepers are standing below it, listening to something clank on the other side.

Maxim looks over at his partner, her face distorted slightly by the clear face plate on her armor, an upgraded model of the same armor she wore aboard the space station they stole Gabe from. She catches him looking at her and winks. "You ready?"

Maxim grins, showing all of his teeth. "You bet." He confirms the charge on first one pulse pistol, then the other.

From above, a faint glow begins to form, a plasma torch cutting through the circular hatch. Within seconds, globs of molten metal begin to fall as a bright white line moves around the hatch.

Zephyr watches the globs of metal hit the deck and begin to cool. "Those will be hard to clean up."

Maxim grunts his agreement. "I wish we had more cover."

Zephyr nods and taps a control on her wristcomm, causing her infiltrator armor to engage its active camouflage system. She wavers and then is nothing more than a vague shimmering shape.

Maxim's HUD shows an outline of his partner so he knows where she is. He follows suit, vanishing. "I wish we had newer gear." He holds up a pistol that appears to be floating.

"True, but this will help. It's better than what we had back then," she replies, recalling the used armor the two of them had bought with Wil's credits before the space station job. She toggles another control on her wristcomm, causing the lights in the corridor to wink out, putting the space into pitch blackness. The only light is coming from the nearly completed circle of glowing metal.

THE LAST OF THE BRIDGE CONSOLES GOES DARK. WIL LOOKS around the bridge. The main display is on, but with the sensors still overloaded and burnt out, the bulk of the screen is static. "Jarvis, launch the boys, set 'em to roam, and keep tabs on the crew."

Four small, spherical drones pop out of the top of Wil's armored pack. Since he last used them, he's painted them: green, blue, red, and a burnt orange color. From the speaker in his helmet, Jarvis replies, "The ducklings and Launchpad are away. I will supervise them," in his crisp sort of British accent.

Wil exits the bridge, and after closing the hatch, instructs the ship's computer to lock the hatch. He turns to the starboard airlock and moves into it. "Ghost team, Ghost One going EVA." The outer doors slide open. A series of green dots on his HUD blink, letting him know the rest of the crew have acknowledged him. "Jarvis, have the folks trying to enter through this airlock given up?"

"Indeed, they have, sir. Also, the port airlock is clear, just so you know."

Wil nods and cycles the airlock. As the outer doors part, he peeks out through the opening. "Fuck me."

Above and behind the *Ghost* are a dozen light freighters with articulated grappler arms mounted on their sides. Several have grabbed onto the *Ghost* at various points along the hull. Small boarding pods are flitting around, several attached to the hull. Wil can see one at the ventral boarding hatch and another on the port side of the lounge and engineering deck. He spots another drifting toward the airlock he's in. He slaps the control to close the outer doors and pushes off to drop below the *Ghost,* using the thrusters in his suit to move under the ship, out of view. As he moves out of view, he looks toward the cargo ramp that is inexplicably lowered. The cargo doors are wide open, a boarding pod moving toward them. "What the hell? Bennie, check in. The cargo bay is open to space. What's going on?"

Bennie replies in a whisper, "We got this, don't worry."

Wil groans. "Gabe, I need you to get to engineering and get the engines online. We can outrun these assholes, but I don't know if we can outfight them. Cyn, can you backstop Bennie and Jarek Ruus?"

Cynthia replies, "Moving."

THAT'S GONNA LEAVE A MARK_

Gabe nods to Bennie and Jarek Ruus, then turns and uses his leg thrusters to jet to the staircase connecting the cargo hold to the deck above. The boarding pod is slowly edging closer to the open cargo bay. Bennie had shut the lights off when they opened the bay to space, and he's behind a cluster of strapped-down crates. Jarek Ruus is hiding on the opposite side of the bay, closer to the open doors, to slip behind the boarding party. Bennie offered the older man a weapon, but he refused, saying Knights use only their beam sabers.

The boarding pod settles just inside the cargo doors, ensuring they can't close. The hatch opens and floods the cargo bay in red light. One by one, a dozen armored forms drift out, moving in a loose formation. The moment they leave their pod, the gravity in the bay takes hold, bringing them gently to the deck. Each boarder is wearing mismatched armor over heavy duty vacsuits. Each has a plasma rifle held at the ready.

Bennie watches as all twelve move into the bay, spreading out to secure the space. Bennie watches Jarek Ruus dart into the boarding pod. He slides from his hiding place and opens fire with a scream that would be deafening if he weren't wearing combat armor with a sealed helmet, and in a vacuum. His two pistols unleash a storm of high energy plasma. Much of the energy is absorbed by armor plates, but a few of his shots find weak spots between plates, burning through vacsuits, killing the wearers. Before the pirates can turn, he ducks back down and crawls to another crate. Plasma bolts strike the crates where he was just hiding. "Wil's gonna be mad," Bennie mumbles as the crate he was behind is shredded by enemy fire. A tub of Red Vines rolls toward the pirates.

A particularly large armored figure steps forward, putting a foot on the tub of licorice. The figure looks first at where Bennie had been and then at the crates nearby. "There's no way you keep us here," he says via Wideband broadcast.

Bennie is about to retort when the boarding pod explodes, sending the remaining pirates scattering to the deck. Bennie stands up just in time to see Jarek Ruus leap from the boarding pod as it drifts from the entrance of the cargo hold as small explosions rip the craft apart. The moment the older man lands on the deck, he's up and moving, slashing pirates, his beam saber cutting through their armor like it isn't there. Bennie closes his mouth and starts shooting at the astonished pirates.

The confusion doesn't last long, however, and before long, Jarek Ruus is near the stairwell using his beam saber to deflect plasma bolts, his arm moving almost faster than Bennie can track, his sword either absorbing the energy weapon's fire or deflecting it. Bennie moves as close as he can toward the stairwell, then stands, firing wildly as he darts across the distance. He looks up. "Time to go!" He bolts up the stairs, Jarek Ruus on his heels.

THE TOPSIDE BOARDING HATCH FALLS TO THE DECK WITH A crash. Right behind it, a pirate in tactical armor drops, visually scanning the corridor plasma rifle at the ready. The pirate looks up and makes a hand gesture, then steps out of the way as another pirate, then another, and another drop into the corridor.

Once five pirates are crammed into the corridor, Maxim sends a chirp to his partner's armor. He grins as he leans out of the bulkhead separating the berths from the stairwell and the public head opposite. Zephyr is across from him at the stairwell entrance. She leans out into the corridor, as well, and they both open fire. The pirates are taken by surprise and mowed down. Their bodies hit the deck, smoking holes dotting them. Another pirate drops to the deck and remains crouching, firing back at the invisible attackers. The pirate falls, but two much smaller beings drop in and open fire, forcing the two Palorians to duck back for cover. One of the beings leaps to the ceiling and sticks there, one hand still aiming a pistol down the corridor.

"Time to go," Zephyr says, pushing open the hatch to the stairwell that leads down to the crew lounge and engineering level. Maxim bolts across the opening in the corridor, taking two hits on his armor, causing the camouflage to ripple. He rushes past Zephyr. She closes the hatch and presses the lock button. "Computer, lock down this deck."

"Acknowledged." The panel inside the stairwell blinks twice and several built-in latches engage within the hatch.

Maxim looks at Zephyr. "What do you think the little ones are?" She shrugs.

CHAPTER 13_

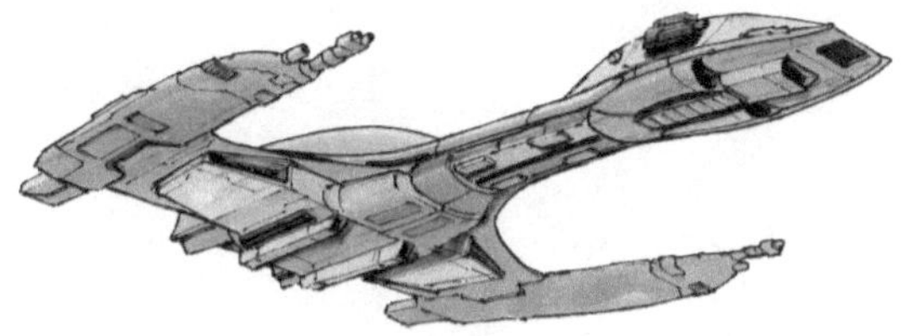

UNWANTED GUESTS_

Cynthia meets Bennie, Jarek Ruus, Maxim, and Zephyr as they exit the stairwell. Before she closes the hatch, two small, spherical probes drift in, one blue and one green. She slams the hatch shut and issues the lockdown command. She looks around. "Wil, we're all in the crew lounge."

"Okay, that's gotta be our last stand. If Gabe can get things running, we can control the ship from engineering."

Maxim and Zephyr, both visible, their active camouflage systems disengaged, are moving the few pieces of unsecured furniture into the corridor. Engineering is located at the end of the corridor, the very back of the deck.

Wil watches the pod that boarded through the cargo bay explode and begin to drift away. "Okay, Jarvis, let's get dangerous." He fires his suit thrusters and heads toward the nearest pirate ship that has latched onto the *Ghost*. "Are they scanning? Doing anything?"

"It doesn't appear so. I'm not detecting any sensor beams or other energy readings," his armor replies.

As he nears the ship, he realizes just how ramshackle it is: hull plates poorly patched, rust everywhere, and several exposed sections of inner hull. He slips a small device from a pouch on his thigh and pushes it inside one of the holes in the outer hull. "How're the ducklings doing?"

"I have Dewey and Louie with the crew, while Launchpad and Huey are in the cargo hold and A deck, respectively. We have lost the cargo hold and A deck. The crew is gathering on B deck."

"What're the pirates doing?" Wil asks as he pulls himself along the hull of the freighter toward its engines.

"Both groups of pirates appear to be regrouping and preparing to move. They have lost significant numbers but still outnumber us. Right now, they are cutting through the hatches keeping them from B deck."

Wil sighs. "Okay. Let the others know." He slips another device in next to a sub-light engine exhaust. He looks around. No sign he's been detected, so he pushes off and thrusts over to a ship a bit farther away. It looks much newer and better maintained than the one he has just left.

"Incoming!" Jarvis says, taking control of the armor enough to twist Wil out of the way of a black blur that shoots past.

"The hell!?" Wil looks around, his HUD highlighting the attacker. It looks like a single being, bigger than Wil, with a plasma rifle. He adjusts his flight so he can draw down on the attacker with his pistol. Jarvis assists by making minute corrections in his aim by taking control of the suit servos. As the pirate spins, taking aim at Wil, plasma rounds flash past, then impact on the pirate's armor, sending them spinning away.

Wil adjusts his flight again, accelerating toward the ship he was heading for. A blaster turret mounted on the top of the ship spins to fire as Wil flies below its firing line. He looks back toward his opponent, who is nowhere to be seen. "Great. Jarvis, any idea where our friend is?"

"I'm afraid not, sir. I will task more resources to find him quickly. His armor is quite stealthy."

Wil crawls up and over the hull of the freighter, staying out of the turret's line of sight. He deposits one of his small devices next to the turret.

"Dodge right!" Jarvis says. Wil doesn't hesitate pushing off with his left hand a split second before two plasma rounds impact the hull.

"Shit!" Wil says as he drifts away from the freighter and toward the firing line of the turret, which seems ready to fire the moment he's in its sights. He engages his thrusters and pulls in tight to skim the hull. He looks back, letting his arm go limp in the armor to allow Jarvis to take over and aim the pistol. The shots don't connect but do force the pirate to dodge and avoid so he can't take aim at Wil. "Let him get closer," Wil tells his armor AI.

As the pirate works his way closer to the freighter, dodging Wil's intentionally not well targeted shots, Wil uses his free hand to grab another device. He waits until the pirate is twenty meters away, then hurls the small cylinder at his opponent. The other man doesn't see the motion, busy dodging plasma rounds and trying to return fire. Wil takes a shot in his midsection that sends him cartwheeling away from the freighter. As he spins, he briefly sees a flash of light.

"Got him, sir!" Jarvis says excitedly, then, "Oh my, hold on!" The armor suit stiffens, forcing Wil's arms to his side as thrusters and maneuvering jets fire, forcing Wil into a series of wild moves to avoid blaster fire from now two ships. "Hold on," the AI repeats.

"Like I have a choice?" Wil groans as he makes a turn that leaves his stomach behind. He watches on his HUD as Jarvis tracks the incoming fire and banks and jukes to avoid being obliterated.

BANG, BANG_

THE SEALED HATCH connecting the crew and engineering deck to the decks above and below is glowing, bright. Maxim is at the hatch that leads to the bridge. "I think we need to split them up." He points down the corridor they call the neck. "Zephyr and I can lure some this way. Make a stand either at the bridge or armory if they'll follow us. The rest of you, hold the engineering corridor."

Zephyr holds her hand up. "I think you and I should split up. Our scout armor lets us move around a bit better. We can use that to our advantage."

The big man nods. "Makes sense, yeah."

Bennie walks towards Maxim. "I got you, big man."

Maxim grunts and smiles at his small, brave friend. "Too bad we don't have a wooden stick for you to use." He winks.

Jarek Ruus looks at Cynthia and Zephyr. "I guess that leaves us." The two women nod.

Cynthia looks at the short corridor between them and the hatch to engineering. It is at best two meters, with hatches on each side leading to the computer core and medbay. No real cover anywhere. "Let's fill the corridor with stuff." She glances at the hatch to the stairwell; a plasma torch is slowly slicing through the thick metal. The hatch is robust, meant to slam shut and contain hull breaches, but it is no match for the plasma torch.

They get to work, the two drones drifting near the ceiling.

Maxim and Bennie watch for a beat, then rush to see what they can fortify near the bridge. As they walk down the length of the neck, Maxim says, "This is not going to be easy."

Bennie grins and runs ahead. "I have an idea."

By the time the stairwell hatch sags and pushes open, the corridor leading to engineering is choked with furniture and anything else the three defenders can find. There's a small path connecting the two side rooms to the engineering hatch. Jarek Ruus is in front of the engineering hatch. His two companions are hiding in the side rooms, their hatches propped open.

One by one, nearly two dozen pirates file out of the stairwell. Half move toward the hatch leading to the bridge; half mill around the lounge looking at the makeshift barricade. Jarek Ruus activates his beam saber, causing the pirates nearby to flinch and shield their faces, the glare of the beam saber overloading their night vision. He's fully sealed in his vacsuit now, his face hidden by a smooth matte black face shield.

While the pirates are off balance, Cynthia and Zephyr lean out of their cover and open fire, dropping several pirates immediately in a blaze of super charged plasma.

Two pirates drop behind the kitchen table taking aim at Jarek Ruus, their plasma bolts deflecting off his saber to ricochet back. One bolt strikes a pirate in the chest, sending her sprawling to the deck, her cobbled-together armor smoking. His beam saber sings as it moves through the air deflecting weapons' fire.

Cynthia ducks back into the medbay as several plasma bolts impact the entry, warping metal. "That's gonna leave a mark," she mumbles as she leans out and fires, spotting several pirates leaving the lounge toward the bridge. "Big man, green bean, incoming." On her HUD two green lights blink. She sees one of Wil's probes dart through the open hatch. She leans out again and hears a grunt. Looking over, she spies Jarek Ruus holding his side. She fires at the pirates then moves to stand beside the older man. His beam saber never stops moving. "Fall back!" she shouts.

Zephyr leans out, her active camouflage engaged so the pirates have a harder time seeing her. She opens fire, dropping another pirate, then another. She crouches down and moves toward her friends. "Go!" Cynthia pushes Jarek Ruus toward the hatch leading to engineering. As the three of them approach, Gabe steps into the opening, his eyes bright red, both forearms transformed into blasters. He opens fire, forcing the remaining pirates to scatter, taking cover. Several are too slow, falling to the deck, armor smoking, charred flesh exposed.

Over the comms, Wil says, "Two more pods inbound. Jarvis and I are trying to stop 'em."

Zephyr, Cynthia, and Jarek Ruus slip past Gabe as the heavy doors to the engineering compartment close. The tall droid returns to his normal mode, eyes turning yellow. "I am almost done, but I need more time."

ALWAYS SOMETHING_

"Okay, I don't want to do that ever again," Wil tells Jarvis once he's behind the engine compartment of what he's decided is the command ship for this pirate fleet. He plants his last small cylinder against the sub-light engine housing and pushes off.

"Captain, three more targets," Jarvis warns, highlighting three more armored figures departing a freighter nearby. Wil takes aim, again allowing Jarvis to make minute adjustments to his arm, controlling the finger of his glove. Plasma bolts streak out, catching all three, sending them spinning. "I believe we took one out. The other two are just wounded, I think."

"You think?"

The AI sounds stricken. "They are quite distant, and there is ragla blood covering one camera pickup and two sensors."

Wil doesn't reply as he pushes off from the ship, careful to remain out of the line of sight of the turret. "Damn." He adjusts his course, selecting an icon for team comms. "Two more pods inbound. Jarvis and I are trying to stop 'em." He angles towards one of the pirates still trying to correct their tumble. He gets close and fires point blank until his pistol's power cell is dead. He releases the dead cell, sending it drifting away while he reaches for a cell strapped to his bicep. The two boarding pods are halfway to the *Ghost* now.

"Captain, your pistol will not do much against those pods. Not in time to stop them from reaching the ship," Jarvis warns. The pod attached to the *Ghost's* ventral boarding hatch disengages and moves away to make room for one of the inbound pods.

Wil angles from the pods towards the freighter attached to the *Ghost*. The one he planted the explosives on. He glances over. The last pirate is moving toward one of the two boarding pods. When he reaches the freighter, he moves quickly to the outer hull breach, grabbing the explosive he had planted earlier. "Okay, time to move things along. Jarvis, I want you to detonate this one the moment it strikes the boarding pod, and detonate the others five seconds later."

"Acknowledged," the AI affirms.

Wil takes aim and throws the small explosive device. It tumbles end over end.

"You must keep your sensors on the pod and the explosive so I know when to trigger the explosives," the AI advises.

Wil pushes off the freighter toward the *Ghost,* keeping the freighter between him and two armed vessels farther out.

"Eyes on the prize, sir," Jarvis admonishes.

Wil turns his head to watch the small canister hit the side of the pod. It bounces off the hull, and before it drifts more than two inches from the hull, it explodes, ripping a hole in the hull and sending the pod crashing into the other pod. Five seconds later, the other explosives detonate, sending four of the freighters spinning wildly, atmosphere venting. One freighter twists, then secondary explosions rip it apart. The freighter that is attached to the *Ghost* by gripping arms rocks. One of the claws releases as the ship shudders from secondary explosions.

THE *GHOST* SHAKES, FORCING MAXIM TO BRACE HIMSELF. "Here they come," he says. He and Bennie are each crouching in one of the staircases that leads from the bridge level to the armory below. Maxim has activated his adaptive camouflage and is keeping his rifle low so the approaching pirates don't notice it. He counts as the pirates creep closer, and when he gets to six, opens fire. Bennie follows suit and the first six pirates fall to the deck, their armor perforated, smoke wafting up. Maxim reaches back and pulls out several softball-sized devices. He presses a button on each, then hurls them down the corridor. One by one, there is a pop sound followed by thuds and crashes.

When no energy blasts streak down the corridor, Bennie stands and walks aft toward the rest of the ship, Maxim behind him. Both have weapons at the ready. Bennie looks up at his big friend, smiling. "Told ya."

"You know, Wil is going to make you clean this up," Maxim says, nodding toward the six or seven—it is hard to tell—pirates encased in semi-rigid foam that has expanded to fill most of the corridor. The pirates are completely immobilized. One is wriggling, trying to get themselves free until Maxim places a plasma round through their helmet. When Bennie makes a face, the big man shrugs. "Don't leave enemies at your back." The Brailack hacker nods and walks on.

"Captain, I have repaired the main reactor," Gabe says over the team channel. "We have sub-light propulsion, some weapons, and shields. However, at best, we can use only two of the three systems at once."

Zephyr says, "Cynthia, Jarek Ruus, and I are in engineering now. What are your orders, Wil?"

"Take out their command ship. You'll know which one it is. I'm coming in from the hold now."

Maxim and Bennie peak out through the open hatch opening into the crew lounge. Several pirates are trying to gain entry into engineering.

Maxim says, "Bennie and I will head to the bridge and get things in motion." He eases back from the hatch, Bennie following him.

NEWSCAST_

"GOOD EVENING," Mon-el Furash says breathlessly. She's standing in the open doorway of the governing council chamber. "This just in. The governing council has voted ninety to ten in favor of the droid civil rights initiative." She waves a hand to take in the massive door and chamber inside. "As you would imagine, the mood here is quite festive." She looks off camera. "Oh, here comes the droid liberation committee now." She turns and the camera follows. "Excuse me, Mon-el Furash, GNO. Do you have moment to speak with our audience?"

One of the droids, a medical model similar to Gabe's original design in many ways, bows its head. "Of course. I am Gentoo." It nods to the other two droids with it. They depart into the governing council chamber.

Mon-el Furash watches them go, then turns to Gentoo. "How does it feel? This outcome is over a cycle in the making. Did you expect the vote to go the way it did?"

Gentoo nods. "While I possess free will, I do not possess emotions; thus, I cannot speak to how this outcome makes me feel." The droid tilts its head. "To your other question, I did expect this outcome. I calculated a ninety-seven point two three one one percent likelihood that the vote would go as it did. However, I did not expect the vote to happen for at least two more cycles, so I am..." The droid tilts its head to the side, searching for the right term. "I am at a loss for the term."

"Surprised," the journalist offers.

Gentoo inclines its head. "As good a term as any."

Mon-el smiles. "What will you do now?"

Gentoo looks into the chamber, then back to the Malkorite journalist. It then says, "Myself and the droid rights committee shall remain here on Tarsis to help the council find a suitable world to become the home world of the droid nation. Our work is not yet done."

Mon-el nods. "Are there any candidate systems yet?"

Gentoo shakes its head once. "Not at this time. If you will excuse me."

Mon-el nods. "Of course, thank you for your time."

Gentoo nods and enters the chamber.

Mon-el turns. "There you have it. Next step, find a suitable home world for the droid nation. I'll be staying here on Tarsis to cover this next phase."

PART FIVE

CHAPTER 14_

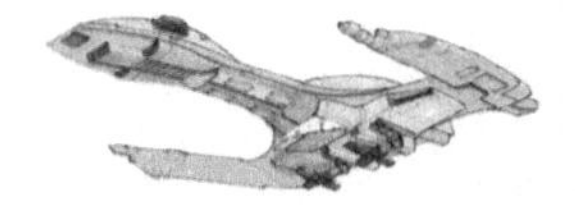

PARTING IS SUCH SWEET_

Wil touches down inside the cargo hold. Dead pirates litter the space. "Damn, Bennie, did you have to let 'em destroy my stuff?" He picks up a scorched tub of Red Vines, shaking his head. He looks around a bit more before heading for the stairs.

Before he reaches the hatch to the deck above, he feels the *Ghost* lurch. Looking out the cargo bay doors, he sees the view shift until one of the ruined freighters comes into view briefly. He taps his wrist-comm. "Do we have comms? Can we hail the lead ship?"

Cynthia answers, "Yes and no. The long-range gear might be burnt out, but short range looks good. Patching you in now."

Wil hears a soft beep and an icon on his HUD indicates that he's live. "Hi, out there. This is Wil Calder, Captain of the ship you're trying to steal. You've lost a lot on this job. Maybe cut bait? Go home while you have a chance?"

The comms crackle, then a gravelly voice replies, "I'll scrap your ship and sell whatever crew survives at the slave market on Zyglon Seven."

The *Ghost* shakes as she takes weapons fire. Wil bolts through the remains of the hatch, letting his armor suit's AI control his gun hand. The few remaining pirates he can see fall to the ground amid a bunch of screams and cries of shock. He looks around. "The ship, such as she is, is secure." He grins, then braces himself against the corridor as the *Ghost* shakes again. He bangs on the engineering hatch. "Hey, in there, mind not getting us shot to hell?"

The sound of the missile magazine cycling under the deck, followed by the distinct racket of missiles launching, answers his question a moment before Maxim says, "Boom," over the team comms.

The engineering hatch opens, allowing Zephyr and Cynthia to come out, weapons at the ready. Cynthia spies Wil and walks over, allowing herself to be folded into his hug. "Glad you're not dead." She smiles as he leans down and kisses her, or at least tries to. Their helmets collide with a loud clang.

Zephyr tuts, "Amateurs." She's grinning.

The *Ghost* rocks again. From inside engineering, Gabe says, "I am capable of many things. Piloting is not among the top one hundred."

Wil releases Cynthia and heads into engineering. The two women look around the short corridor and the common space beyond it.

Cynthia says, "This might be the worst shape I've seen the *Ghost*."

From the bridge, Maxim replies, "Don't forget when we crashed on Harrith Prime. Half the ship was missing."

Bennie grunts, "True." He adds, "How come Jarek Ruus isn't on comms?"

Zephyr slaps her forehead. "Dren!"

WIL MOVES TO STAND NEXT TO GABE, WHO HAS GLOWING DATA tendrils extending from all of his fingers into the control panel next to the reactor. The droid turns. "It is good to see you, Captain." He nods to a section of the control panel. "I have reconfigured that section of the panel. It will be rudimentary at best, but you have flight control. Maxim is on the bridge and has tactical." The ship shakes. "The lead ship is crippled. They managed to shoot one of the missiles before impact, but the other was a direct hit on their engines." The ship shakes again as Wil attempts to maneuver between two of the disabled freighters. "There was more than one armed vessel," Gabe points out.

Wil nods as the *Ghost* shudders as he pushes the sub-light engines to half power. "Yeah, I know there was at least one other ship with a blaster turret. We don't have to give up shields to launch missiles, right?"

"That is correct." Sparks erupt overhead. Gabe focuses his attention on whatever systems he's working on, his optic sensors dim.

Wil pushes a button. "Okay, this is weak. I need actual flight controls. How'd they do this on *Star Trek*?" The *Ghost* shakes, and something inside the engine room clatters to the deck. An indicator flashes red, and Wil watches as Maxim launches another missile salvo. The sound of the missile magazine working confirms what the small display says.

"Jarvis, put this out on local broadcast: 'Sorry, you had your chance. Now, even crippled, I'm gonna pick your forces apart. Too bad, so sad.'"

"You miserable kreb—" The comm is filled with static. On the too-tiny-for-Wil's-taste display, he sees one missile strike the wounded command ship and the other destroy the second armed freighter.

AFTERMATH_

"How is he?" Wil leans into the medbay. It fared better than most of the ship but was still heavily damaged. The autodoc is throwing errors, and one of its telescoping limbs is broken, dangling by a bundle of wires. Despite that, the unit is working. The table Jarek Ruus is on beeps quietly as it monitors his vitals. The autodoc checks the wounds on the older man's torso, then raises to the ceiling to make room.

Bennie turns from Jarek Ruus to Wil and shakes his head once. Zephyr steps out of the small compartment. "Several plasma rounds burned through his vacsuit. Severe organ damage."

Wil groans, palming his face. After rubbing his temples, he asks, "How long?"

"Hard to say. He's a tough oldster. We can put him in a medically induced coma, let the autodoc manage him. That'll buy us time," the Palorian woman offers.

Wil turns to head into engineering. "Time is definitely not something we're swimming in." He takes the five steps needed to enter engineering. "Gabe, status report?"

Gabe comes from around the reactor. "Would you prefer the bad news, the less bad news, or the mostly bad news, first?"

"No good news? I'd settle for just okay news."

"I am afraid not," the droid apologizes. "I am an engineer, not a miracle worker."

Wil sighs more dramatically than normal. "Okay, start with the worst. Let's end on a slightly high note." He leans against a panel that he recalls normally has blinking lights all over its face but is now totally dark.

Gabe inclines his head. "Very well. The worst of the news is that our power generation system is operating at thirty percent, and that is the best I can do. Until we find a shipyard, it will be an either-or situation with weapons and shields."

"We have missiles, though," Wil interjects.

Gabe tilts his head, staring at Wil for interrupting. "We have four left." He turns to look at something on the reactor, making adjustments. "The last part of the quite bad, is that we will not be fully airtight until a—"

"Shipyard," Wil interrupts, making a *go on* motion.

"I have been able to patch this deck and the deck above; however, I would advise, at a minimum, vacsuits when not in your berths." Gabe continues, "The bad news is that I have made as many repairs as I probably can. I have saved a few things for once we are en route to wherever we decide to go, but for the most part, the *Ghost* is as repaired as she is going to get until we find a —" He stops when Wil makes a face, then adds at a much lower volume, "Shipyard."

Wil nods slowly. "Okay, the less bad? High note time."

"As bad as the damage is, none of it is life- or vessel-threatening. Hull integrity, while not one hundred percent, is sufficient to continue our mission." The droid holds a hand up, finger pointing up. "Oh, and the damage to the sensor array was minimal. While not at full capacity, we will have sensors shortly. The diagnostic cycle requires one more tock."

Before Wil can answer, Maxim walks in. "I've got the surviving pirates gathered up. Right now, they're in the port airlock, since that was closest."

"Space 'em," Wil says before turning to his tactical officer.

Maxim does a double take. "Wait, what? Really?"

Wil nods. "Yeah. Space 'em. They're all in armor, right?" Maxim nods. "Top off their air, slap a beacon on a few, and space 'em. They attacked us, gravely wounded Jarek Ruus, and when offered an out, didn't take it. There were at least two ships still intact enough to rescue their people." His face is red. "Then have Zee resume our course."

Maxim says nothing. He nods and leaves engineering. Wil turns back to Gabe. "Okay, so...wait." He turns to the open engineering hatch. "Hey, Max?"

"Yeah?" the big man says from somewhere in the crew lounge.

"Have Zee broadcast that the beacon is their people, and that if we ever see one of their ships anywhere, we'll destroy them." He gets a grunt of acknowledgement then turns back to Gabe. "Let's make getting the *Ghost* airtight our priority for now. Then the internal hatches. I don't like the idea that a single breach could decompress the whole ship." The droid nods.

REPAIRS OR SOMETHING_

Once the diagnostic on the sensor suite is complete, the sensors end up having good news to deliver, more or less. The pirates' trap was set up just beyond the heliopause of system P3X-595. They apparently had set up massive gravity well generators that pulled any inbound traffic to their kill zone. Wil assumes there's a similar setup on the opposite side of the system, maybe four all equidistant? Either way, the one they got sucked into is mostly ruined. Only two ships are still functional, barely.

Wil looks around the bridge. It is just him and Zephyr, while the others work with Gabe on making repairs or generally trying to clean things up. Bennie is spending equal parts of his time in the medbay and scraping his capture foam off the bulkheads in the *Ghost's* neck. "Damn, that thing is ominous looking," Wil says as the gravity generator comes into view on the main display.

"This may not be exact, but looks like it's three kilometers in diameter, give or take."

Wil looks over at his first officer. "Give or take?" He smiles.

She nods. "Sensors are fuzzy."

Wil turns back to the main display. He's easing the *Ghost* toward the massive construct. Mostly, he's moving the *Ghost* away from the jettisoned pirates so that their friends can pick them up without worrying about the angry pocket warship nearby. They made sure the survivors left the *Ghost* with some delta vee so their friends would be pulled farther away from the *Ghost*.

Zephyr says, "No shields that I'm seeing. No bio signs."

"Good," Wil growls. He pushes a few buttons and a tactical overlay appears on the main display. "Been a while since I've flown the *Ghost* like this. Kinda fun." The targeting reticle moves over the large sphere. "Stay on target. Stay on target," Wil murmurs. The reticle blinks red, then stays a solid angry red as a low tone comes from the console. A small cover on Wil's right flight control pops open, revealing a trigger. "Like shooting womp rats in a so and so." Bolts of brilliant green energy streak out from the engine nacelle-mounted disruptors. On the main display, the energy bolts leap from the sides of the screen, stitching along the sphere.

The energy bolts impact the sphere, ripping in to it. Wil howls as the sphere first cracks in two, then is further ripped apart by secondary explosions.

"Gravity field is gone. Normal space as far as the sensors can detect," Zephyr reports.

THE AUTODOC LOWERS TO CHECK JAREK RUUS' BANDAGES AND administer meds. Bennie steps back to make room.

The older man's eyes flutter as the machine works on him. He tilts his head. "Hello, my little friend." His voice is thin, weak. "We may need to put further training off for a bit." He smiles.

Bennie rushes across the short distance between the two bio-beds. "How are you feeling?"

"Like I've been shot several times," the older man says weakly. He grins and says, "Have you seen my flask?"

Bennie beams. "I've been holding onto it." He offers the container up. "I found it under a pirate in the cargo hold."

Jarek Ruus takes a sip, waving the autodoc away with his free hand. "Leave me be, you beeping annoyance." The autodoc beeps several times, then retreats back to the ceiling. Jarek Ruus tries to sit up, wincing as he moves to a half sitting up, half lying down position.

"That doesn't look comfortable."

"It isn't. I'll be dead soon, though, so..." He trails off, then takes another sip from his flask.

Bennie frowns. "Maybe we can get help on the planet? We're almost to P3X-595-C. Should be there in a few more tocks."

"Okay, then leave me. I'm tired." He waves toward the autodoc. "Come back down here, beepy." The autodoc makes a happy sound and descends on its articulated arm.

Bennie walks out, bumping into Gabe. "Hello, Bennie. How are you doing? How is Sir Jarek Ruus?"

"Grouchy," Bennie says, heading into the crew lounge.

"That's promising," Gabe offers, following Bennie.

LIGHTS OUT_

WIL DROPS down onto the bed. He's covered in grease and sweat and a few things he can't remember coming in contact with—they're blue and green mostly, some troubling brown. "Well, this is truly fucked." He takes a deep breath.

Cynthia sits next to him, putting an arm around her exhausted and seemingly beaten boyfriend. "I'd say we've been through worse, but yeah, this is pretty grolacked." She leans her head on his shoulder, wrinkles her nose, and sits up straight. "You're disgusting." She pushes him off the bed, noticing that whatever it is he's covered in, now covers part of the bed. "You shower, I'll change the bed." She wrinkles her nose again. "What is this?"

Wil moves to the refresher in the corner of their berth, getting out of his jumpsuit. "Beats me. I don't even remember where I got it on me." He steps into the small shower area. Over the sound of the hot water he says, "Given the reception, I'm not sure what to expect when we reach the planet. Ruus insists we get this last archive cube before heading back, though. Not that we could just turn around now and leave. We'd never make it anywhere."

Cynthia has the bedding wadded up and shoves it into the small cleaning device set in the wall. She picks up Wil's shipboard jumpsuit with as few fingers as possible and shoves it in behind the bedding. "So gross."

When Wil comes out, wrapped in a towel, he drops back down onto the newly cleaned bed. "What're we gonna do, babe? Ship's shot up, we don't have FTL, Ruus doesn't look like he'll make it a few days, let alone weeks. We don't even have long range comms to try to call in a favor or anything."

Cynthia looks Wil in the eyes. "We'll do what we always do: barely scrape by." She smiles when he grins at her joke.

"We're definitely in our sweet spot," Wil says, dropping back to lie down.

Cynthia purrs, "We'll find a way. We always do." She looks at the ceiling. "Lights."

"What is this?" Zephyr asks, holding Maxim's shipboard jumpsuit up to inspect. She leans in to smell, then leans back, putting the garment at arm's length. "We might just have to burn this one." She turns it around. "Is this?" She retches. "Nope." She puts the offending garment in the cleaning unit, selecting the recycle option, not the clean option. The device whirs, then clunks three times.

From the refresher, over the sound of the shower, Maxim says, "Yeah I think the green stuff is foam solvent. I was helping Bennie clear the neck out." He's silent, then says, "It was a great idea, but messy as wurrin."

The cleaning unit thuds once before quieting down. "How's he doing? He hasn't come up to the bridge since this all started." She strips out of her own much less disgusting jumpsuit, shoving it into the cleaner and selecting *clean*.

"He's taking Jarek Ruus' injuries hard. I think the two of them bonded much more than we thought. I know he's been trying to keep himself busy." Maxim walks out and falls into the bed.

Zephyr starts rubbing his shoulders. "Great googa mooga, my

love." She leans in, putting pressure on a knot that feels like a rock under his skin. Maxim groans like she's bending him in half. "Oh stop, you big baby."

"You'll pay for this," he groans, then slurs, "Lights."

CHAPTER 15_

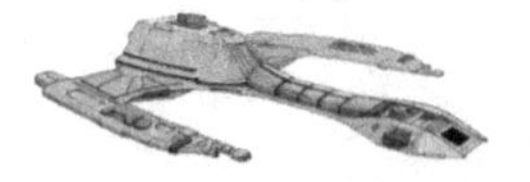

INFORMATION ISN'T CHEAP_

"Who'd have guessed we'd find a planet more shit than Fury?" Wil says, walking down the cargo ramp.

Cynthia walks next to him. "According to what I got from the space control operator, the Shrike's Nest is the place to find information."

Two hover vans approach. Zephyr points. "Must be the repair crew we hired." She looks up the ramp at Maxim, Gabe, and Bennie. "You sure you're good staying here?"

Maxim nods and looks at the other two. "Yeah, I don't know how much help I'll be, but I'll keep an eye on our guests at a minimum."

Bennie nods, as well. "Yeah, you guys get supplies and see if you can figure out where the archive is. We'll have the ship put back together when you get back." Something in the cargo hold falls to the deck, making a metallic clank. Bennie hunches his shoulders at the noise. "Mostly."

The two vans pull up and an assortment of beings hop out, led by a lanky Trenbal woman. She looks Wil, Zephyr, and Cynthia up and down, then focuses on Zephyr. "You the one I spoke with?"

Zephyr's head tilts back, surprised this woman rightly picked her as the point of contact. She'd reached out based on the spaceport administrator's recommendation to Cynthia. She nods. "Yeah, this your whole crew?"

The scaled woman blinks rapidly. "Yup." She looks past the trio to the *Ghost* behind them. "Wow, that's a piece of dren."

Wil puffs his chest out. "Hey, she's a damn fine ship. She's just been through a lot." He points an accusing finger. "Maybe some public notices about the pirates intercepting ships at the heliopause?"

The lizard-like woman tuts, "Ah, you're the ones that caused the ruckus, then? Good for you." She pushes past Wil and the women walking up the cargo ramp. She points at Maxim, then thinks it over and points at Bennie. "Show me around, tiny."

Maxim looks at his shipmates, eyebrow raised. Wil shrugs, then turns to walk away. "All right, let's go, ladies."

The Trenbal woman looks down at Bennie as they approach the stairwell. "So, what's your name?"

Zephyr looks around as they exit the spaceport. "Wow, busy market." The market just outside the spaceport is busier than most. Beyond the market is a mid-sized city.

"You know Bennie will be mad if the archive ends up being in the city. No swamps or jungles," Cynthia says.

Wil approaches a stall selling some type of fried creature on a stick. "Excuse me?"

The squat Trollack looks up. "Yeah? Want a fried lumpsucker?"

Wil makes a face. "Yeah, not even a little. We're looking for information." The vendor holds out a purple, three-fingered hand, fingers wiggling. Wil holds his wristcomm up. The fish-like face of the vendor scrunches. "Hard currency."

Wil sighs and digs in a pocket, removing a metal disc about the size of an Earth quarter. He holds it up and drops it into the creature's palm. The Trollack looks at the piece of metal, then slips it into a pocket on his tunic. Wil asks, "We're looking for information on a

Knight of Plentallus. They would have lived a few hundred years ago. Somewhere here on this planet."

The fish-like seller blinks his huge eyes rapidly as he thinks. "Doesn't ring a bell."

Wil glares and brushes aside his long brown duster to reveal one of his pulse pistols. "Try harder."

The little man stammers, then runs his hands over his bulging eyes. "Wait, wait. Knights of Plentallus? Laser swords, cloaks, kinda mysterious?" Wil nods. "My parents moved here when they were children and used to tell me about an old legend. An old woman used to live in the Flend District. People used to talk about her." Wil makes a *go on* motion with his free hand. "They used to talk about her being part of some cult or something. They said she had a laser sword. She used to run a temple or something."

"Sounds right," Cynthia murmurs.

Wil nods. "Okay, so is there a shrine or museum or anything? Her temple still standing?"

"For a crazy old woman? Why would anyone build a museum for a crazy old lady? The planet would be packed with museums if they did." Wil is about to say something when the man says, "Besides, as far as I know, she's still alive."

A LITTLE HISTORY LESSON_

THE TRAM that connects the spaceport and market to the city beyond is crowded but not so crowded there aren't seats. As it trundles along the elevated track, Wil watches what looks like slums pass by below.

Cynthia and Zephyr are sitting together while Wil stands next to them. Wil looks down. "So, somehow this woman is still alive." It's not a question, just a statement, as he works through what the Trollack food vendor told them. "How is that possible?"

Cynthia and Zephyr both shrug. Cynthia offers, "There are a number of races that are long lived. The Tragalallan live to what? Five hundred, if I recall?"

Zephyr nods. "Jarek Ruus never said what species Sir Prenta Zulii was. Is."

Cynthia looks past Wil. "We're nearing the city."

Wil looks over his shoulder. "All right, according to our fishy little friend back at the spaceport market, she's in some type of old-folks home near the city center."

The tram slides between buildings of varying heights, leaving the slums behind. Trees with purple leaves line streets below. Wil points. "Was that a CVS Aid?" Both women look at him, expressions bland.

As the tram slows down, the two women stand up. A chime sounds. "Now arriving, Flend District. Mogon Street."

"That's us," Wil says. The doors slide open, and the three of them depart the tram mixed in with a few dozen random beings from all across the Commonwealth. Cynthia leans over to Zephyr. "Does this planet have its own people? So far I've seen only races from GC member states."

Zephyr shrugs. "I don't know, but you're right. I haven't seen anyone yet that I haven't seen elsewhere."

Wil points. "Let's ask over there." He's pointing to a cart and its Brailack proprietor.

Cynthia reaches the cart first, and the small blue Brailack man smiles. "Hi, what can I get you?"

Zephyr and Wil join her. The Palorian woman says, "We're looking for an elder care facility."

The man grins. "I'm sure an order or two of qorrum fries will jog my memory." He holds a hand out.

"This whole fucking planet..." Wil grumbles, swiping on his wristcomm. The Brailack's wristcomm beeps, and he goes about scooping qorrum fries into baskets. When he finishes, he hands a basket each to Zephyr and Cynthia. "The only elder care facility in this part of town is two blocks that way." He points. "It's one of the ritzier ones."

"These are good," Cynthia says, offering Wil the basket. She nods to the vendor. "Thanks." Wil opens his mouth to ask his question. She puts her hand on his arm. "Come on."

MAXIM IS IN THE CREW LOUNGE MOVING FURNITURE AROUND when the Trenbal woman comes in from the hatch to the stairwell that connects all three decks of the *Ghost*. "Those drennogs did a number on your ship."

Maxim grunts, "Yeah. They paid for it, though. There's now a safe route in and out of this system."

The woman nods. "Not sure if you guys know this or not, but those pirates are all one organization. I'm guessing the other checkpoints are jumping up and down mad." She grins. "Those gravity well generators aren't cheap, as I understand it."

"They're welcome to send an angry letter. How does this planet survive with pirates perched all around the system?"

The woman hunches scaled shoulders, wiping a hand on her grease-stained tank top. "This planet was initially settled by the Burzzad, but they found it too dry, so they left, every last one of them. Folks started moving in, a loose government formed, trade started to pick up, on and on. This was about, oh, I guess, four hundred cycles ago or so. Then about fifty cycles back, I'm told, the Crimson Sun moved in. They brought those big gravity generators and just waited. They only intercept about thirty percent of the inbound traffic, but it's enough to make it worth their while." She walks to the sink and pours a glass of water. "Normally, they board a ship, take half its cargo, then leave. Guess they got really unlucky with you lot."

"How come the government doesn't shut them down or call in the Peacekeepers?"

"The Sun has its fingers in the government, and like I said, they hit just enough shipping to make being here profitable but not so much that commerce has stopped." She waves a hand to encompass the planet outside the *Ghost's* hull. "Habitable planets aren't so numerous folks can just pack up and leave when things get tough. So, we all make do here." She shrugs, then drains the glass and starts for the hatch to continue whatever she was doing.

"Very unlucky," Maxim agrees, watching her go. He turns and heads toward engineering.

VISITING HOURS_

Wil whistles as they enter the massive building. It's at least ten stories tall and takes up most of the block it's sitting on. There is a small market on the corner that seems to have held out when the owner of the retirement building bought everything else on the block.

"Do all the old people of the GC come here?" Wil wonders aloud as they walk through a lobby that would make many hotels jealous. Oldsters of various races sit on benches and at tables talking to each other and playing games. Wil looks at one group around a wide table. "Hey, space puzzles, cool." He steps to the side quickly to avoid a fist intended for his midsection. He tuts at Cynthia when she realizes she missed. She darts in quicker than he can react to deliver her blow.

As he coughs, he bumps into an elderly Quilant man, his fleshy catfish-like whiskers wrinkled and rather beef jerky-like to Wil. "I'm so sorry," he stammers, reaching for the old man to steady him.

"You'd better be, youngling. Running around knocking people down, that's just not polite." The old man shakes his fist, the webbing between his fingers loose and as wrinkled as his whiskers.

Wil releases his grip on the old man, awkwardly patting him down until the oldster swats him away with a flurry of choice expletives.

Zephyr sighs and increases her speed so that she arrives at the check-in counter first. "Hello," she says as two Durbrillians look up at her. Their big eyes blink as their fan-shaped ears wave.

The closest clerk smiles. "Greetings. Are you here to visit one of our residents?"

Wil leans over to Cynthia. "Is there another reason someone would come here?" She suppresses a chuckle, then elbows him.

Zephyr nods. "Yes, we're here to see Sir Prenta Zulii."

The other clerk looks at the first. "Zulii? She hasn't had guests in some time."

"Since I've worked here," the first adds.

Zephyr just watches them converse, then says, "Floor? Room?"

The first small furry clerk coughs. "Sorry, floor ten, room one zero one eight." He points a tiny little hand toward a bank of elevators. Zephyr nods.

"I'm not gonna say this is too easy, but...you know," Wil says as they enter the elevator.

Cynthia and Zephyr both turn on him, the Tygran woman saying, "Are you insane? There aren't loopholes for jinxing us."

A chime sounds a second before the lift doors open. Wil wrinkles his nose. "Guess old aliens smell like old humans." He pinches his nose closed, motioning for the women to exit the lift first.

Zephyr looks up and down the hall, then turns to an elderly Rigellian sitting in a high-backed chair. "Excuse me, we're looking for room one zero one eight. Can you point us in the right direction?"

At first, it seems the old man doesn't hear Zephyr's question, until his eyes snap open. He looks at each of the three of them intently, then closes his eyes again, lifting a bony arm to point down the hall. Never once does the elderly Rigellian make a sound.

"Creepy," Wil says, leading the way down the indicated hallway.

The door with one zero one eight on it is ajar. An overpowering smell of cinnamon drifts out through the gap. Zephyr knocks softy and says, "Hello?"

"What's taken you so long?" A thin, reedy voice calls out. "Come in, come in."

Zephyr looks at the others and shrugs, pushing the door open.

"YOU AND YOUR TEAM HAVE DONE A SURPRISING AMOUNT IN such a short time," Gabe says to the Trenbal work crew leader. He, Bennie, and the team lead are standing atop the *Ghost*'s hull where a boarding pod had breached the upper boarding hatch. Gabe had welded a piece of steel plate over the hole to keep the ship airtight. Now the steel plate is gone, and a new circular hatch is installed. Gabe leans down to inspect the work, then turns, smiling. "Well done."

The team lead's tail swishes back and forth. She gives Gabe a thumbs up, then says, "We're about halfway done, but I figured it made sense to focus on structural things first."

Bennie nods. "Good call. I checked your guys' work on the cargo deck hatch. Looks good."

She nods. "We're the best. We'll start on the crew berth deck now." Gabe and Bennie nod. The hatch irises open, and one by one, they all step in, dropping into the ship.

MEAN OLD PEOPLE_

The room is dimly lit, the only light coming from a single window, the sheer curtain half pulled open. There is a bed in the middle of the room, like the bio-beds on the *Ghost* but wider and more comfortable looking. It's on wheels and has guards on the side to keep its occupant from falling out. Lying in the bed is a pale green creature that resembles a praying mantis. She's propped up on a pillow, looking towards a wall-mounted vid screen.

"Woah," Wil says as they enter the room.

A thin green arm reaches out, pressing a control on the bed, raising the creature's triangular head as the bed turns on its own to face the newcomers. Large compound eyes turn toward them as frail mandibles flex. "I've been waiting," she rasps. Her arms end in clawed hands. The rest of her is under a bulky blanket that mostly hides the thin insectoid outline of the body beneath.

"Uh, hi," Wil says, hand raised to wave.

Cynthia and Zephyr both smile and incline their heads.

"Sir Prenta Zulii?" Cynthia asks.

The old woman nods. "None of you look like Knights. Have they begun admitting in lesser beings into the order?"

"Lesser?" Zephyr growls.

Wil chuckles. "We're not Knights."

The old woman exhales. "That's disappointing. I've been holding on so long, I was hoping I was done." She turns to Wil. "So what? What do you want? I don't like visitors. What are you? Multonae? Are you selling things? They're supposed to stop solicitors at the front desk." She reaches a frail arm out, hand grasping a small comm unit.

"Human," Wil replies, making a motion to stop her from making the call she's about to make.

"Never heard of them," the cranky bug woman says, lifting the comm unit again.

Wil frowns. "Well, I've never encountered a race of cranky praying mantis people, so I guess we're even."

The pale green arm shifts, pointing at Wil. "I like you." She might be about to say more but a fit of coughing takes over.

Wil inhales. "We're traveling with a Knight, Jarek Ruus."

"I don't know that name." She moves a stick thin arm, the chitinous exoskeleton pale and cracked in places. Lying next to her on the bed is the hilt of a beam saber. It doesn't look like the one Jarek Ruus carries. Prenta Zulii's is thicker with some type of blood red crystal mounted at the bottom. It's shorter, as well, nearly half the length of Jarek Ruus' saber hilt. "You've seen a beam saber before?" A thin-fingered hand grasps the hilt, lifting it. She moves to hold it in both hands, then activates it. The beam that leaps out of isn't white. It's bright red. While the hilt design and blade color appear to be unique to each Knight, the hum the saber makes seems to be universal.

"We're here in search of an archive cube," Zephyr says.

The beam of energy retracts into the hilt. "I know that. It's why I'm still alive."

"What does that mean?" Wil asks. "How are you still alive? You've gotta be, what? A couple hundred years old."

"It's rude to talk about a woman's age," the older woman chastises. She breaks into a coughing fit, her mandibles clicking.

Cynthia whispers to Zephyr, "I don't recognize her species." The Palorian woman nods her agreement.

"This Knight you're traveling with, he's a good man?" the elderly insectoid woman asks.

"He's a cranky drunk, but otherwise, yeah," Wil replies. He adds, "You'd like him."

Prenta Zulii coughs. "Interesting. How do I know you're here with a Knight?" Cynthia opens her mouth but stops when Prenta Zulii continues, "You know what, I don't care. I'm tired, I'm old, I've been in this dren hole since they built it." She points to a floor to ceiling bookshelf against the far wall.

"Great, secret room behind a bookshelf," Wil grumbles, turning toward the bookshelf.

"What? No." The triangular head shakes back and forth, compound eyes glittering, one of her antennae bent halfway along its length. She points to the top shelf. "It's in that box." She coughs up something wet, her mandibles clicking. "The wooden one." She mumbles something about hidden rooms and no one having time for that.

Wil reaches up to remove the box from the shelf. He opens it. "Well, I'll be damned." Inside is an all-too-familiar glowing cube. This one is glowing pink.

Cynthia is about to join Wil, but a hand grasps her forearm. She looks down and sees that their host has a second set of arms that she has until now kept under her blanket. She turns to look at the old woman, who dips her head, then with the other hand on the same side offers Cynthia her beam saber. Cynthia opens her mouth to ask a question, but the grip on her arm tightens, then releases. The hand holding the hilt also goes limp, forcing Cynthia to quickly stoop to catch the falling device.

Standing, she looks around the room, then at Zephyr, and shakes her head. She turns to Wil. "We should go."

Wil looks up from the box in his hands to Cynthia and the beam saber hilt she's holding. "Shit," he says softly, walking back to the bed.

Wil stares at the body until Cynthia says, "What are you doing? What are you waiting for?" She holds up a hand before Wil can answer. "You're waiting to see if she vanishes, aren't you?" When he looks up sheepishly, she sighs and pushes him toward the door.

CHAPTER 16_

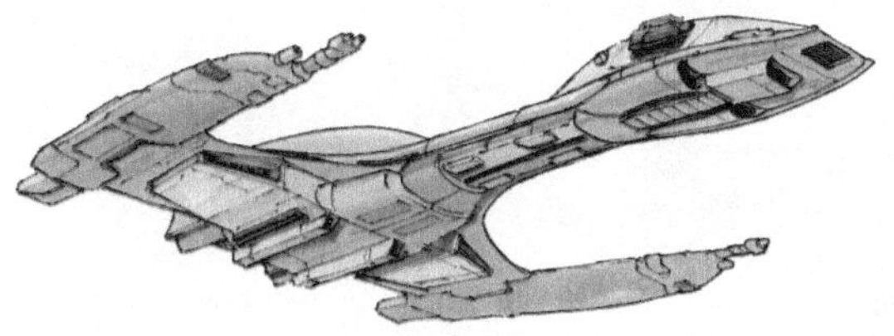

COMPLICATIONS_

"How're things going?" Wil's voice comes through Maxim's wristcomm.

Maxim looks around the crew lounge. "Actually, pretty well. The hull is patched, stairwell hatches are replaced. The damage to the reactor and power systems is almost repaired. Comms are back online. Sensors, too."

"Damn," Will replies. "That's great news. We're making our way back to you now."

"Success?"

"Yeah, we got it," the Captain of the *Ghost* replies.

Maxim can tell something isn't quite right by the tone of his voice. "What's wrong?"

Wil sighs over the line. "Nothing. We'll fill you in when we get there. How's the patient?"

Maxim looks at the door to the medbay, repaired and currently closed. "About the same. Stable-ish. The sooner we get him back to civilization, the better."

"Roger that," Wil says. "See you shortly." The channel closes with a beep.

Maxim looks around, then heads for the bridge. The crew that's working on the bridge is mostly Quilant. One looks up from under Zephyr's station. "We should be done in another tock or two." His catfish like whiskers twitch.

Maxim nods. "Okay, great. Anything I can do to help?"

Another catfish-whiskered face pops up from underneath Cynthia's station right next to the big Palorian. "Actually, yeah. Grandal could use help with some of the wiring trunks behind the main display. Maxim looks to the front of the bridge, noticing for the first time that the large display is hinged open to allow access to the mass of wires and equipment that live behind the display. The Quilant next to him shouts, "Grandal! Sending some muscle!"

From behind the large display someone shouts, "Great!" Then, "Dren! Dren! Dren! Ouch!" A cloud of smoke wafts from behind the main display. Maxim turns to the Quilant nearest him, eyebrow raised. The other man shrugs and crawls back under Cynthia's station.

AFTER STOPPING TO TELL THE TWO DURBRILLIAN CLERKS ABOUT the passing of Sir Prenta Zulii, Wil, Zephyr, and Cynthia exit the sprawling elder care facility. On their way out, the elderly man Wil tangled with earlier watches them pass, then shakes a wrinkly old fist in their direction.

Wil looks up at the sky. "That's enough old people stuff for a while." He holds the archive cube up, examining the intricate designs that cover every side. "Have to admit, they're pretty."

"The tram stop is this way," Cynthia says, pointing down the street in the general direction of the station they had disembarked at earlier.

Wil puts the cube in a bag he's brought with him. He nods. "Off we go."

The tram ride back to the spaceport is no more eventful than the ride into town. Cynthia and Zephyr persuade Wil to do some shopping at the market outside the spaceport, to restock the larder, on their way in. After all, Maxim said it'd be a tock or two, and the ride from town was only half a tock long.

Wil has both hands full with an overstuffed shopping bags and asks, "You know, we're trying to hurry and get the hell off this planet, right? Dying Knight of Parallelogram and all that."

"Plentallus," Zephyr corrects, even though she knows that Wil knows the right word.

Cynthia puts down a bundle of root vegetables. "Okay, fine. No lipnal tonight, I guess."

Wil looks at Zephyr, shrugging. She returns the gesture.

A ship roars overhead, departing the spaceport and causing many in the market to look up and point. The ship is a bit bigger than the *Ghost*, some type of mid-sized freighter with a lot of weapons bolted on. Zephyr taps the Stiltin next to her. "Excuse me, who does that ship belong to?"

The insectoid clacks its mandibles. "Crimson Sun. It came in about a tock ago."

Zephyr spins to the other two. "We gotta go, now," she growls.

Wil drops the bags of groceries and they take off at a run into the spaceport. Wil raises his wristcomm. "Bennie! Max! Report! Jarek Ruus! Come in!" Nothing.

"Fuck!" Wil shouts as they pass through the high wall that encircles the spaceport and contains administrative offices, mechanics bays, and various import-export businesses.

The *Ghost* is standing where they left her. The two hover vans that brought the work crew are still parked near the starboard engine nacelle.

Wil is out of breath by the time they get close enough to the ship to see the body. A Quilant man is sprawled at the foot of the cargo ramp, two plasma blasts burned into his back.

"Oh dren," Cynthia swears as she kneels to check the being. She looks at her friends and shakes her head once. The three of them draw their sidearms and walk up the ramp slowly. Zephyr is in the lead. At the top of the ramp are two more of the work crew, a Quilant and a Trollack.

They find another body in the crew lounge, this one still alive, barely: the work crew team lead, the Trenbal woman. Orange blood is pooling around her. Her dinosaur-like face is twisted in pain.

Wil rushes over, dropping to his knees. "Don't move, we'll get help." He looks up at Zephyr. "Check medbay!"

The Palorian woman darts past Wil and opens the hatch to the small medical compartment. She turns. "Empty."

Wil scoops the wounded woman up and rushes her to the medbay. A bloody hand reaches up and grabs Wil's shoulder. "It was... Crimson Sun... took your people."

PARTY CLOTHES_

Wil throws the PADD across the room. It impacts the bulkhead next to the hatch that leads to the bridge. The device explodes into hundreds of small pieces.

Zephyr asks Cynthia, "You copied the message?"

"I did."

"Fucking fuck fuck!" Wil screams. "Those dickheads walked right in here, killed the work crew, the innocent work crew, and took our people!"

"We know," Zephyr says, standing next to the entertainment screen.

Cynthia puts a hand on Wil's shoulder, but he shrugs it off violently. She grabs him by the shoulders and spins him around. "Babe. You need to calm down. Breathe. We can't save our friends or kick those drennogs' asses with you throwing a tantrum. Breathe."

Wil inhales and holds his breath, looking at the ceiling. He exhales. "Okay, you're right." He walks over to the refrigeration unit and removes three bottles of grum. "Okay, let's get our friends back." He looks at Cynthia. "Cyn, you copied the message, I hope."

She smiles, placing another PADD on the table. The screen comes to life, showing a message. "Not much to copy."

YOU OWE US.

"CERTAINLY NOT THAT INFORMATIVE," WIL GRUMBLES. He walks to the medbay. "Maybe our guest can help."

The work team lead, Jenice—she finally gave her name—is lying on the bed. The autodoc is retracted up to the ceiling, out of the way. She flicks her tongue as Wil walks in. "Hi."

"How're you feeling?" he asks, making room for Cynthia and Zephyr to stand in the doorway.

"Like I've been shot a bunch and almost died." She looks down at her gown. "I'm not going to die, am I?"

Zephyr smiles. "No, you got lucky. Trenbal are pretty hardy, and whoever shot you didn't aim very carefully."

"I don't feel lucky," the wounded woman quips, then frowns, or at least frowns as best as her facial features allow. "I guess I am, though. I'm alive. My crew ain't." She looks down.

Wil puts a hand on her shoulder. "I'm so sorry about your crew."

"This isn't your fault," she says.

His face takes on a grim set. "I dunno about that. But I do know that they're going to pay." He reaches back for the PADD. Cynthia drops it into his hand, and he shows Jenice the screen.

She looks at the screen then up to Wil. "When they're planet side, they hang out in a bar on the far side of downtown, The Rusty Ruknak." She coughs. "They have a small private spaceport over there."

Cynthia looks at Zephyr. "Who names these places?"

The other woman shrugs. "Explains why they took off, private place to park."

Wil nods to the Trenbal woman on the bio-bed. "Stay aboard the

Ghost. When we leave, I'll button her up and activate the self-defense system. No one will get close to you. If you need anything, ask the computer. It's moderately helpful."

She nods. "Thank you, Captain."

Wil turns, ushering Cynthia and Zephyr out of the small medical center. The hatch closes behind them. "Let's suit up. We've got pirates to kill." He heads for the hatch leading to the forward section of the *Ghost*.

After discovering the dead work crew, Wil and the others watched the security feeds. It was gut wrenching to watch so many innocents be slaughtered and their friends hauled off, but it confirmed what they were up against. It also confirmed that the pirates hadn't planted any booby traps or surprises in or around the *Ghost*.

"I know they were in a hurry, but those idiots should have searched the ship," Cynthia says as she attaches armored bracers to her forearms. One has an opening in it to allow access to her wristcomm.

Wil is half into his armored combat suit. "We're lucky they didn't. We're gonna need all of this." He waves to take in the wall of the armory with weapons of various size and design mounted on it. He checks his wristcomm. "Jarvis, we good?"

From a speaker mounted somewhere on the armor, the suit's AI replies, "Yes, sir. All systems are functional. Power cells are fully charged. The ducklings and Launchpad are charged. It is fortunate you asked Gabe to make repairs to the suit. Also, thank you for cleaning me." Wil nods and finishes closing the armored suit around him.

Zephyr is in her old scout infiltrator armor. She holds out her arms to examine them. "I guess it's time I got an upgrade."

Cynthia looks at her. "Can you even active the camouflage?"

The other woman shrugs and taps a command on her wristcomm. The active camouflage system engages and her legs and right arm waver, then become invisible. Her left elbow also fades from sight, leaving the rest of her left arm and most of her torso completely visible.

Cynthia chuckles. "Okay, sneaking in is off the table."

"Gabe said the damage was too severe," Zephyr offers.

THE RUSTY RUKNAK_

"Team Ass-kickers," as Wil has decided to call them, ride the tram back into town. Wil looks around. "I admit I'm glad they've got this tram. Would suck to keep having to hire cabs." It's much later in the day, the tram is not very crowded, and the sight of armed and armored people has kept their car pretty much empty.

Cynthia looks around the empty car. "Yeah, but we lose the element of surprise." She looks down at her armored torso. "We kind of stand out."

The tram slows. Wil shrugs. "This is our stop." They've crossed town, passing the stop they got off at last time, some time ago. In the distance they can see a much smaller spaceport, enough for 2-3 vessels at most. Unlike their first trip into town, this stop is in a decidedly seedier part of town. "Why don't pirates and sleaze bags set up shop in nicer parts of town?" Wil grumbles as they exit the tram station. "Say what you want about Xarrix, but he at least set up fronts in the nicer areas."

Cynthia tuts, "He operated out of Fury. The whole planet was the dren part of town."

Zephyr tuts, "Besides, the good parts of town have better police service."

Wil smiles, "Good points, both." They walk around a corner and Wil consults his wristcomm. "That's it there." He points to a windowless single-story building. "I can see why it's called The Rusty Ruknak. Well the rusty part, at least."

"Quite funny, sir, well done," Jarvis says. Cynthia and Zephyr smile, eyebrows raised.

Wil sighs. "Launch the ducklings. Keep Launchpad though, in case we need him."

"Very good, sir," the AI replies as three small spheres pop out of the armored pack on Wil's back. Each small probe takes off on small grav lifts towards The Rusty Ruknak, guided by Jarvis, looking for ways to sneak into the building.

"Jarvis, patch in to team comms and narrate anything interesting from the ducklings."

"Of course, sir," the AI replies. On Wil's HUD, a map of the bar ahead of them begins to form as the small baseball-sized probes infiltrate the air ducts. The HUDs on Cynthia's and Zephyr's armor update in real time with Wil's.

After taking a side alley to get to the back of the building, Wil looks around. "Must be almost trash day." He kicks an overflowing bag of refuse aside. Turning to the two women, he points to the door that, according to Dewey the probe, leads to the kitchen. Kneeling down, he extends a finger, and an arc of cutting plasma leaps out to slice through the locking mechanism. He pushes the door open. "Let's get dangerous."

"Captain, according to Huey, our missing crew are in the basement. There are three guards outside the room they are locked in," Jarvis reports as they enter the kitchen. They're in a small storage room.

Cynthia consults her HUD. "Two cooks, both Multonae."

Zephyr pulls a stun grenade out of a satchel she's carrying. She holds up a hand, the two thumbs tucked in, three fingers up. She counts down to one, then tosses the grenade into the kitchen. There's a soft puff and a bright flash of light, followed by two thuds as bodies hit the floor. She leaves the small storage room. "Clear." Wil and Cynthia rush to follow.

Wil points to a door that blends in with the far wall. "Stairs are there."

Zephyr looks at the camouflaged door. "Guess they don't like guests."

"Clock's ticking," Cynthia says. "Someone will notice those two sooner rather than later."

Wil deploys his plasma cutter, making quick work of the locking mechanism on the door. He motions the others to follow as he descends the steep stairs.

"Sir, there are two guards at the bottom of the stairwell," Jarvis whispers on the team channel.

Wil consults his HUD. There are indeed two guards stationed on either side of the stairs. The stairs empty out into a mid-sized room, five meters to a side, roughly. The room with their friends in it is off to one side. There are three more doors closing off rooms the duckling probes couldn't get into. Jarvis has parked the probes out of the way so they don't get shot or noticed.

Wil looks over his shoulder as Zephyr offers him a stun grenade. She and Cynthia nod once, their faceplates going matte black. "Jarvis," he says, causing his own faceplate to shift to matte black.

Wil tosses the grenade, rushing down the remaining steps. He enters the room as the grenade detonates, dropping the two surprised guards, both Malkorite. Wil points toward the door their friends are behind just as one of the doors opposite them opens.

"Hey Kilb, Cwen, what's going — who the wurrin are you?" a big Ruknak woman asks. She's in a loose-fitting jumpsuit that's covered in stains. The logo for a cola company Wil isn't familiar with is emblazoned across the front.

"Joe sent us," Wil says, aiming his pulse pistol at the woman. "Hands."

WHO'S JOE?_

"Who the wurrin is Joe?" the Ruknak woman asks, stepping into the room, reaching for her sidearm.

"You know, the skinny guy with the hair," Wil says.

She looks at the two unconscious guards. "What happ—"

"Hey, Jaru, what's going on?" someone behind her inside the other room shouts.

Jaru turns to answer and Wil groans, shooting her twice in the chest, sending her flying back into the room she just left. He looks over his shoulder. "Secure our friends." He charges into the room that Jaru the pirate just flew back into. "Leroy Jenkins!" he screams.

The room he runs into is big. Clearly, this underground lair extends beyond the edges of the street level footprint above. The room is some type of barracks, a barracks full of Crimson Sun pirates. One of the probes, covered in green paint, Louie, zips through the doorway and toward the far wall of the large room.

"Oh shi—" Wil says, diving behind a footlocker set just inside the door. It takes the occupants of the room a second to realize what is happening, but only a second. Plasma bolts rip the wall behind Wil apart, followed by shouts. Wil snakes along the floor. "Little help here?" He leans up and returns fire blindly.

"On it," Cynthia says a split second before she leaps through the open door right behind two stun grenades. Several thuds sound as pirates closest to the doorway fall to the ground.

Jaru sits up, her hands feeling around her torso. "What the grolack? You shot me!" She turns to look at Wil, who's crawled to the corner of the room behind some crates, hidden from the rest of the pirates but in plain view of the angry Ruknak woman. Cynthia lands next to her and rolls away to sit up facing the other woman. "You shot me!" she screams again.

Cynthia scoots backward. "No, I didn't." She points toward where Wil has gotten to a crouch behind a storage crate. "He did!" As Jaru turns, Cynthia shoots her twice more, then again two more times. The woman falls back dead. "Sorry," Cynthia murmurs as she scrambles to find cover now that the large Ruknak woman isn't sitting up making an obstacle of herself.

As Cynthia darts to Wil's rescue, Zephyr pushes open the door that Jarvis has outlined in yellow on her HUD. She has two stun grenades left after giving Cynthia two before she went off to save her boyfriend. Zephyr has the rough lay of the land, thanks to one of Wil's probes, so she kicks the door open and tosses the grenades in gently so they stay near the front of the room. She dives in just as the twin flashes go off. Her HUD tells her that one of the guards has dropped, but the other two were out of range.

Before she lands, she feels the burning of plasma bolts hitting her in the side. Her scout armor does its best, but she really should have replaced the armor some time ago. A small icon in the lower right of her HUD, a humanoid outline indicating suit integrity, is flashing yellow.

"Team! Down!" she shouts as she stands up, taking aim on the pirate, rushing toward her friends for cover. The pirate, a Trollack in mismatched armor, stumbles and falls to the ground in front of

Maxim, several plasma burns across his back. Maxim kicks the dead pirate. Maxim and Bennie both have their hands in cuffs and were until now sitting in chairs next to a bed of crates holding Jarek Ruus. Gabe is standing in the far corner of the room, de-activated. Some type of bolt-like device is spot-welded to his chest.

The other pirate, a Kilden, gets behind the crates that Jark Ruus is lying on. He stands and fires at Zephyr, striking her in the shoulder. She grunts, falling over and sliding into the wall. Bennie turns and charges the Kilden pirate, crashing into him before he can turn to take aim at the handcuffed Brailack. As the two smaller beings collide, they hit the crates that are serving as a bed for Jarek Ruus, knocking the old man to the ground with a grunt. He sits up, rubbing his head.

Zephyr calls out, "Sir Knight!" She removes the beam saber that Sir Prenta Zulii had given Cynthia, tossing it to the man. He reaches up and catches the device in mid-air, activating it and quickly plunging the blade of energy into the Kilden pirate who has gained the upper hand on Bennie. He quickly cuts Bennie's and Maxim's bonds, then walks up to the motionless Gabe. A quick slice, and the small device that has been welded to the droid's chest falls off.

Immediately, the droid's optic sensors turn on, then shift to red as his forearms shift into combat mode. "Thank you. That restraining bolt was unpleasant." The old man nods.

"We have to go!" Zephyr urges.

CHAPTER 17_

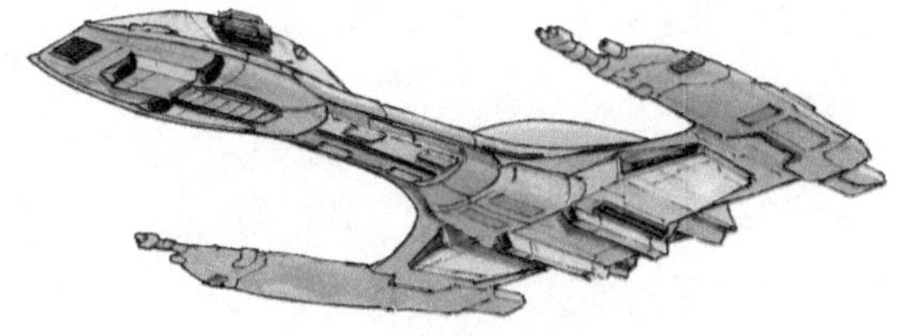

THIS ONE TIME AT PIRATE CAMP_

"Is this like pirate summer camp?" Wil shouts, firing at a lanky Sylban with a lush canopy tied back with a bandana. There are at least thirty pirates pushing toward Wil and Cynthia's not very sturdy cover. A plasma blast strikes the wall directly over his head, causing him to flinch.

"Incoming," Zephyr says a moment before a shadow falls over the door. Gabe.

The droid walks in, firing rapidly into the ranks of Crimson Sun pirates, causing them to dive for cover, turning over bunks and shoving footlockers into piles.

Behind him, Jarek Ruus enters, a bright red bladed beam saber in his hand. He moves to stand in front of Gabe, his blade moving fast to deflect or absorb the plasma rounds meant for him and the taller droid. The blood red blade sings and hums as it gracefully deflects incoming fire. Gabe doesn't stop firing.

Wil and Cynthia crouch and run out into the antechamber. Cynthia leans down and hugs Bennie, as Wil fist bumps a bloodied and bruised Maxim.

Gabe backs out of the room, followed by Jarek Ruus and a small green sphere. The door to the barracks room slides shut. Gabe fires a single shot into the door control. He turns to the others. "That will likely not hold them for long."

Jarek Ruus' beam saber deactivates and he drops to a knee, gasping. Wil rushes over to the wounded man. Blood is soaking his midsection.

"That doesn't look good," Maxim says.

Bennie rushes to the older man's side. "Let me help you." He moves the other man's arm over his shoulder. When it's obvious he's nowhere near tall enough to actually help, he points at Maxim. "You help him!"

Maxim smiles and kneels to help the other man stand. Jarek Ruus groans. Cynthia and Zephyr both rush to his side to inspect his wounds.

Gabe moves to the other doors, securing them. "We should depart posthaste."

The three small probes return to Wil's armored pack. He looks around. "Let's go." He turns for the stairway. Maxim, supporting Jarek Ruus' full weight, follows. Jarek Ruus' head dips and lolls to the side. His hand goes limp, releasing the borrowed beam saber hilt.

Bennie rushes to catch the device in midair and then bolts back into the room where they'd been held captive.

"What the hell?" Wil says, watching his small friend vanish. There's a commotion from inside the room, then the familiar sound of a beam saber activating, followed by a scream.

Bennie emerges, two pulse pistols nestled in the crook of one arm, the other holding the white bladed beam saber of Jarek Ruus. He quickly moves to hand Maxim one of the blasters, offering the other to Cynthia. She quickly fusses with the controls, setting the device to overload and tossing it toward the barracks door that is about to fail, if the glow of the metal is an indicator. Bennie looks at the door, then says, "Now, we go." He doesn't deactivate the laser sword.

The kitchen is bustling when Wil pokes his head out from the doorway. He almost gets a plasma blast in the face for his troubles, falling backward in time to avoid dying but still feel the heat of the blast. He leans out and fires indiscriminately, then looks at his friends. "Ready?"

There's a pop and low rumble from behind them, the pulse pistol's power cell going critical and exploding. Jarvis, on his own initiative, launches all four small probes, sending them hurtling out into the kitchen to distract and attack the gathered pirates. "Sir, there are twelve hostiles," the AI reports.

Wil rushes out of the stairwell, followed by Cynthia, then Bennie. The small Brailack rushes towards the pirates, his appearance momentarily confusing them. He leaps onto a food prep counter, beam saber whistling as he slices through pirate after pirate. His battle cry drowns out the shocked shouts of the pirates as they are cut down.

Gabe enters behind Maxim, bringing up the rear. He looks at the unfolding carnage, then looks at the others. Wil shrugs, then fires several plasma bolts into an Olop pirate that is trying to make for the door to the alley. Gabe fires three quick blasts, eliminating the last two pirates.

Two of Wil's probes zip in from the window that food is typically passed through, and Jarvis reports, "There are six beings in the dining area, but I cannot tell if they are pirates. They do not appear to be, as they are not moving in this direction." The two probes dock on Wil's back, followed by the two that remained in the kitchen area.

"Let's get back to the *Ghost*," Wil says, heading for the door to the alley. He turns to Gabe. "Can you book a ground car?" The droid nods.

NOT YET OVER_

THE RIDE back to the spaceport is uneventful, but when they arrive at the port, they see a dozen assorted beings standing just outside the *Ghost's* defensive perimeter. There are three bodies inside said perimeter. All of them but one is armed.

Everyone gets out of the ground car, arranging themselves in a wide arc. Wil walks toward the group of beings near the *Ghost* until they see him, weapons coming up. "Woah there, fellas." He looks around. "Sorry, fellas and ladies." He nods to an Olop woman with a heavy rifle aimed at him. "Look, I'm sure you know where we're coming from. I don't know if you know how it ended, but do the math. The number of us that went in, is the same number that came out." He spreads his arms wide. "This doesn't have to escalate." The rest of the crew is still arrayed behind him, their weapons drawn. Bennie comes forward to stand next to his Captain.

The leader of the group, so Wil assumes, takes a step forward. "We've got orders. You don't leave this planet." The Trenbal man has a heavier than normal accent, sounding raspier than most Trenbal.

Wil looks at the man, then to his friends, then back to the man. "Be realistic. We just left the bar you all call a base. The place you had my friends stashed in the basement of. There aren't more than a handful of folks left alive back there. Why join them for no reason?"

The female pirate, the Olop with the heavy rifle, growls, "Let's kill 'em and be done, Kelsot."

Bennie activates the beam saber of Sir Prenta Zulii. The snap hiss sound draws all eyes to him. He points to Maxim and the gravely wounded Knight of Plentallus. "He's dying. Nothing is going to get in the way of me getting him to our medbay. You have ten microtocks." He scrunches up his face in his most menacing look, helped by the red glow of his borrowed beam saber.

The Trenbal pirate looks around, then says, "They're all dead at the Ruknak?" Wil and Bennie nod once. He looks over his shoulder. "Stand down." A few of the assorted pirates grumble but are silenced by a hand gesture.

Wil holds up his wristcomm, issuing the command to open the cargo doors and lower the ramp. He looks at the Trenbal man as he passes. "Good call." The other man smirks as best as his reptilian physiology allows.

"Get Ruus to the medbay, then get to the bridge," Wil orders as they enter the cargo bay. Bennie and Maxim head for the stairwell. Wil presses a button on the control podium next to the cargo doors. While the ramp raises and the heavy doors slide towards each other, he says, "I don't know if this is over."

Cynthia nods. "I don't know anything about Crimson Sun, but yeah, by now the ships at the other interdiction points are certainly in orbit, if they didn't land."

Gabe looks at the three of them. "We are lucky that the work crew was mostly done when the Crimson Sun attacked us. While not one hundred percent, the *Ghost* is in better shape than when we landed."

Wil nods. "Better than nothing." He nods to Gabe. "See if there's any outstanding repairs you want to make, but we leave here as soon as possible." The droid nods and heads for the stairwell. Wil follows with Cynthia and Zephyr. He says, "Call Duch, see if he has any pull with Crimson Sun." Cynthia nods.

"I am afraid you're stuck with us for a bit," Maxim tells Jenice, the work crew lead, as he gets Jarek Ruus situated on the second bio-bed in the small medbay. "We're leaving, and the spaceport is crawling with Crimson Sun. I doubt they would be interested in letting you walk away."

She nods. "Guess we'll see how good my team's work was." She nods toward the old man. "He gonna make it?"

Maxim steps back to allow the autodoc to deploy from the ceiling. Its multiple spidery arms begin moving over the man's body, cutting away clothing, and treating plasma burns. He looks at the machine, then at Bennie, who is standing near the door, then to the woman, and shakes his head once. She nods, saying nothing.

ONLY WAY OUT IS THROUGH_

"Captain, we are ready to lift off. Reactor is at one hundred percent, repulsor lifts online, atmospheric engines are primed," the voice of Gabe says over the ceiling-mounted speakers. He adds, "We have only four missiles, but all beam weapons are fully functional and shield emitters are showing green across the board."

Wil nods. "Copy that." He looks around the bridge. Maxim and Bennie are at their stations now. The entire crew is present.

Cynthia says, "Duch doesn't have much to offer, says he doesn't work much with the Crimson Sun and has no pull." She wrinkles her nose. "He did make sure to warn us to stay away from them. They're 'dangerous.'" She adds air quotes around the last word.

Wil nods, grinning. "Worth a shot." He turns to Zephyr. "Anything up in orbit?"

She consults her console, then says, "Yes, but no idea who's who. Apparently, while overall the Crimson Sun are a nuisance, it seems the locals aren't in a big hurry to piss them off. Space control isn't sharing any data."

"The hard way, then. Awesome," Wil says, working his console to start the repulsor lift power up. He presses a button on the arm of his chair activating the ship wide comms. "Okay, everyone, strap in. This is gonna get rough." He turns to Maxim, "Our guests nice and snug?"

Maxim nods. "Jenice is keeping an eye on Jarek Ruus." He glances at Bennie, still wearing both beam saber hilts on his belt. "I don't think he's going to make it, Wil." The small Brailack's shoulders droop.

Wil nods once, slowly, then turns his attention to his console. "Here we go." He pushes the power lever for the repulsor lifts to half power. The *Ghost* leaps off the landing pad, leaving everyone's stomachs back on the ground. The telltale boom from the back of the ship, followed almost immediately by enough force to make most of the crew grunt as they're forced into the backs of their seats, indicates that the atmospheric engines are engaged at significantly higher power than normal for departure from a spaceport.

Zephyr looks at Wil and decides from the look on his face that now isn't the time to point out protocol. The *Ghost* roars up and out of the spaceport as several incoming comm requests blink on Cynthia's console from the spaceport and space control. She taps each one, denying the connection request.

"I'm getting better readings on the orbital traffic," Zephyr announces.

While Zephyr, Maxim, and Wil coordinate their strategy to get past what looks like an orbital blockade, a text alert appears on Cynthia's console, from Bennie. She looks up and over at the Brailack's station. He's looking at her and nods toward her console. She reads the message and looks up, nodding.

"Okay, here's what I'm thinking," Wil starts, then adds, looking at the ceiling, "Gabe, you on? I want your input."

"Acknowledged, Captain. I am here and have the main display mirrored on one of my displays," the droid says.

Wil nods to Zephyr, and the main display switches to a tactical view. Wil has the *Ghost* flying in a gradual climb for now, the repulsors at full power while the atmospheric engines are only at three quarters. In orbit over them are what look like three dozen, at least, vessels. Several read as similar to what they encountered in the outer system on their way in: a mismatch of light and medium freighters, with armor plates welded on and assorted weapons systems attached. At least two are larger light cruisers. The ships seem to be tracking the smaller Ankarran *Raptor*, keeping themselves positioned over the *Ghost*. The two light cruisers highlight in bright green. "We thread the needle."

"That's gonna be a rough ride for sure," Maxim says. He taps a control, and wireframes of the two dated, but still dangerous, light cruisers appear. Next to each is a read out of assumed weapons. "They're not new, and likely not well maintained, but if even half their weapons are functional," he pauses, "won't be fun."

From overhead, Gabe says, "It is unfortunate we no longer have access to XPX series missiles." When Wil is about to respond, the screen updates with a projected flight path. "I propose we make our escape attempt here. I believe we can fool the Crimson Sun vessels into thinking we're charging for the cruisers, then at the last moment change course." Wil looks at Maxim, who's nodding along as Gabe explains, "At our current separation, changes in our course are easy to mirror by the vessels above. If we can get our relative speed up and reduce our separation drastically, then last minute maneuvers are harder to mirror for the larger vessels."

"I like it," Wil says. Maxim and Zephyr nod. He looks at Cynthia, then swivels to look at Bennie. Both nod.

NEWSCAST_

"GOOD MORNING, I'm Klor'Tillen, and this is *Good Morning, Commonwealth*." The Brailack journalist smiles. "I'm standing on a planet that until recently had no name, was un-colonized. Today, that's changed. The Galactic Commonwealth governing council, in a unanimous decision, has agreed that this planet, now called Arcadia, will be the official home world of free sapient artificial lifeforms."

CHAPTER 18_

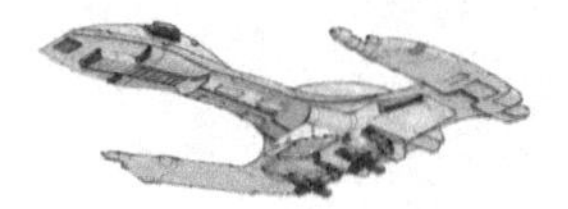

UP, UP, AND AWAY_

"Tʜᴇʏ'ʀᴇ ᴍᴏᴠɪɴɢ," Zephyr reports. The atmospheric engines are roaring to push the *Ghost* out of the atmosphere of P3X-595-C. The repulsor lifts are powered off, and the *Ghost* is flying close to vertical to escape the gravity of the planet. The small pirate fleet overhead is adjusting to match the small pocket warship's course. On the main display, Wil can see the sensor data overlay showing the outlines of the pirate fleet, despite the cloud cover.

Wil keeps his eyes on his displays. "Ready?"

"In five," Zephyr says.

"Jenice, hold on," Cynthia says into her commset.

"Go!" Zephyr says.

Wil pushes the sub-light throttles forward, activating them. The *Ghost* rumbles. The additional thrust pushes the *Ghost* to atmospheric speeds she isn't rated for. "Here we go!" Wil says, pushing the flight controls over, forcing the ship into a turn far tighter than she is meant to handle. Metal groans as the ship banks sharply starboard while still climbing. On the main display, the two light cruisers rapidly slide away from the *Ghost's* new trajectory, moving in the opposite direction the *Ghost* is now moving.

"Max, ready?" Wil asks, holding on to the controls tightly.

"Yup, targets locked," the big Palorian man says, hands gripping the edge of his console tightly.

On the main display, the clouds thin until it's just the growing blackness of space. The outlines of the midsized freighters of the pirate blockade come into view. Once the *Ghost* clears the planet's mesosphere, Maxim's console emits a tone. "Firing," the big man says. From deep inside the ship, the sound of the weapon's magazine shifting is followed by the hunk of missiles loading into the launchers, one after the other, four in total. "All birds away. All on target."

From the bottom of the screen, an unimpressive two pairs of missiles streak out ahead of the ship before veering off into groups of two.

Several indicators on Wil's console begin to flash red. "Shit," he hisses. He powers down the atmospheric engines, then looks at his display. Fewer red lights, but still several. One is the sub-light engine on the port side.

"Captain, I am reading an overload in the power converter in the port side sub-light engine," Gabe says from the overhead speaker.

"Yeah, I see it. Anything you can do?" Wil asks.

"Unknown," Gabe replies.

Gabe turns from the main situation display in engineering and grabs a large toolbox. Behind the reactor is an access panel that leads to a small crawlspace and access to the sub-light engines. When the panel slides open, thick black smoke fills the engineering compartment. Fans overhead kick in whirring loudly to clear the air.

Gabe peers into the crawlspace, then kneels down to lower himself into the cramped space. The equipment is scorched, and several melted components need to be replaced. Gabe reaches the port side sub-light engine access panel. Sparks and flames leap out of the opening.

"Oh my," he says out loud, then realizes he's beginning to take after his biological colleagues. He reaches in, data tendrils extending from the fingers of his right hand while the left feels for the burned-out power converter.

The device is fused, so Gabe withdraws the data tendrils and puts his right hand on the bulkhead above the access panel. His arm shifts, reinforcing his elbow joint, then he pulls. His left shoulder reconfigures, as does his bicep. Metal groans, and with a shriek, the fused power converter comes free. There's a right-handed indentation on the bulkhead above the access panel. Gabe examines the device, then looks at the ceiling. "Captain, I do not have good news. The power converter fused beyond repair. I removed the damaged component, but it did considerable damage to the engine itself."

"Shit, Gabe, we need that engine if we're gonna outrun these guys," Wil says through the overhead speaker.

"I will do what I can."

BOOM BOOM_

"I will do what I can," Gabe says from the overhead speakers.

Wil looks at the main display just as their missiles begin impacting the freighters, ripping several to pieces. Wil beams, pushing the controls to slide the *Ghost* between two burning hulks that are falling into the atmosphere.

"Those cruisers are coming back this way," Zephyr announces.

Wil looks over. "Can we outrun them on one sub-light engine?" The Palorian woman shakes her head.

"Christ on a cracker," Wil exhales. He looks at the small side display next to the main display screen. It shows a tactical view of the battle space, including the rapidly gaining light cruisers.

Bennie turns around. "I've been able to hack their battle network, if you could call it that. It's primitive as grolack. They've got two more cruisers coming in from behind the fifth moon. They parked 'em there in case they needed 'em." He grimaces. "Guess they need them."

Zephyr looks at her console. "I don't see them yet." She looks up. "That's a good thing, at least."

Maxim turns to look at Wil. "Without missiles, I don't like our odds."

"I don't like our odds even with a full magazine," Bennie says. "Not against four light cruisers, even old ones."

Wil adjusts their course. "I'll buy us time. We're on a course away from the planet and as oblique as we can be from the fifth moon."

"Missile launch!" Maxim reports. "The two cruisers just lobbed a handful of missiles, extreme range. Impact in sixty microtocks."

"Deploy countermeasures," Wil orders while looking at his command console uselessly. They're flying as fast as their single sub-light engine can push them. "This sucks."

Several clanks echo through the ship as missile countermeasures eject from the aft of the *Ghost,* doing their best to confuse the inbound missiles.

"In the clear, all missiles detonated by countermeasures," Maxim reports but then swears, saying, "More missiles. These drennogs may just pick at us from a distance. We don't have an unlimited supply of countermeasures, nor are they guaranteed to work every time." The sound of more countermeasures deploying fills the ship.

Wil growls, "We're not going out like this, not tail tucked running from pirates." He brings the *Ghost* around in a wide arc.

"Wil, what're you doing?" Zephyr asks, watching the missiles on the small tactical display veer away from the countermeasures toward the icon that represents the *Ghost.*

"Disruptors, now!" Wil shouts.

Maxim does a quick double take, then hunches over his console. "Hate you!" he grumbles, working his console, selecting targets as fast as he can. On the small tactical display, the incoming missiles wink out one by one. Maxim turns to Wil. "You suck."

Wil smiles and points at Maxim's console. "Not done yet." On the main screen, the two light cruisers are now rapidly closing the distance. "If we're close, they won't fire missiles."

"No, they can just rip us apart with energy weapons," Zephyr points out.

"Well, yeah, there's that, I guess," Wil says, then pulls the controls hard to the right, forcing the *Ghost* into a tight spin as repulsor blasts lash out from the two larger ships.

"I don't think this is a good idea," Bennie groans, clutching the side of his console.

"I've got contacts on long range sensors," Zephyr announces.

"About time," Bennie and Cynthia say at the same time, looking at each other in surprise.

Wil looks first at Bennie, then turns to look at Cynthia. He's about to ask a question when the ship rattles and something outside the bridge hatch makes a metallic grinding noise. Wil's focus returns to the main display as the *Ghosts* blasters lash out toward the two cruisers.

As the ship rattles and twists to avoid incoming fire, Zephyr starts, "It's—" She looks over to Cynthia. "—the Burzzad."

FRIENDLY FACES_

Seven beautiful, swan-like ships drop out of FTL. As the ships drop out, their majestic wings spread to over two hundred meters, wingtip to wingtip. At the end of the long elegant neck is a powerful particle cannon.

The *Ghost* slips from between the two cruisers, exchanging disruptor fire until out of range.

"Those are pretty," Wil says. "I don't remember seeing anything like that over Burrziira."

"They keep them stationed at a base in the outer system. The Burzzad Navy is mostly ceremonial now: escorting dignitaries, exhibitions, that sort of thing," Zephyr says. She looks at her feline featured friend. "How did you arrange this?"

The ship shakes as Wil brings her around, doing his best to stay out of the weapons range of the closest cruiser.

Cynthia nods towards Bennie. "It was little green's idea."

On the main display, two of the swan ships fire on one of the cruisers. Their powerful beams slice through the cruiser's shields, then its hull. The ship breaks in two.

"Woah," Maxim says. He turns to Wil. "Can we get one of those?"

"The other two cruisers are burning hard. They're engaging the Burzzad," Zephyr announces.

Wil adjusts their course to move into the pack of *swan ships*. He looks at Bennie. "And?"

The Brailack is beaming. "I remembered how much the Burzzad revered Sir Jarek Ruus and the Knights. So, I figured they might be interested in helping us." He spreads his arms wide, still beaming.

"We're being hailed," Cynthia says. "It's the lead Burzzad ship."

Wil nods to the main display, and a window appears with a Burzzad man in a military uniform. "Greetings, Captain Calder and crew of the *Ghost*. I am Captain Wu'Tan of the Burzzad Ceremonial Navy vessel *Glorious Heritage*." The long-necked Captain bows his head slowly, his three eyes blinking in unison. "We know of your mission; we will take care of these rabble. Are you able to make FTL?"

Wil grins. "Hi there, Captain Wutang. Thanks for the assist. You sure you're good?"

The Burzzad man tilts his head, which causes his neck to sway. "This system has long been a problem. My government has decided this is the perfect opportunity to address it. Two squidles with one stone, as it were."

Wil's eyebrows shoot up his forehead, but he says nothing. "Well, I won't look a gift horse in the mouth. I've set our course. We'll be gone shortly. Thank you." He dips his head slightly before hitting the *end* button to close the communication.

Once the *Ghost* is clear of the immediate danger, Wil puts the ship on auto flight. They won't be clear of gravity wells for thirty minutes. "Guess we should check on our guest...er, guests.

THE *GHOST'S* MEDBAY IS FAR TOO SMALL FOR THE ENTIRE CREW to fit inside, especially with the second bio-bed occupied. Jenice looks at Wil and Bennie when they walk in, her reptilian face a mostly unreadable mask. She catches Wil's eyes and shakes her head. He looks over at Jarek Ruus' body and puts his hand on Bennie's shoulder. "I'm sorry, man."

Bennie shrugs off Wil's hand and moves between the two bio-beds. He places a hand on the deceased man's arm. He looks up at Wil. "You didn't expect a body to be here, huh? You thought there'd be a pile of clothes." He grins.

Jenice looks from Bennie and the body to Wil, and back. "Why would you expect there to be no body?" She gets a disgusted look on her face. "Did you think I'd eat him? That's grolacking offensive!"

Wil holds both hands up. "No, nothing like that." He turns to Bennie. "No, I knew his body would be here. That old bug woman died right in front of me." He makes a hand wave gesture. "She didn't vanish."

The Brailack hacker looks at the deceased old man next to him. "We should get him on ice. We've got four more days at FTL."

Wil nods. "I'll take care of it." Bennie nods and leaves the medbay.

When the door closes, Jenice says, "He gave me this." She holds up the never-runs-dry flask. "Oh, and gave me coordinates." She points to a PADD lying on a small shelf between her bio-bed and Jarek Ruus'.

Wil takes the flask, slipping it into a pocket on his leg. He looks at the PADD, studying the coordinates.

Wil puts the PADD down and turns his attention to the bio-bed controls. He taps a few controls, mumbling to himself before the bed and the autodoc come to life. A thick membrane rises up from the edges of the bed, slowly enclosing the body. The autodoc adjusts the material as it moves.

Jenice asks, "So, uh, where are we going? Recognize the coordinates?"

Wil turns to look at their guest. "Yeah, I'm sorry you're stuck here tagging along with us." He looks at the display above her bed. "You don't have to stay in here. Looks like you're as good as we can get ya with what we've got. We're heading to a planet called Nexum. Heard of it?" The woman shakes her head. "Me, either. We'll be there in five days, though, once I get up to the bridge." He smiles. "At least we were already sort of heading in the right direction."

CHAPTER 19_

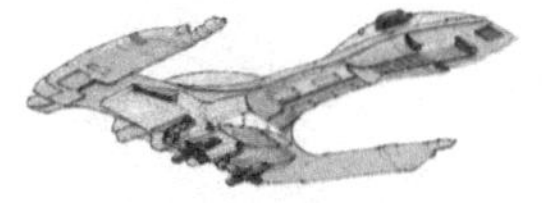

WELCOME TO NEXUM_

"Welcome to Nexum," a droid says from the main display. Wil has never seen a droid like this one before. He's seen plenty of models designed to look and act as close to a biological being as possible, but this one is different. From a distance, in the dark, Wil might assume it was a human or a Multonae man. The mirage would fade the closer you got to it. Its face is featureless but shaped like it would have eyes, nose, and a mouth. The entire body is matte black.

"That thing is weird looking." Bennie voices Wil's thoughts in a whisper.

Wil scowls, then says to the display, "Hello. I'm Captain Wil Calder. We're carrying the remains of Sir Jarek Ruus. Prior to his passing, he provided coordinates for this planet."

The droid dips its head. "That is grave news. I will transmit landing directions and meet you planet side." The screen goes black, then returns to the view of Nexum slowly rotating ahead of them. The planet is beautiful: several oceans visible, snowcapped mountain ranges spanning continents, and lakes of bright pink water.

Zephyr says, "According to the internex, Nexum is technically a protectorate of the GC." She pulls up a star map on her console.

"Weird. We're very much inside the GC, but sure enough, this system is technically not a member state."

Cynthia wonders out loud, "Could this be where the Knights started?"

Bennie nods. "It must be. Sir Jarek Ruus talked often of the beauty of the home world of the Knights." He points. "That's pretty damn beautiful." Everyone nods.

Wil says, "I've got the landing co-ords. Here we go."

During the five-day trip from P3X-595-C to Nexum, Gabe has been busy making what repairs he can. The damaged port side sublight engine is still damaged but now functioning at thirty percent. Better than nothing, as far as Wil is concerned.

They fly over cities that would put any Earth metropolis to shame: towers reaching into the clouds, transit ways spanning kilometers connecting every part of the massive cities.

The spaceport they land in is twice the size of their usual haunt on Fury and is busy with ships coming and going.

As the *Ghost* settles on her landing gear, metal groaning and popping, Wil puts his station into standby mode. "Let's get this done." He looks at Jenice, who has been standing near the bridge hatch. "You don't have to come with us if you don't want to."

The Trenbal woman nods. "Thanks, I'll see if I can find transport from here. Seems like a pretty busy spaceport for a planet none of us has heard of."

Wil smiles. "Right?" They all exit the bridge.

As the cargo ramp hits the duracrete, the crew walk down to greet their host. Wil extends a hand. "Hello, I'm Captain Calder."

The droid looks at Wil, then his hand, then back up to Wil. Wil lowers his hand. The droid looks over Wil's shoulder to where Maxim and Gabe are guiding a grav sled with the cocooned form of

Jarek Ruus on it. It says, "Please follow me to the temple," then turns and heads for a large hover van. The back is open, waiting for the grav sled.

The ride to the temple is silent. Thankfully, the temple is located only a few kilometers from the spaceport, on the outskirts of a large metropolis, near a lake.

The temple is stunning. A squat circular base of at least three stories supports an obelisk that reaches at least a kilometer into the sky.

As they disembark the vehicle, two other droids similar to their guide but bronze colored approach. Their guide says, "My associates will take possession of the body." It extends a hand toward a massive wooden door carved with intricate designs. "Please follow me."

"Forgive me for not introducing myself," the matte black droid says once it and the crew of the *Ghost* are inside a foyer that is larger than the *Ghost's* cargo hold. It places a hand on its chest. "I am C7K2, head custodian and curator of the Temple of the Knights of Plentallus."

Wil takes in the foyer. It is lined with ten-foot-tall stone statues of what he presumes are past Knights of Plentallus. A few of them are the same race as Jarek Ruus, but the rest are as assorted as the GC: two Burzzad, a Palorian, three Harrith. At the end of one of the rows is a Brailack. Wil looks at C7K2. "Are there other Knights here?"

The droid shakes its head. "No. Sir Jarek Ruus was the last." It dips its head in reverence. When it looks back up, it explains, "Over the last several hundred cycles, fewer and fewer beings sought to become Knights. Most systems no longer teach the history of the order, so their populations are largely ignorant of the existence of the Knights. Those that do know of them consider them legends, historical curiosities."

It turns and leads them deeper into the temple, explaining as it walks, "I do not know how much Sir Jarek Ruus explained, but in an attempt to combat the exclusion of the Knights from modern culture, many left, taking teachings and knowledge with them on missions of education and recruitment." They arrive at a large lift. The moment the door closes, the lift accelerates upward. "Many Knights were never heard from again, while many others were able to remain in contact, albeit briefly, with the order. In the end, none returned, so it is unknown how successful they were."

The lift doors open to reveal a room of floor to ceiling windows. A circular table sits in the center ringed by almost two dozen chairs. Each chair is a different design and physical arrangement. C7K2 leaves the lift. "This is the council chamber. Here the eldest and most experienced Knights guided the order. When it was clear to Sir Jarek Ruus that he was the last, he left on a mission to bring the knowledge of the order back here to Nexum."

Wil looks over his shoulder and nods to Bennie, who pulls a satchel he's been wearing around to open it. The hacker slowly removes the three archive cubes, placing them on the table next to him. After that, he removes the beam saber hilts of Sir Prenta Zulii and Sir Jarek Ruus and places them on the table.

C7K2 looks down at the assorted devices, then looks at Bennie, then Wil. "Thank you. I feared Sir Jarek Ruus would not complete this most sacred, final mission."

Maxim raises a hand. "This wasn't his first outing to collect those doodads?" He points at the cubes, each glowing a different color.

C7K2 shakes its head. "No, this was, in fact, his seventh outing into the galaxy." A section of floor begins to rise, revealing a three-meter-wide section of shelving. Dozens of square openings fill the display case; all but three are full. Cubes glowing every color of the rainbow sit on small clear pedestals.

"Wow," Zephyr and Cynthia say in unison.

C7K2 picks up the three cubes from the table and places them in the empty cubbies. It turns back to the crew. "Now that the collected knowledge of the Knights of Plentallus is complete, we will be able to fulfill our last responsibility."

"Which is?" Cynthia asks.

The droid comes to stand next to them again, the case of archive cubes returning to the floor. "This temple will become an institution of learning and memorial, open to any who seek knowledge." It turns to the table, picking up Jarek Ruus' beam saber, then turning to Bennie. "I believe you should have this."

Bennie stammers, "Why? How—?"

STATE FUNERAL_

"You are marked," C7K2 replies. It continues, "When a Knight is in the field and interviewing potential apprentices, they mark them." Bennie cranes his neck, trying to look all over his body, holding his arms out wide. Everyone else leans down to inspect the freaked out Brailack. C7K2 says, "It is nothing visible."

Gabe interrupts, "An isotope." The other droid nods. Gabe continues, "I have been detecting a radioactive—"

"Radioactive?!" Bennie screeches.

Gabe puts his hand over Bennie's mouth. "The radioactive signature is far too weak to cause you harm. Until now, I was unable to locate the source."

C7K2 looks up at Gabe. "If you adjust your optic sensors to see in the 445-nanometer range, you will see it."

Gabe looks at Bennie. His optic sensors don't visibly change, but he says, "Indeed, I do." He taps Bennie on the forehead between his large eyes. The angry Brailack bats the droid's hand away.

C7K2 holds out its hand, the hilt of Sir Jarek Ruus' beam saber in it. "As I said, you should have this. Having known Sir Jarek Ruus for quite some time, I am certain he would want you to have it. I am afraid there is no one to train you, however."

Bennie blushes a deep shade of green and reaches out to accept the ancient weapon.

C7K2 looks at Wil. "We can coordinate repairs to your ship while you attend the funeral."

Wil looks at the droid, then to Gabe, who uncharacteristically nods vigorously. He turns back to the matte black droid. "We'd be honored to attend the funeral and grateful for the repairs."

THE FUNERAL FILLS THE MASSIVE FOYER. APPARENTLY DESPITE their waning popularity among the larger Galactic Commonwealth community, among the people of Nexum, the Knights of Plentallus are still quite popular. Hundreds fill the foyer while thousands fill the courtyard outside the temple, and according to C7K2, nearly every sporting arena on the planet is simulcasting the event.

C7K2 leads the event, while several presumably politicians and patrons of the Knights speak both about the order and its history but also about Jarek Ruus, the last member of the order.

The crew of the *Ghost* is given seating in the front row and are dressed in the best clothes they have. Thankfully, after the Galactic Corporate Congress summit, everyone owns something formal and more or less fitting, except Bennie. At the crew's urging, he went into the city to have a less ostentatious suit tailored. He insisted on keeping the hat and its accompanying feather.

After the ceremony, Gabe excuses himself to oversee the final repair work.

Wil looks at his crew and his friends. "Just got a message from Jenice. She's almost home. She sends her regards."

Maxim raises an eyebrow. "She going back to P3X-595-C?"

Wil shakes his head. "No, she decided to head back home to Baal."

"Makes sense," Cynthia says.

Wil looks down at Bennie. "You doing okay, green bean?"

Bennie isn't really paying attention to the conversation and blinks rapidly as he looks up at Wil. "What? Yeah, I'm fine."

"Captain," Gabe says over the commset in Wil's ear, "the repairs to the *Ghost* are complete."

Wil nods and tells the others, "Repairs are done."

Before he can say anything else, Bennie says, "Let's go, then. I'm tired of being sad."

Wil makes a face but says, "Okay, then. I'll go say goodbye to C7K2. Meet you all outside."

Wil approaches the droid, who is standing off to the side of the large space observing the guests. It turns its head as Wil arrives. "The repairs to your ship are complete. I assume you are departing?"

Wil nods. "We are, unless there's anything else you need from us?"

The droid tilts its head. "There is not. I paid your invoice and the funeral is essentially over. Once the guests leave, my team and I will begin the work of converting the temple to a place of learning."

Wil nods. "I look forward to visiting when you're done." As he turns, a matte black hand rests on his shoulder. He turns back to the caretaker droid.

C7K2 offers him a data card. "This is for Ben-Ari Vulvo. While he is not officially an apprentice, I have decided to extend the benefits to him. This data card contains everything he will need to access the temple's database. He will have access to the collected knowledge of the Knights of Plentallus and all of the training materials needed, should he choose to continue his education."

Wil is speechless. A few beats later, he finally says, "That's very kind of you. Thank you. I'm sure Bennie will appreciate it." The droid nods but says nothing, then turns back to watching the ever-thinning crowd.

WHAT'S NEXT?_

ABOARD THE *GHOST*, everyone is at their station. Gabe is in engineering. Wil powers up the repulsor lifts and guides the ship out of the spaceport before activating the atmospheric engines.

Cynthia looks up from her station. "Hey, Gabe?"

"Yes, Cynthia," the ceiling replies.

"Congratulations." She's grinning wider than Wil has seen in a while. She taps a control, and a window on the main display appears with the broadcast of *Good Morning, Commonwealth.*

"Hot damn," Wil drawls. He looks at the ceiling. "That's awesome, pal! Congrats!"

Maxim adds, "Indeed, that is excellent news."

For a moment there's silence from the speakers, then Gabe says, "Thank you, all of you. I am excited to see the droid nation flourish on Arcadia."

Everyone on the bridge exchange looks, then Zephyr says, "Okay, then."

The small video window closes. The *Ghost* is hurtling up and out of the atmosphere of Nexum. Wil looks around the bridge. "Okay, what's next?"

THANK YOU_

Thank you so much for reading Space Rogues 7: A Guy Walks Into a Bar

If you enjoyed it I'd love it if you left a review. Seriously, reviews are a big deal. They help readers find authors. They help authors show how awesome they are.

Reviews are social proof and go a long way to encouraging other readers to take a chance on an unknown author.

OFFER_

As they say, there's no harm in asking, so here we go.

If you can help connect me with someone who can get Space Rogues on a screen (Big or Little) I'll cut you in for 10% (Up to $10,000) of whatever advance is paid.

Send me an email and we can discuss.
rights@johnwilker.com

Want to stay up to date on the happenings in the Galactic Commonwealth?
Sign up for my newsletter at
johnwilker.com/newsletter
Lots of goodies await you, just sayin'

Visit me online at
johnwilker.com

If you like supporting things you love by sporting merch, well you're in luck! I've launched a Space Rogues Shop, take a look.

Coming Spring 2021
Space Rogues 8: Probably in Space (Working Title)
Pre-Order it now!

ACKNOWLEDGMENTS_

I couldn't do this without an amazing group of people who sign up to beta and/or ARC read for me. The Beta readers in particular have to suffer through an early draft to help shape the story.

Below are some of these awesome people (If I missed your name, email me and you'll be in the next one :D)

- Robert Allsup
- CJ Boyd
- Alice Clark
- Mike Connelly
- Barrie Davis
- Penelope Lind
- Meenaz Lodhi
- Dale Parker
- Stephen Rakoczy
- Viet Thanh

Thank you so much, all of you!

The Space Rogues Series. Wil Calder and a bunch of alien misfits somehow keep finding themselves in the thick of it. No one ever checks qualifications when it comes to saving the galaxy!

The Grand Human Empire Series. Jax, Naomi and the droids are just trying to get by. New droid parts ain't cheap after all.

www.ingramcontent.com/pod-product-compliance
Lightning Source LLC
Chambersburg PA
CBHW051638180726
48284CB00006B/1774